Little Welsh Wanderer

– CATHRYN ANNE –

An environmentally friendly book printed and bound in England by
www.printondemand-worldwide.com

Mixed Sources
Product group from well-managed
forests, and other controlled sources
FSC www.fsc.org Cert no. TT-C
© 1996 Forest Stewardship C

PEFC Certified
This product is
from sustainably
managed forests
and controlled
sources

This book is made entire

FastPrint Publishing
www.fast-print.net/store.php

Little Welsh Wanderer

This book is based on some true events that mostly concern the character 'Lucky.' However, it has been fictionalized with incidents, characters and timelines being changed for dramatic purposes. Certain characters and events are composites or entirely fictitious.

ISBN 978-178035-341-8

First published 2012 by
FASTPRINT PUBLISHING
Peterborough, England.

For all my family, but in particular Mam and Dad,

who have taught the importance of friendship, family

and the value of childhood and beyond

Thank you… for everything

Contents

Chapter 1

Swansea Dogs' Home

'Now, you must promise me something, Carys,' Evan said to his daughter as he drove slowly east along the M4 motorway. He was driving well below the speed limit for once because he was in no hurry to go home and face the inevitable consequences from his wife. 'Whatever you do when we get back. Don't tell your mother.'

'But, Dad won't she notice we have a dog now?'

'Of course she will, but it will be too late. What I mean is, don't tell your mother that this was what we set off to do this morning. You get me?'

Carys' eyebrows pulled together and she pursed her lips as she looked down at the tiny, scruffy terrier in her lap. He was struggling against her tiring grip with his breath wheezing in fits and starts as he choked himself on his new collar, straining to follow a strange instinct to stick his head out of the glass window beside him. He did not know why but he was sure that this was going to be the best experience of his short life so far.

'I don't understand, Dad.'

Evan thought carefully about his next words. He was in enough trouble already but there was no need to put his daughter in the firing line as well.

'I mean that if your mother knows we left the house this morning to get a dog we will be in trouble. But if we just say that we went for a walk in Singleton Park and found the dogs home by accident, she might not mind as much.'

'Oh Dad, is she going to make us take him back?' She tightened her grip around her new puppy. He did not like that and added a body wriggle to his incessant pulling.

'I'm certain that she won't make us take him back,' Evan lied. 'Anyway, he's ours now so Swansea dogs' home expect us to keep him.'

'But she knows that we know where Swansea dogs' home is. We've been there before, remember?'

He clucked his tongue against the roof of his mouth. His studious, nine-year-old daughter had a better memory than he did. He tried again.

'Not accident then, coincidence. It was a coincidence that we walked by the dogs' home and just went in for a little look.'

Carys nodded her head in agreement and on another day she might have analysed why her father was making this strange request of her. Instead, she started to bounce her new tiny terrier up and down on her lap, chatting to her father about the animals she has read about in books. Her favourite stories were the ones about dogs who were loyal and well-trained and accomplished great feats such as saving people's lives. Carys wondered aloud what her little puppy would be able to do with her.

While his daughter's imagination ran riot, Evan silently pondered his fate. His wife, Jayne, was the practical one in the family. She had lists for everything; lists of things to get for Carys, lists of places to take their son, Daniel and lists of things for him to do, get, shop for or mend. Evan might have argued that sneaking Carys out of the house on New Years Day to buy a dog while his wife lay in bed with a hangover was a spur of the moment decision, but that would have been untrue. It had been well over a week since he had seen the advert in the evening post newspaper just before Christmas 1989. A full page spread of black and white photos of dogs and cats all peering out to him with longing eyes from the rough, recycled paper.

He had also considered telling Jayne that the dog was for their daughter, who was besotted with any animal she came across. But while Evan regularly did things his wife did not approve of, honesty was not a fault of his and he would be truthful with her eventually. His actions this morning stemmed not just from his daughter's, but his own desire to get a canine companion. His own childhood dog had been a large, majestic and completely snow-white Alsatian called Rusty. He had been everything that Evan could have wanted in a dog and much more. The pet budgie could land safely on his back and preen his long white fur but Rusty's bark was deep and menacing enough that no one had ever dared to say a wrong word to Evan in his presence. Rusty was the one who had sat patiently on the sand zealously guarding the little possessions Evan had carelessly strewn on the shell-saturated ground, while he surfed high breaker waves at Aberavon Sands beach.

Evan liked the thought of a dog that would help to protect his children but his own childhood musings and hopes faded when he turned his attention to the motley mongrel sitting on his daughter's lap. The little puppy was an exemplary example of mongrel breeding, his back being too long for his little stumpy legs and huge ears that folded over gently at the top. He had endearing dark brown eyes with soulful depths and thick black lashes curving perfectly around them. The soft fine hairs of his muzzle were a dark, rich chocolate colour and stuck out like static and his tail was so long that when he wagged it from side to side it thumped against his sides. His tail was not moving now though; it was curled up tight and tense, just like the rest of him.

For the first time since Carys had literally stumbled against his kennel in the dogs' home a few hours ago, the tiny terrier was still. He was staring with glazed eyes at the floor of the car with his ears flattened onto the back of his head. He belched quietly and swallowed loudly as he tried to understand the new and unpleasant feelings in his body. Evan jolted to attention and stomped his foot onto the accelerator, lurching the car forward.

'What's the matter with him?' Carys asked, her voice high with panic.

'Nothing's wrong with him, I just should have taken up the offer of a travelling cage,' Evan replied regretfully.

The old and rusty but serviceable Ford Escort family car barrelled its way along and Evan counted the seconds until he saw signs for Baglan. He swung a sharp left off the two-lane motorway and then immediately right into the respectable Pentwyn estate where they lived. Modest sized houses with well-tended gardens and council kept grass verges whizzed by as Evan speeded home. Meanwhile the tiny terrier's stomach continued to grumble uncomfortably and his head felt light and disorientated. Every few minutes his stomach heaved upwards into his rib cage and his nose sank even lower into Carys' lap.

The car squealed to a stop and the front tyres bumped against the pavements curb at the front of their house.

'Quick Carys, get him outside, the fresh air will do him good,' Evan said as he leapt out of the car and ran around to open the door for his daughter. When the fresh air hit the tiny terrier the scents of his new neighbourhood stunned his senses. His vision blurred and his bones felt as if they had become disjointed, only being held together by the under developed limbs and muscles of his puppy frame. He fell limp in Carys' arms.

'OK, Dad I think he's all right,' Carys said when she did not feel her new puppy heave again. It was a slow progression up the front path and in through the front door, Carys fearful of upsetting the little puppy further and Evan apprehensive of his wife. Carys was still bundled up in her Christmas present, a thick woollen winter coat with unused mitten gloves hanging from the pockets but Evan, as always, was wearing shorts and a light t-shirt.

Carys and Evan froze when they entered their porch area. They were confronted by Jayne, half way down the stairs in front of them. She had one hand clamped to her aching forehead and the other held out in front of her, palm facing outwards as if to ward off the vision before her. Her dark, shoulder length brown hair hung limply around her face, which had drained of colour and emotion and her eyes were squeezed shut.

Evan was silent

Carys was silent.

The tiny terrier was silent until his stomach heaved one final time before he retched up a white, lumpy liquid. It proceeded to dribble down Carys' coat and land on the new royal blue carpet with gentle, irregular thuds.

Jayne's eyes snapped open.

Chapter 2

Hangover

'What is that?'

'It's a dog, Jayne.'

'I can see it's a dog, Evan. What's. It. Doing. Here?' It was never a good sign when Jayne spoke that slowly.

'Yeah well.... he might need a bit of a clean up... before he settles in that is. You're up early anyway. I thought you'd be in bed a bit longer, do you want me to get you anything, luv?' This was not the way Evan had wanted Jayne to find out about their new dog.

Jayne's mouth snapped shut and her usually full lips hardened into a straight line. She squared her shoulders and shuddered because this was not the first animal to arrive as a result of her husband's devious behaviour. She was regretting the decision to combine cider with cheap red wine last night and if it had not been for the persistent thumping inside her head and the parched, dryness of her mouth, she might have felt frustrated that she was giving up so easily.

'Well, that is your responsibility, not mine, and I strongly suggest you clean up his homecoming present to us and get me another glass of water!' Jayne pirouetted on the stairs, wobbled and then stamped back up to her bedroom slamming the door behind her. She flopped into bed and pulled the duvet over her head, preferring to nurse her hangover than accept the reality of the last ten minutes.

The tiny terrier wriggled in Carys' arms. He felt much better after having got rid of the contents of his stomach but a squeeze on his groin was alerting him to his primitive needs. Carys carefully stepped over the milky mess on the floor and bent over slowly so she was able to place, rather than drop her little puppy on the floor. As she stood upright to examine the damage to her new coat, the tiny terrier tried to unsuccessfully cock his leg before peeing over himself and one of Carys' trainers and then dashing out of sight into the living room. Carys stared at her leg with speechless horror. This was not how any of the dog stories in her books started. Evan took charge.

'Carys, quick, get upstairs, clothes in the wash and change before your mother sees you.' Carys hopped upstairs, grimacing when her left foot squelched with every step. She was quick to return, washed and changed just in time to find her father chasing the tiny terrier around the dining table in an attempt to retrieve a chewed piece of plastic that somewhat resembled their television remote control. Daniel was still sitting cross-legged in front of the television, the cartoons he so loved watching blaring out at him. He had actually torn his gaze away from the screen to watch the strange looking terrier dog completing circles around the furniture with Evan close behind.

When the remote control was eventually wrestled from his tiny, pointed teeth the little puppy propelled himself around the downstairs rooms with all the mania of a dog possessed. He replenished his stomach from Daniel's untouched breakfast, chased a big black cat from underneath the sofa and, in trying to run into the garden, smacked into the glass patio doors at the back of the house. The tiny terrier sat on his haunches and paused after doing this, making a mental note that there were obviously some invisible walls in this house, so running in circles was best. He proceeded to chase his tail but with it being so long he caught it easily.

Jayne re-emerged from her safe haven a short while later, her curiosity winning over her headache, just in time to see the new arrival race past her six-year-old son, nipping his hand as Daniel attempted to pet him.

'OOOOOOOWWWWWWWW' and as Daniel began to sob Evan thought how unfortunate it was that Jayne had witnessed this particular event. The tiny terrier was completely oblivious to Daniel's distress. The little quiet boy was obviously the smallest and weakest link in this place and so he thought it perfectly acceptable to treat him in such a way. He had heard people scream louder in his previous life and he certainly did not attribute the noise as pain inflicted by his own teeth. He made a lap of the room and headed back towards Daniel again.

'For goodness sake, Evan. What have you brought home?' Jayne demanded of him as she rushed over and threw her arms around her wailing son.

'Don't worry, Jayne,' Evan said reassuringly. 'He's just settling in, he'll learn.' As the tiny terrier tried to playfully sink his teeth into Daniel's other hand, Evan grabbed him by the scruff of the neck and lightly smacked him on the rump.

The tiny terrier stopped dead in his tracks and threw himself to lie on the floor, his back towards Daniel and his tail curled up tightly besides him. His eyes were wide open and his ears glued to the back of his head. It did not matter that it had been the larger man who had hit him and it was not relevant that it had not hurt, much. The tiny terrier knew in that instant that he had been humiliated because of the little, screaming boy.

Daniel stopped sobbing when Jayne pretended to wipe the invisible teeth marks from his hand. The tiny terrier forgot about sulking and instead became engrossed in playing tug of war with Carys, testing her defences and willingness to let him do as he pleased. Jayne watched helplessly as he tore small holes in the tips of her socks while her daughter giggled uncontrollably. She inhaled sharply and sighed deeply in defeat.

'Are you sure about this, Evan?' She said and gestured towards the little puppy with one hand. 'We haven't exactly had much luck with pets.'

'What do you mean?' His eyes were wide as he looked at his wife, adjusting his thin-rimmed glasses so they were higher up his nose.

‘I am saying,’ Jayne said (she was speaking slowly again, determined to get a grip on her frustration). ‘We haven’t had a hamster or gerbil, or pet mouse, rabbit or guinea pig live to even half of its life span because the cat keeps eating them or they die for reasons unknown. And the hamsters that the cat doesn’t eat, we lose underneath the floorboards.’

‘Yeah, I thought I heard something last night,’ Evan mused. He had still not managed to retrieve the hamster that Carys had received for her birthday a month ago and lost a week before Christmas. The scratching late at night was evidence that the rodent was still alive and well, somewhere under the floorboards of house. ‘The budgies were O.K. though, Jayne and the kids loved them.’

‘Evan, do you remember that we had the budgies six months before you put them out the garden in their cage so they could enjoy the feel of the wind in their feathers…?’

‘Yes, they loved it.’

‘And then the wind blew the cage over and the cage broke and they flew away?’

‘Yeah, well, they worked out fine before that happened…’ Evan muttered.

‘And that cat your sister gave us went and tripped Carys up on the stairs and she broke her arm in two different places when she was only two and a half. I’m sure the hospital staff thought I was abusing my own daughter when I gave that explanation.’

'Yes but apart from that the cat hasn't caused us any problems, has he?' Evan demanded and he crossed his muscular arms across his thickset chest.

'Well...' Jayne paused as she thought about the little kitten that she had been assured was a female, until the kitten grew up to be the biggest and most aggressive feline in the neighbourhood, regularly coming home with bloody battle wounds. It had been a vet who had informed Jayne when she took the cat to be spayed that he would actually have to be castrated and while she was at it, she should change his name from Julie-Ann to Julian. Instead, the big black cat became known as 'Big Black Cat' and despite losing his manhood continued to fight off anything that challenged him.

Jayne shook her head and decided that ruminating over past pet problems was not going to help or change the situation now. Big Black Cat had been with them for six years and was still alive and well. It was clear from the way Carys was engrossed in playing with the strange looking terrier that he was not going anywhere. This was the sort of unexpected situation that Jayne dreaded but living with Evan, happened a lot. Now, without any proper planning time, she had to reorganise the family's whole routine around the demands of what looked like a mischievous and untrained puppy.

'Well, that's the last time I listen to you when you say 'Have a lie in, Jayne' she muttered, doing a bad impersonation of her husband. Her interest was slowly getting the better of her frustration though. 'So, what is he then?'

‘It’s a dog Jayne,’ he was sure they had already had this conversation.

‘I can see it’s a dog, Evan, but what type of dog.’

‘Terrier.’

‘Funny looking terrier, never seen one quite like him before,’ Jayne said but she was an optimist if nothing else so she decided to try and brighten the mood by encouraging Daniel to forget about his little teeth scraping incident and detract from her own reservations. ‘OK then, what are we going to call him?’ she asked.

‘I’m going to call him Lucky,’ Carys said proudly. ‘Because I just know he’s going to be a lucky dog and we are lucky to have him.’ Evan snickered, sure that his wife would not think the same way.

‘But I wanted to give him a name,’ Daniel whinged and a few theatrical tears threatened to escape.

‘Well,’ Jayne said, her eyebrows still half way up her forehead from her daughter’s last comment. ‘It’s only fair we all get a say in what he is called, since only you two got to pick him.’ Jayne’s green eyes were blazing as they bored into her husband, but Evan was now completely unabashed by his actions and ignored his wife. Carys however was not going to let anyone have anything to do with naming her dog.

‘No way. I named him ‘coz I picked him and…’ Carys glared at everyone in turn as she vehemently protested. Jayne sighed again, Evan smirked and Daniel rolled his eyes at his sisters temper tantrum, he was used to it. ‘He’s my dog and I've already named him.' Carys persistently repeated.

The tiny terrier pricked his ears at the little girl who was now trembling, her hands clenched tightly into fists and her back as unnaturally straight as the side of his old kennel. He forgot about trying to pull Carys' socks off and he rose to stand over her, his two front paws placed firmly on her thighs while he monitored the other people in the room with wide open and alert eyes. He had no idea why the little girl was now so angry but he had already made allegiances to her and the large man, not to the screaming boy or doubtful woman.

Jayne's persistence was such that Carys agreed to a naming ceremony for the tiny terrier. Jayne rushed to her bureau where she kept her methodically organised papers and pens and made a mental note to start a dog-shopping list. She also rummaged through a stack of newspapers and when she returned to her family she had pens, pieces of writing paper, a newspaper and a gleeful glint in her eye. Jayne had found the same advert for Swansea dogs' home that Evan had read a week earlier. In the middle of one of the pages and set amongst various other pictures and written adverts for dogs and cats, there was a picture of a little, fluffy puppy with large, dark eyes and over-sized triangular ears that folded over gently at the tips. It was the same tiny terrier that had so far been sick on her new carpet and bitten her son (Jayne was still oblivious to his urinating on her daughter).

Underneath the picture was the caption

'Tiddles has been kindly sponsored'

'Obviously not as friendly as he looks in the picture' Jayne murmured as she eyed Daniel's recently grazed hand. 'But Tiddles is a good name?'

'Oh my gosh,' Carys cried out. 'We are not calling him Tiddles. That's so lame.'

Carys' parents laughed at the scowl on their daughter's face which was easily her most dominant feature in that moment. Jayne handed out slips of paper to everyone and then handed another piece to Daniel as the tiny terrier bounded off Carys' lap, snatched the slip from Daniel's hand and bolted across the living room, halting abruptly when he slammed into the glass patio door - again. Undeterred, the little puppy flopped to the floor and proceeded to rip the paper to shreds.

Jayne instructed everyone to write a name and put it in a bowl that she had also brought. The name that was written the most, she declared, would be chosen or if it was tied, everyone would each vote again with the winning names. Jayne thought it was highly unlikely that anyone would write the same name and she suspected that her daughter would get her own way in the end, but she always felt comfortable with democracy.

Four slips of paper were completed, crumpled and thrown into the mix. When all the scraps were carefully unwrapped there were four completely different names of 'Lucky,' 'Tiddles,' 'Whiskey' and 'Moocher.' The name Tiddles was scrawled in Daniel's untidy handwriting, something that Carys was sure he had written just to annoy her. Carys stood, stamped her foot and loudly voiced her objections to the suggestions of Tiddles, Whiskey (courtesy of Evan) and Moocher (Jayne's idea). It was an outburst worthy of any nine-year-old child and Daniel quickly became bored and returned to watch his cartoons. Evan adjourned to the kitchen for a late breakfast and Jayne sacrificed her attempt of social equality for the sake of some peace from her daughter. Carys once again smiled with delight, the tantrums and scowls forgotten.

The tiny terrier watched the drama with mild curiosity while he meticulously shredded and ate his stolen piece of paper. He sat still long enough for Carys to officially christen him as 'Lucky.'

Lucky was then promptly sick on the carpet again.

Chapter 3

Public Place Prohibition

'Grrrrrrrrr, grrrrrrrahhhhhhhh,'

'Carys, Daniel, get the dog,'

'Grrrrrowwwwwwww, wow wow wow,'

'Carys, Daniel, did you hear me?'

'Grrrrrow, wow, Grrrrrow, wow.'

'I said get the dog before he…'

'Arrrrrrrooowwwwwwwww,'

'Too late,' Jayne muttered.

Lucky was on guard duty, his lips drawn back over his tiny teeth and his eyes narrow and challenging. His hackles were raised, giving the impression that he was twice his usual size. In the absence of effective leadership and training since his arrival, Lucky had quickly risen to become the self-designated leader of the family. They were all put in danger twice a day when intruders came to his territory and threatened them with some unknown but highly dangerous device. It was that time of day now.

He leapt from his watchful position in the large bay windowsill at the front of the house and sailed buoyantly through the air. Daniel was running towards Lucky through the dining room when Big Black Cat emerged from underneath the table, tripping him up and sending him sprawling face first onto the carpet. Carys was upstairs when she heard her mother call. Her bedroom door slammed open and shut as she scampered to the top of the stairs.

Lucky landed on the dark wooden laminated floor and skidded, his tiny legs a blur as he struggled for traction. Daniel squinted and scrambled to his feet, ignored his fallen glasses and continued with his pursuit while Carys thundered down the stairs. Lucky reached the carpet in the hallway and the sudden grip propelled him towards the front door. Daniel dived for Lucky the same time as Carys jumped the last two steps. They crashed into each other falling to the floor in a tangle of arms, legs, screams and shouts. Lucky neatly evaded the human cannon balls and sprang into the air, deftly catching the newspaper before it hit the floor.

Carys and Daniel stumbled to their feet just as Lucky was shaking the newspaper, a shower of confetti around him as he ripped and tore it apart. When Carys and Daniel tried to wrestle it from him he darted between their legs and ran into the garden determined to destroy the danger and protect his pack.

Lucky had a 'danger list' and anything that was bigger than him constituted a threat. Of course, given his tiny size, that is a lot. The most hazardous items on his list though were the newspaper, the newspaper girl, letters and parcels, the postman, Big Black Cat, any other cat, the vacuum cleaner, the ironing board, plant pots with decorative markings on them, the hair dryer, lawnmowers, the hosepipe, footballs, tennis balls, any other type of ball, the next door neighbours, people with hats, people on bikes, people getting into cars, people getting out of cars, seatbelts, the milkman, anyone who rang the doorbell and any one in a uniform. At the top of Lucky's 'danger list' were big dogs. German shepherds, Boxer dogs, Great Danes and Rottweiler's all became immediate targets for his wrath.

When Lucky was inside the confines of his large, three bedrooms, three-reception room house he easily matched the little people's energy. He would pounce, bounce, bound and circle them tirelessly and when they were too tired to play he would head off in search of Big Black Cat. He allocated Carys as his female alpha equivalent and for him she could do no wrong. He laid quietly while she dressed him up in sunglasses and a range of weird and wonderful hats and clothing. He slept on her bed while she tickled below his ears with one hand and held a book she was reading with the other. When Carys talked intently to him she was delighted when he spoke back to her. 'Aaaarrraaaroooogh aaaarrraaa.' What he was really saying was 'when are you going to stop making funny noises so we can go search our territory.'

Evan was Lucky's second in command. Together they would venture into unknown lands so Evan could investigate strange buildings where lots of other people were coming and going from. Lucky would guard the car to show any passing dogs and people that he was in charge, squeezing his nose through the tiny gap in the window that Evan always left for him, barking and scrabbling his claws against the glass. He also chewed and shredded the seatbelts until Evan would reappear from inside the pub and Lucky could relax, knowing he had defended their territory with his life.

Jayne had always refused to have a dog on the grounds that she knew she would be the only one in the family who would look after it properly. Lucky's arrival only served to confirm her fears. She was the one who fed him every day, every week and he depended on her to let him outside in the morning. She was further down Lucky's chain of command, only one above Daniel and so she did not fare as well as her daughter and husband. Lucky chewed her hairbrushes like dog biscuits and if she shouted at him he simply cocked his head, then his leg and peed, usually on the corner of the sofa.

Daniel, although still under Lucky's protection, was at the bottom of the pecking order in Lucky's pack and as such Lucky saw it fit to sometimes put him in his place with a surly snarl or quick nip. Fortunately, Daniel was oblivious to pretty much everything apart from his basic needs, school and his computers, which he played on constantly.

The Pentwyn estate became Lucky's territory and he pulled Carys around it in endless circles. She puffed behind him, struggling to keep up with his short and stumpy but quick little legs. She still carried childish puppy fat that most of her peers had long shed, her long dark blonde hair bouncing around her waist as she struggled with the exercise program that owning a dog had imposed upon her. Pentwyn was a decent estate in Baglan, one of the villages in Port Talbot. In a working class town with pockets of deprivation and low-income families, Baglan is considered by its residents to be respectable and perfectly middle class. A huge fuss had broken out when an adult only shop had opened in a neighbouring village and the community wasted no time in mobilising councillors and local members of parliament to address what they saw to be a serious drop in retail standards.

Lucky was barely aware of the broad leaved deciduous woodland on the Dinas mountain that overlooked his immediate home. Neither did Lucky consciously notice the dark green conifer covered Baglan Mountain, that extended up steeply from the Pentwyn estate. Lucky's world was very small but he came to know it well, defending his family and his territory from all the dangerous and perilous hazards they encountered. Carys struggled to hold him whenever he saw something on his ever-growing danger list. He would throw his weight against the end of his lead, barking, yelping, twisting and growling at whatever had offended him. He fell asleep every night satisfied that his family were safe for one more day.

Margam Country Park was a favoured family day out because Jayne and Evan reasoned that the one thousand acres of fields, woodland walks and other attractions provides plenty of scope to tire two children and a dog. On Lucky's first trip there the sights, scents and amount of activity assailed him and he strained and struggled against his lead so determinedly, that Carys quickly passed him to her father. Evan grinned as he easily stopped the persistent tiny terrier from attempting to scamper off in every direction apart from the way the family were heading.

Jayne and Evan initially set out to accompany Carys and Daniel as they ran around the magical, miniature houses and castles in Fairyland, where a range of life sized plastic, popular Disney characters posed. However, Lucky enthusiastically attempted to leave his urinal mark on every front door of every miniature house. After soaking the welcome sign to the house of Snow White and the Seven Dwarfs and adding some fluids into the Koi carp fishing lake, Evan dragged him over to the entrance to wait for Carys and Daniel to complete their tour of make believe.

When the family took a leisurely stroll up to the café area Lucky continued to relieve himself on anything that stood more erect than he did. This included the twelfth century chapter house, every five feet along the majestic eighteenth century orangery and the artistic stone sculptures and woodcarvings that line a series of steep stone steps.

'This dog can pee for Wales, Jayne,' Evan shouted over to his wife with amusement.

'Good. Hopefully he won't have any left to piss on my sofa,' she said dryly.

By the time Lucky was led to the majestic Gothic Tudor Mansion, affectionately known in the local area as Margam Castle, Evan was wise enough to keep him away from the nineteenth century Grade 1 listed building. The impressive, large mansion with its irregular towers and steeples had been undergoing restoration since the late nineteen seventies and Evan knew that no one would appreciate Lucky being close to the distinctive stone architecture with so much fluid to lose. He dragged Lucky over onto the large grassed area at the front of Margam Castle while Carys and Daniel went to explore the exhibitions that line the inside grand hallway with the stone, marble emulating staircase.

It was nearly mid-day when Lucky's family joined him and Evan at the front of the castle. The bright, strong sun was the only colour in an otherwise perfectly blue sky. The grassed grounds were packed with couples, families and groups of friends enjoying the welcomed hot weather. Many were lounging on the grass tucking into picnics, laying back on blankets or lazily kicking a football around. The bray of the pet corner donkey echoed over the grounds while petite fallow deer grazed on the horizon. Lucky was tense and alert as he surveyed the scene.

Amongst this, an enemy grabbed Lucky's attention from afar. His coarse body hairs rose vertical and a low growl started in his stomach and emerged from his panting mouth. A red mist clouded Lucky's sight and he threw himself against the end of his lead, yelping, barking, twisting, jumping, growling. All his thoughts were focused on one big thing and one big thing only. Protect and defend, attack if needed.

Evan followed the direction of Lucky's eye-line and also saw him. He was a large, stocky, chocolate coloured bullmastiff with a perfect white star on his head. His shoulders were nearly as wide as the well-built man sitting in an upright position behind him. This man was clutching the thick chain lead of his massive dog in one hand and holding the hand of a woman Evan could only presume was his girlfriend in the other. The bullmastiff was positioned in front of them both, alert but calm, guarding his owner.

Lucky was stood on his hind legs, straining against his lead. Evan tugged on him and to his horror, Lucky fell back, twisted to the left, rolled over to the right and slipped his neck from out of his collar before gleefully propelling his little legs faster than even he would have thought possible. Lucky scampered through a chaotic crowd of people, weaving and darting in between the legs of running children, sitting parents, groups of friends, past a spaniel, golden retriever and another terrier dog. He covered thirty metres in less than thirty seconds and when he came within reach of the unwavering Bullmastiff he launched himself into the air, straight towards the thick neck encased in a silver studded, leather collar.

Carys, Jayne and Evan watched in horror as Lucky failed to sink his teeth into the massive neck of his enemy and dropped ungainly to the floor. The bullmastiff remained like a statue until Lucky, undeterred, jumped from the floor and launched himself at the stocky mass of fur and muscle again. He was unable to open his mouth far enough to grab the neck of the massive dog so he satisfied himself instead with sinking his teeth into the dog's collar. Lucky hung there, all four feet off the ground, growling, his little body writhing in anger.

The Bullmastiff slowly lifted a gigantic paw and pushed Lucky from around his neck. He pinned him to the floor and had a good look at the squirming source of his minor discomfort. Lucky found himself being picked up by the scruff of his neck and shaken from side to side before being thrown ten feet away.

'No' Carys screamed.

'Lucky, come here' Evan was running towards him.

'Oh no' Jayne sighed.

Daniel was oblivious.

Evan and Carys raced over to their tiny terrier who had been shaken like a rat and tossed through the air before bouncing twice, rolling over, landing on his feet and heading back towards the big dog for another go. Anger coursed through Lucky as he flung himself at the neck of the dog again and once more hung from his collar, growling ferociously. Once more he was pushed and pinned to the ground before being picked up and flung across the picturesque setting of Margam Country Park.

Evan intercepted Lucky before he could run back to the bullmastiff for a third time. Lucky was still growling, shaking, writhing and baring as much of his teeth as possible. Crowds of people, Jayne, Carys and even Daniel, who had finally realised what was happening, waited with baited breath as the enormous owner of the Bullmastiff slowly got to his feet to confront Evan. Cautious anticipation from eager spectators quickly turned into relief and giggles as the bullmastiff owner turned out to be only a little taller than his dog but just as wide. Evan, being only five foot ten inches, towered over him as the stocky man held up his hands in a gesture that said,

'It's your dog attacking mine.'

'Sorry 'bout that, mate,' Evan nodded to the short and stocky man, secretly thinking how appropriate the saying, like dog like owner. He wrestled Lucky's tiny struggling body under his armpit and walked away from the scene of disaster.

There were titters from children, parents and friends as Evan strolled back to his family with Lucky in his strong underarm grip. Other more responsible dog owners reached out to draw their dogs closer to them, out of sight and out of harm's way from the tiny brown terrier attacks. As Lucky's growls continued to escape from him, a random man turned to Evan with a lopsided grin and asked

'What's his name then, Tyson?'

'No it's Lucky.'

'I should think he's very blooming Lucky to still be walking after that.'

Jayne and Evan gave more thought to the time, date and venue of the next proper family outing. They decided on Kenfig Nature Reserve, one of the finest wildlife habitats in South Wales, known for its unique fen orchids, insects and bird watching. The vast sand banks used to belong to sand dunes that once stretched along the South Wales coastline from the River Ogmore to the Gower peninsula. Now they only run from the west end of the tourist town of Porthcawl and alongside the long and rocky Morfa beach, until they halt at the massive industrial Steelwork site in Margam, Port Talbot.

Jayne's master plan was to stroll the short walk from the car park to Kenfig pool, a huge seventy-acre freshwater lake that glitters peacefully amongst a network of rough sandy footpaths that snake through dense patches of grassland and scrub woodland. Then they were going to head to the quieter part of the reserve where the sand dunes are high, with narrow tracks at their summit giving far-reaching views across the beach where the rough, grey sea pounds against the rocky shore. They would have to avoid the areas where farmers graze sheep in fenced off areas because Lucky would only chase them. She also hoped that this time they would not come across any naked hikers strolling between the soft folds of the sand dunes. The last time they had seen a naturist as they headed towards the beach, Carys had been thoughtfully silent for longer than usual and it had triggered a talk between mother and daughter about unusual lifestyle choices and the male anatomy.

The morning stared well. Lucky was so consumed by the scent trails of rabbit and dogs that he was entrusted off his lead, he glued his nose to the path and quietly sniffed his way towards the lake. Carys and Daniel ran ahead to the water's edge where small ripples lapped gently against a sandy shore. Evan did not see the wooden bird hut hidden in the foliage around the lake, nor did he see the glint from two sets of binocular lenses.

'Carys, Daniel, throw this in for the birds,' Jayne said as she pulled a stale loaf of bread wrapped in a plastic bag from her practical and well-used rucksack.

Daniel grabbed the food and ran to the waters edge with Carys close on his heels. As the first pieces of bread left Daniel's hand, the serenely peaceful water parted in a dozen places and a herd of ducks zoomed to the shore to fight for a surprise breakfast. Two large, majestic swans gracefully glided to the water's edge and joined the frenzied chase. Lucky froze when he saw them approach, his mouth partly open with his ears pricked forward and one front paw raised in front of him.

These odd, water-based creatures were the strangest and most unfamiliar animals that Lucky had ever seen. Necks too thin and long to be like any other dog he had come across before and an uncanny ability to glide on water. Lucky sized them up and decided he did not care what kind of animal they were, they were big and that meant they were dangerous and to top it off they were heading towards his little people. Protect and defend, attack if needed. He propelled himself forward, took a running leap into the air and dived with a splash into the shallow water.

Lucky bounded through the flock of wildfowl that dispersed loudly around him, heading for one of the large, white swans. They easily turned and swam away from him. Lucky became out of his depth and with a final spring submerged himself completely underwater.

'No' Carys screamed.

'Lucky, come here' shouted Evan as he ran towards the waters edge.

'Oh no' Jayne sighed.

Daniel continued to throw bread into the water.

Lucky was unconcerned when the cold water washed over his head and soaked through his thick coarse fur. An ancient instinct kicked into his conscious being and he began to move his legs just as if he was running on the ground. He executed the time old doggy paddle technique to get back to shore where he vigorously shook the cold water from his coat, soaking Daniel's trouser legs.

'Grab the dog, Daniel, don't throw any more bread,' Jayne shouted but Daniel did not hear her. The swans returned to the shoreline and Lucky turned and sprang into the air before darting back into the water. The water parted and ducks erupted from the surface in all directions, flapping to a safe distance from the tiny brown terrier bouncing through them. The large white birds pirouetted on the water, tantalisingly out of Lucky's reach.

The nearby bushes shook vigorously and two short, plump men emerged wearing identical green camouflage clothing. Each of them was carrying a pair of binoculars. They spoke as one person.

'Get that dog…' one started

'Out of that lake' the other finished.

Evan, Carys and Jayne startled at the sudden appearance of two almost identical men but Daniel continued to throw bread into the lake. The two men continued lecturing, bobbing their red-cheeked faces in unison.

'This is a nature reserve….'

'Not a common play park…'

'It's just not funny…'

'Or acceptable…'

'Get that dog ON A LEAD.'

'ON A LEAD.' It was impressive when they finished in unison.

Evan quickly grabbed Lucky and hooked a lead onto him.

He grimaced as the cold droplets of water Lucky was shaking from himself pelted him in the face. Lucky was dragged away in disgrace by Evan with Jayne, Carys and Daniel following. He mentally added these strange large white animals onto his danger list.

When the family reached the western side of Morfa beach it was almost deserted. The salty, sea breeze stung Lucky's nostrils, rejuvenating his muscles and senses. He was off his lead for five minutes when he saw two large, brown animals thundering along the edge of the sea. Two small men sat astride the beautiful, powerful racehorses, training on one of the most natural resources available. Protect and defend, attack if needed.

Lucky bolted towards the sea to meet the majestic animals. The two horses and jockeys ignored the tiny terrier approaching them and they all but thundered over the top of him. Undeterred, Lucky flew up the beach, yapping close on their hooves.

'No' Carys screamed.

'Lucky, come here' shouted Evan but he stood glued to the spot.

'Oh no' Jayne sighed.

Daniel was trying not to get sand in his shoes.

That evening, Lucky slept sprawled across Carys' bed while she lay perched on the edge of her mattress. He was blissfully ignorant to the conversation downstairs as Jayne and Evan relaxed into the soft and worn fabric of their cushioned sofas. Jayne tried to reflect on the day's disastrous events.

'You know what, Evan?' she mused thoughtfully. Evan grunted but his eyes did not leave the television. 'If that dog was any bigger we would have a real problem with him.'

Evan grunted again.

'I mean, if he was a big dog, he could really hurt another dog. He could hurt someone.'

'Good job he's not a big dog then' Evan replied pragmatically.

'Well,' Jayne continued insistently. 'At least we know what the problem is. I mean, if you know what the problem is, you can fix it, right?' Evan raised one eyebrow. 'There's no way we are going to take him to dog training classes anyway. He would be a liability.' Jayne closed her eyes and shook her head with horror at the very thought of Lucky in such close proximity to other dogs. Evan raised his other eyebrow. He had no intention of taking Lucky to dog training classes, groups for dangerously disturbed dogs or being part of any other bright idea Jayne could conjure up.

'I don't know what you're so worried about, Jayne. I think he's funny and he's only trying to protect us.'

'Oh yeah, I'm sure that those birdwatchers, and those jockeys on the beach today and the man last week who owned the biggest dog I have ever seen think he's hilarious.' Jayne drew breath before starting again. 'So, we'll have to do something ourselves. It can't be that hard, for goodness sake. After all, he is just a little dog… and we both work for the council.' Jayne's chin jutted out with pride and determination written all over her face.

'You're the Crime Prevention Officer, Jayne, whack him with a warning.'

'Ha ha, very funny. You're just going to have to take Lucky out more, Evan. Really get him used to other dogs.' Jayne paused and eyed her husband expectantly.

Silence.

'Evan, are you listening to me?'

Evan grunted.

'O.K. From now on you must take that dog out every day. Take him out properly. Not just leave him in the car for an hour while you have a pint with one of your mates.'

Evan's eyebrows disappeared into his hairline. He wondered outside which pub Jayne had seen the car parked with Lucky in it. She had certainly kept that one quiet until she needed to spring it on him.

'So I've drawn up an exercise list,'

'Surprise, surprise,' Evan grumbled.

'You and Carys have the main responsibility for doing this since you two went and got him. From now on, that dog is not going to embarrass us again in public or put anyone, any dog or any other thing in danger. If this is the only problem we have got with him we are just going to have to work a bit harder to solve it.'

Jayne resolutely promised herself that Evan was going to take the dog out every day. Evan resolutely promised himself that he would not park the car in the pub car park again when he was supposed to be walking the dog. Maybe a nearby street...

Jayne and Evan were blissfully ignorant that the problems associated with their tiny terrier's protection over them was going to pale in comparison with the new challenge he was about to present them with. Even worse, it was a problem that was going to re-occur for many years to come.

Chapter 4

A Policeman Calls

Lucky was stretched out in the warm autumn sun rays, enjoying the delicate feel of the grass ticking his belly and the soft breeze that carried the scents of the neighbourhood. His head was laid comfortably on his front paws but his eyes were open and flickering to and fro. He was waiting for some sort of activity to give him an excuse to spring into action. It was quiet though, only the deep tenor and monotonous song of a lawn mower being walked laboriously up and down a neighbouring garden and the distant tinkling of children laughing as they ran along a paved street.

It was tough being the top dog but Lucky was confident he was up to the job. When he looked in a mirror he saw a big dog, with big paws and sharp teeth and when he pounced at the reflective glass he saw a humongous scary dog pouncing back. Lucky rarely looked into mirrors for long because he was content with the animal he thought he was. When his family looked at him they saw a tiny terrier that had grown a bit in height since his arrival and doubled in length. His ears were more in proportion with his face and no longer folded over at the top but pricked upwards, always attentive. His legs were still too short for his body and his tail was still far too long. His fluffy puppy coat had grown and thickened into a double layer of dark and sandy brown, coarse and wiry body hair. The only things that remained unchanged were the soft, dark hairs around his muzzle, which permanently stuck out with static.

Lucky was always restless during the day. It was a time when his pack disbanded and he was left alone, never an easy thing for an alpha. He had recently become clearer about his job as the leader of his family. There had been a sudden increase in the amount of times he was required to leave the house, surveying, marking and defending his territory. From this Lucky inferred that he had to check out the local area, guarding it against any one who could pose a risk. Lucky considered himself to be more than a companion and a leader for his family, he was a working dog and this required a level of independence if he were to complete his duties properly.

The children in Lucky's family left most days to go to a building where lots of other little people congregated. He knew this because sometimes they required him to escort them safely there and back. Lucky had a routine that mostly made him very happy. When the weather was dry, he walked to school with Carys and Daniel and was dragged back to the house by Jayne. Sometimes he was allowed to wait in the back yard for Carys to return but Lucky had long bored of exploring the three-tiered garden.

He knew every footstep along the dilapidated fence. He could see the difference between the original older panel wood with faded peeling paint and the newer plywood pieces. Lucky had checked out the nooks in the five-foot stone wall separating the top two tiers of the garden. He knew he could detect the shadow of the next door neighbour's dog through the tiny gaps in the woven hazel wattle fencing on the ground level and he knew where the neighbourhood cats were likely to enter into his territory. As fast as Big Black Cat meticulously killed Carys' hamsters, gerbils and fish and Carys meticulously buried them in the soft earth by the fishpond, Lucky meticulously dug them up again. It was an exciting part of his routine that he looked forward to, but it did not happen often enough for him. Lucky was restless.

It took him a while to find out that he had not searched the garden as well as he should have and that the fence was not as impenetrable as he had thought. Lucky realized that he did not need to wait for someone to come and take him to perform his duties. He could take himself. Carys came running into the house from school one day and raced up to her bedroom to get changed while Daniel dawdled in behind her to settle in front of his computer.

'Mum, where's Lucky?' Carys shouted when she ran back downstairs and realised that Lucky had not run to greet her.

'Outside,' Jayne yelled from the next room where she was engaged in negotiations with Daniel about going outside to play instead of staring at his computer screen for the next two hours. Jayne found Carys ten minutes later searching behind the fir trees at the top of the garden.

'Can't find him?'

'No.'

'Well, he's not going to be there.'

'How do you know?' Jayne shrugged and joined in to look for their tiny terrier but in such an open plan garden there were few places to look. She was bewildered because Lucky was easiest to find when he was being called to go for a walk. Their search was interrupted by a high-pitched bark from outside the front door. When Jayne opened it, Lucky raced inside straight to Carys, jumping up on her and tugging on the lead in her hand.

Jayne shrugged, thinking she must have let Lucky out through the front door earlier by mistake and went to resume her previous discussion with Daniel about getting some fresh air. When Carys arrived home from school the following day though, Lucky had gone again. After only ten minutes of calling him he was outside the front door barking to come in. Carys was dismayed that over the next two weeks Lucky was not in the house more days than he was. Lucky on the other hand was particularly pleased with the added addition to his routine.

Every time Lucky escaped from the garden, Evan would scour the fence for holes, gaps or any hint that a terrier could disappear through. Whenever he thought he had found Lucky's latest escape route he would hammer some more plywood onto the fence and saunter into the house confident that he had solved the problem. A few days later and Lucky would be gone again.

'We are going to get a phone call one day, Evan, and you are going to have to deal with it because you were the one who brought him home,' Jayne said to Evan one evening, her hands on her hips and her eyebrows pulled together.

'If he was going to get in trouble he would have done so by now, Jayne,' Evan replied without looking up from his book.

'You can't trust him when he's out on a lead with supervision. I dread to think what he is doing without one. I'm waiting for the phone to go any minute now.'

'I'll answer it if you want, luv,' Evan said as he turned the page and continued reading. He was not really sure why his wife did not want to answer the phone but if it kept her happy he would speak to who ever she was expecting.

'I think you're missing the point.'

'Ok, that's fine, I'll sort it out.' Evan re-read the last line again, having been distracted by his wife. Jayne knew a lost cause when she saw it but she still left the telephone handset on the coffee table next to Evan.

Lucky was not escaping just to go wandering anywhere he was trying to find the place where he left Carys and Daniel every morning. Unfortunately though, although he always headed in the right direction towards the school grounds there was always something that distracted him along the way. He merrily chased cyclists along the roads, finally got to sink his teeth into a few footballs being kicked around on the local pitch and peed on every lamppost he passed.

The day that Lucky found his way to Baglan Primary school it was early afternoon and the concrete playgrounds were deserted so he proceeded unnoticed to explore the school grounds. Mr. Llewellyn was a pleasant and mild mannered headmaster and he could see the strange dog tracking scents around the playground as he sat in his office labouring over paperwork. Stray dogs rarely stayed long in the school but as the afternoon break drew closer he decided it was too risky to allow hundreds of children outside when there was a stray. He could have called the caretaker to get rid of the dog but paperwork was not his favourite past time so the tiny terrier became his excuse to stretch his legs. Mr. Llewellyn strolled out of the building and Lucky was only too pleased to allow the friendly man to read his nametag. Jayne received a telephone call and she arrived at the school fifteen minutes later.

Mr. Llewellyn remained a gentle, mild mannered man for the next twice Lucky turned up at the school. His calm demeanour started to erode after the fourth time of having to chase Lucky around the rugby pitch and he would have gladly stayed in his office doing paperwork but the caretaker was now off on sick and all other members of staff always seemed to be busy whenever the tiny terrier made an appearance. Lucky made the association between the nice, softly spoken man coming into sight and Jayne arriving to collect him so he avoided capture at all costs. Carys and Daniel thought it hilarious to look out the classroom window and see their dog scampering through the playground with Mr. Llewellyn streaking furiously after him.

Jayne became very proficient at apologising to the headmaster and the other teachers and even more adept at moaning to Evan in the evenings of her being called to the school. Her frequent trips to Baglan Primary school also meant that Mr. Llewelyn or any other teacher had ample opportunities to inform her of her children's progress. She was thankful that the extra time she and Evan spent with their children on their homework in the evenings was paying off because they both did very well and more importantly, loved being at school. But there was the occasional time when the feedback was less than exemplary.

'Lucky couldn't have picked a worse day to go to school today,' Jayne complained to Evan one evening. 'The headmaster had great delight in telling me that Daniel volunteered to feed back about his weekend in assembly this morning.' Jayne blushed and shuddered at the memory and her subsequent silence piped Evan's interest.

'Please tell me that he didn't tell them that I can't beat him on the computer yet?'

'I wish. He stood up and first told everyone how he had played hide and seek with his mother and sister from the milkman because mammy had no money,' Jayne paused to allow Evan to recover from a combined fit of giggles and coughing. 'Then in the next breath he told them how he could not paddle in the paddling pool because his mammy and daddy were using it to keep their cans of cider cold.' It took a while for Evan's red face to pale back to his normal healthy complexion.

'I'm surprised that Daniel even noticed let alone remembered. He's always so busy in his own little world that nothing much seems to sink in' Evan said, secretly glad that he was too busy in work to be making regular trips to the school to pick up Lucky.

'You are going to have to have a look at that fence again tomorrow, Evan. That dog is getting out somewhere.'

'Don't worry, Jayne,' Evan smirked. 'I've sussed it. I've got the boys from work bringing me some stuff tomorrow. Lucky won't be going to the school again unless he's in a car or on a lead.'

'What boys are bringing some stuff over Evan?' Jayne's eyebrows narrowed and her eyes half-closed suspiciously.

'Don't worry about that, I'll sort it out, OK?'

'Evan. I'm concerned, what are you going to do with this stuff some boys are bringing over and how are you going to afford it when only a few weeks ago I didn't have enough money to pay for milk delivery?'

'I said don't worry, a few weeks ago is a long time and we've been paid since. I'm going to finish work early tomorrow and sort the problem out once and for all. So take the car tomorrow and pick the kids up from school. Lucky will be here waiting, I guarantee it.'

Jayne closed her eyes and her head sank into her open palms.

'Evan, you do remember that I am a crime prevention coordinator, don't you? So if whatever your planning tomorrow isn't ethical I don't want you doing it.'

'What on earth has ethics got to do with a garden fence?' Evan snorted with laughter. 'You take your job too seriously if you're worried about things like that.'

'Someone has to worry, did you know that the theft from gardens and garages in Port Talbot has gone up by 4% over the past year. The neighbourhood watch committee is besides themselves.'

'I'm telling you that you don't have to worry, it's already taken care of.' Evan jumped up from the sofa, lazily stretched his arms out wide then threw them around his wife shoulders, planting a kiss on her cheek. He was telling the truth because even though he could get what other people could not and for half the price at that, it was perfectly legal. He just enjoyed teasing his serious wife. 'And maybe you should tell the neighbourhood watch committee to do more watching and less talking and then they might lose less of their belongings.' Jayne chuckled and playfully slapped her husband off her but the worry lines on her forehead remained.

Jayne, Carys and Daniel arrived home the following afternoon to find Evan slumped on the sofa watching television.

'Well…' Jayne asked tentatively.

'Well what?' Evan said.

'What have you done?'

'What do you mean?'

'I mean are you going to tell me what you have done in the garden to stop Lucky escaping? In other words, Evan, dare I look at what you have done outside?' Evan looked up at Jayne with innocent, wide eyes and his hands flew to his chest as he mocked a hurt expression.

'Dad, where's Lucky?' Carys asked, peering out the patio doors and into the garden.

'Outside where I left him, he won't get out now.'

Jayne and Carys ventured out into the garden and Jayne groaned when she saw the planks of wood that had been badly nailed onto the existing fence. Evan had got a dozen ten foot by one foot planks of wood from goodness knows where and had obviously spent the afternoon tacking them to the bottom of the wooden fence surrounding the garden. Each plank was a different colour, size and thickness. 'Ummmm, Mum.' Carys said to her mother, careful to make sure she was out of her father's earshot 'I don't think its worked 'coz Lucky has gone again.' Jayne sighed and went to deliver the bad news to Evan. As she did she heard a familiar, high-pitched bark from the front of the house. Lucky had returned for his daily walk.

In the weeks that followed, Jayne became increasingly concerned about Evan's behaviour. He became obsessed with finding out how Lucky was escaping from the garden. It did not matter how many holes or gaps he nailed up in the fence, Lucky would always find another way out a few days later. The original fence became decorated with more plywood planks of wood and even pieces of sheep wire loosely attached to the top of it.

Lucky started to dig holes in the garden which led Evan to believe he was tunnelling his way out. Lucky was only actually trying to find some more dead rodents to toss around but Big Black Cat had not eaten any of late. Soon, paving slabs started to appear on top of the grassed areas next to the fence in an attempt to stop Lucky from digging at all. Evan was adamant that he had re-covered, nailed and strengthened every bit of fence in the garden and Lucky was still getting out.

'I just don't understand it, Evan,' Jayne moaned one afternoon after another disastrous attempt to find the secret escape route. 'I mean we don't ill-treat him, he gets whatever he wants and he does at least seem to be happy here, why is he running away all the time?'

'He's tired of you nagging him all the time.'

'Don't be such a smart arse. Anyway, I have been doing some research that I think might help us.'

'OK, enlighten me.'

'Well, based on the dog books I've been reading I think that Lucky might be a cross between a Cairn Terrier, Jack Russell, Highland Terrier, Border Terrier and a Yorkshire Terrier. They each have different temperament traits and some of them sound like Lucky. For example,' and Jayne opened the book on her lap to one of the numerous pages with the corner folded over and started to read. 'Border Terriers are small, rough coated dogs and are good with children, but that's about where the similarities end because they are also supposed to like to sit, watch and observe their environment and Lucky doesn't stop to observe anything for long.'

Jayne was interrupted when Big Black Cat came streaking into the living room with Lucky in hot pursuit. Both executed two perfect figure eights at the top end of the living room but whereas Big Black Cat managed the tight turns, Lucky spun out and crashed into the small coffee table, tipping it over and throwing to the floor two television remote controls, Jayne's make up bag, a box of tissues and a pile of metal coasters. Lucky picked himself back up, shook his head from side to side before resuming his chase of the black feline and disappearing from sight. Jayne continued as if nothing had happened but felt slightly smug that her theory so far seemed correct.

'Jack Russells are working dogs described as sturdy, tough and tenacious, which he definitely is and his legs are also short like theirs but he's not the right colour and his head is the wrong shape. Westies can be aggressive towards other dogs and snappy with children and he is awful with other dogs but he is good with the kids, unless its occasionally Daniel, well… mostly Daniel, OK, always Daniel but to be fair he does tease the dog a lot.'

'Well, that's positive, getting along with children' Evan said. He felt an overwhelming loyalty to defend the dog that was bringing so much entertainment to his children and him these days.

'The only resemblance between him and a Yorkshire terrier is that he barks and yaps constantly but I think the Cairn terrier is the most promising. He's not the right shape but listen to this,' Jayne held the book aloft so she could read it word for word. 'Cairn terriers are often referred to as a 'big dog trapped in a small dog's body, they will defend their territory with courage and devotion and will stand their ground if they are challenged. They are good with children and are suitable family dogs but are wilful and need comprehensive training.' She slammed the book and eyed Evan sceptically.

'Well that explains a lot' Evan said. 'Big attitude for a little dog. He's not being naughty, he's being loyal, I told you he was protective.'

'I think the key point in here is that he needs comprehensive training' Jayne was trying to be stern. 'You haven't even taught him to give you his paw.'

'How on earth is that going to solve anything?'

'It might make him look good when we have company.'

'I don't think so, Jayne. But good job researching, that's very useful information.' Evan shook his head and the corners of his mouth tugged into a smile. Jayne doubted that anything she had just said was going to make any difference whatsoever but she felt better now she understood some of their little dog's persistent behaviours, although it did not explain why he kept escaping and going for walks by himself.

Lucky was very clear why he had to leave the house on a regular basis so he continued to do so but one Saturday he had been gone longer than was usual for him. Carys went out on her bike to look for him. Her parents had restricted her to staying on the Pentwyn estate so all she could do was ride into each of the cul-de-sacs, calling Lucky as she went. She could not find him and he did not return at all that afternoon. Evan agreed that if he had not come back home by the evening he would take Carys out in the car and cover more ground. Carys decided to have one more ride around the houses on her bike but with no more sign of Lucky she reluctantly and despondently returned home.

He was lying quietly in his basket when Carys rushed past him. Only his eyes followed her as she ran to find her father. Lucky was still, he dared not move.

'Dad, I still can't find him, Can we go out now?'

'He's back, Carys, no need.'

Carys froze to the spot and stared down around her ankles, her puzzled expression was almost comical as she looked around expectantly. Lucky always ran to greet her when he was in the house and she arrived home. Evan tore his attention away from trying to shamelessly beat Daniel on their favourite computer game and his heart sank when he saw Carys' eyebrows creased together and the edges of her lips turned down. He spoke kindly and softly

'He's in his basket in the hall, but I would leave him alone if I were you. I think he's hurt his leg.'

Lucky was glad when Carys came to see him but he was only able to wag the tip of his tail feebly. Carys sank to her knees and playfully ruffled Lucky's head but pain shot through him, just as it had happened earlier. He reacted instinctively and snarled before immediately retreating his head and whining pitifully. He had not meant to do that to his favourite little person, his equal at that. He tried communicating an explanation to Carys through his soulful eyes but she could not understand him. His back left leg was lying awkwardly to one side and looked distinctly out of place. He licked his lips and bowed his head meekly onto his paws as a violent shudder shook him. He was hurt like never before.

'Carys, I said leave him alone.' Evan shouted from the front room. 'If he hasn't improved by tomorrow we'll take him to the vets.'

Lucky did not move from his basket that evening. He was quiet for the longest period of time since his family had known him and despite the peace, the atmosphere in the house was flat without his usual antics.

'I think I'd better take him to the emergency vet later, Jayne,' Evan told her over breakfast.

'It's not just his leg that needs seeing to, by the looks of things,' Jayne snorted, her lips pursed.

'What do you mean?'

'Don't tell me you haven't noticed. Have a good look. The damn dog's got a black eye. He's probably got concussion.'

'Don't be stupid, Jayne' Evan scoffed. 'Dogs can't get black eyes....'

Evan thought otherwise when he studied Lucky later because the tiny terrier's left eye looked abnormal. His eyelids were swollen, pink and puffy and even though Evan knew that the hairs around both his eyes were usually the same colour, the left one definitely looked darker. Lucky did indeed have a black eye.

Evan and Carys drove to the nearby Spar shop to get some bread and milk for Jayne before they took Lucky to the emergency vets. Shortly after they left Jayne heard three loud, decisive, raps on the front door. She greeted two officers in community police uniform. Navy trousers, heavy black boots, black waistcoats with a decorative display of truncheons, shiny silver identification badges and alarms. Lucky saw the two men and wanted to spring out of his basket to warn them away from his territory, protect his third in command, but he could not. He could not do anything but lie there completely still. The best he could do was let out a low warning growl that not even Jayne could hear.

Jayne was speechless as she confronted the law standing outside her house.

'You wouldn't happen to have a small brown dog, would you?' one of the policemen sternly enquired of her. Jayne was immediately tempted to disown Lucky, but knowing she was a bad liar and guessing that the police had already seen him in his basket not far behind her, she reluctantly opted for telling the truth.

'Yes, we do, he's sleeping,' Jayne moved aside and indicated behind her towards Lucky in his basket. 'Is there a problem?'

'We have had a complaint,' answered the same policemen 'that a small brown dog matching the description of the one in the basket behind you, ran into the front of a car yesterday outside the shop.'

The other policeman was unable to completely suppress a smile when recognition dawned and he remembered Jayne from her day job based at the police station. Jayne remained unaware of who he was as she stared at the leading officer with fixated horror.

'The gentleman whose car this dog hit wants to claim from the owner for a broken licence plate and pain and suffering' he continued. Jayne shuddered as a vision of how Lucky had got his damaged leg and black eye flashed before her. The car must have hit him with some force in order to break a license plate.

'All accidents involving dogs' the policeman continued dutifully 'have to be reported and we are investigating.'

Silence.

'Excuse me, Miss. Do you understand what I am saying?' The policeman politely asked Jayne who remained silent as she processed the second part of the information. She took a deep breath and rolled her shoulders back, squaring up to the officer.

'OK. So. Let. Me. Get. This. Straight.' The policeman had no idea how dangerous Jayne could be when she talked like this. 'You. Are. Trying. To. Tell. Me… That some person who was obviously driving like an idiot not to have seen a dog in the middle of the road, knows that he has knocked a dog down, has probably hurt that dog and is more concerned about a license plate that you can get for a fiver at the local car shop?'

'And pain and suffering, Miss.'

'Pain and blinking suffering. He should have been looking where he was going!'

Jayne gripped tightly onto the front door frame and took a deep breath. She was furious because even though Lucky was a complete nuisance and she often wished that Evan and Carys had never brought him home, he belonged to them and his incessant attempts to attack everything and everyone did seem to stem from a natural instinct to want to protect them. Some one had hurt him badly and reported it to the police not out of concern for the welfare of the dog but for their own selfish gain.

'Well… This is a clear case of mistaken identity. There are lots of brown terrier dogs on this estate, and I don't think it can be our dog because he was in all day yesterday.'

'We have to...' the leading policeman started to protest but Jayne continued talking over him in an attempt to stall him further.

'And anyway… he's always on a lead when we take him out so he wouldn't have had the chance to run out in front of a car now, would he?' This was partially true. Lucky was always on a lead when he was actually with someone.

'And he's not hurt either. He's fine,' Jayne finished lamely. She turned to look at Lucky and nearly doubled over as she realised his black eye was getting blacker by the minute.

'Well, he does seem very quiet,' the leading policeman said slowly.

'Yeah, don't worry about it, Jayne,' the other officer said. 'We'll tell the person we don't think it's this dog.'

Jayne's knuckles went white on the doorframe when she recognised the second policeman as someone who saw her in work on a regular basis. Her initial fury turned to embarrassment and she was secretly glad that her cheeks were already flaming red with anger so she could not blush any more. She made a mental note to stay out of the canteen in work for a few weeks in the hope that the officer would forget this incident.

Jayne stuttered a pathetic thank you and then listened impatiently, tapping her foot and bobbing her head while the leading policeman lectured her about always keeping dogs in the garden or on a lead when they are being taken for a walk. Finally, the policemen left the house and Jayne turned to look at Lucky. Lucky half whined, half yelped and wagged only the tip of his tail as if to say

'Well done Jayne, very smooth.'

'Well,' Jayne muttered to herself, 'I should be thankful they were here for the dog and not the children. I must be doing something right.'

The vet's verdict on Lucky was a mixed bag of news. His eye was nothing to worry about but Lucky had torn the ligaments in his left hind leg and needed an operation to repair the damage. The vet assured Carys that Lucky would be fine but he would need to stay in their care until they operated. They would telephone when Lucky was ready to come home. As promised, Evan had a phone call to say they could pick up Lucky on Wednesday. The operation was a success and Lucky was ready to start his rehabilitation.

When Evan and Carys picked Lucky up Wednesday afternoon though Evan noticed some unexpected and rather confusing charges on the bill.

'Excuse me' Evan politely asked the receptionist 'I think you've made a mistake with my bill, can you check it for me?'

'There's no mistake' she said. 'They are vandalism charges.' Evan looked at her as if she had spoken in a different language other than Welsh and English.

'Hang on a minute, I'll get the vet to talk to you,' she said hastily and made a quick phone call to someone in the back room. The vet came out to speak to Evan and explained that Lucky had behaved so well that the staff had decided there was no need to put him in a cage overnight. After all, he had just had an operation on his leg and had not wanted to move from his basket since his arrival. When the cleaner came in the morning she found two shredded newspapers all over the floor. Further investigation revealed a chewed chair-leg.

Since Lucky was the only animal that had been left loose, he had guilt written all over his face. He had dragged himself out of his basket on his three good legs the moment the newspapers had been posted through the door and ripped them to shreds. For good measure, he had chewed as far as he could reach up a wooden chair leg.

Evan left the vet's reeling with indignation over what he felt were trivial charges. Carys bounced out with a smile on her face and Lucky in her arms knowing that her dog was going to make a full recovery. Lucky had reverted to his usual self. He immediately launched himself at the seat belt, chewing through it happily now that he was pain free.

'Lucky, no,' Carys groaned as she attempted to pull him securely onto her lap. 'The vet said you have to rest your leg for a month or it will never heal properly.'

Jayne and Daniel were in the hallway to greet Lucky on his homecoming. Carys carried him into the hallway and Lucky was promptly sick over her and her jumper. It proceeded to dribble down Carys' coat and land on the not so new and faded blue carpet with gentle, irregular thuds.

'Oh look,' Jayne muttered. 'Bloody déjà vu.'

Chapter 5

Framing Lucky

Lucky's homecoming was triumphant. He had so much pent up energy after being forced to lie still during days of unbearable pain that he was unable to contain his excitement at being in his territory again. He did not understand what the vet's instructions were but even if he could, he would have refused to abide by them anyway. He was only allowed out in the garden supervised to ensure that he did not escape but this suited him fine because as long as he had company, he had no inclination to leave.

Evan was still obsessed by finding out how and where Lucky was escaping from so he finished work early one day to execute a cunning plan. He started by laboriously digging up the earth by the fence on the second tier of the garden. When there was a substantial mound of soft loose soil, Lucky threw himself on top of it and rolled around. All he needed now was a couple of dead rodents and he would be in his element. Evan was muttering manically as he dug

'Blinking dog… like to see him get out now… dig all he likes… won't do any good though… can't dig through steel now can he?'

The lower level of the garden had an impenetrable, fourteen-foot high fence and the upper level could only be accessed by climbing a stone wall that had holes through it. A tall person could swing himself or herself up over the wall and onto the sloping grass. Carys and Daniel had to climb up it using the holes as hand and footholds. Evan reasoned that there was no way Lucky could get up onto the third tier of the garden let alone escape from it, so that only left the middle section.

When Evan felt satisfied by his trench he cut several pieces of barbed wire the same length as his hole. He carefully laid a piece of wire at the bottom of the trench and covered it with soil, packing it down hard. He repeated this process until he had re-filled his hole and buried all the barbed wire. As he stamped down hard upon the last of the loose soil the final product was out of sight. Only Evan knew how deep he had created the hidden barbed wire fence. It was a steel extension of the wooden fence only under the ground. He turned to Lucky who stared up at him, head cocked to one side as usual and his ears pricked attentively to the sky, Evan's dirt still clinging to his shaggy coarse coat.

'Right then.' Evan exclaimed triumphantly. 'Get out of that, boyo!'

Evan walked tall and confidently into the house, shutting the back door behind him and locking Lucky out in the garden.

'Ummm... Evan' Jayne asked him, her eyebrows raised. 'Haven't you forgotten the dog?'

'Don't worry, Jayne, I've sussed him now, he will never get out.'

'I've heard that before, I don't think we should take a chance with his leg...'

'Oh come on, I've definitely got him. He's only got three good legs and he's confined in a garden made of steel.'

Jayne shook her head and let the last comment pass unchallenged. She did not know why Evan had come home early to spend it kneeling by the garden fence and she did not want to know. She would go and make sure there was no visible damage later when he was not looking.

Evan was sure that Lucky's vanishing days was over. He led a reluctant Jayne into the living room to spy on Lucky from behind the patio doors. Evan watched keenly and Jayne looked on with bored scepticism, her arms crossed and one eyebrow raised. Lucky had watched Evan disappear into the house and decided there was nothing in the garden of any interest to him so he was going to go for a long awaited tour of his territory. Jayne got bored watching Lucky sniff his way slowly across the garden

'Come on, Evan, I've got tea to cook, can I go?'

'Hang on a minute now,' Evan had his eyes glued to Lucky through the glass. Jayne sighed but continued to wait and watch. As she stared at Lucky it occurred to her that he looked slightly different.

'Does that dog look darker to you, Evan?'

'Of course he isn't.'

Evan startled as Lucky ran on three legs to the other side of the garden and out of their visibility.

'Come on, Jayne, this window now,' Evan shouted in his excitement as he ran from the patio doors that overlooked the east side of the garden to the smaller window looking onto the western part. Lucky was just visible ambling around this area.

'Ha. I've got him.' Evan shouted triumphantly and punched the air. 'I knew that was where he was getting out. I just knew it!'

'Well, that's lovely, luv,' Jayne replied, bored. Evan continued to look proudly out of the window and Jayne turned to leave the living room. She froze when Evan let out a cry of dismay.

'No, I don't believe it.' Jayne ran back to the window and looked past Evan's shoulder. Her jaw dropped open at the sight before her.

Lucky was climbing up onto the third tier of the garden using the holes in the breezeblock wall just as Daniel and Carys did. He quickly scaled the vertical five-foot hike and scrambled onto the sloping grassed area at the top of the garden. Without a moment's hesitation, Lucky ran full speed, still on his three good legs, from one side of the garden to the other. Jayne and Evan nearly tripped over each other as they rushed back to the glass patio doors. They were just in time to see Lucky at only twelve inches high launch himself from great height straight over the wooden fence on the middle tier that Evan had spent all day digging by. He disappeared into their next-door neighbour's garden.

'Right.' Evan shouted. 'That's it' and he marched from the living room, through the dining room and straight out the front door. Without invitation he ran into the next-door neighbours garden just in time to grab Lucky as he was limping his bid for freedom.

'Got you.' Evan shouted as he swung Lucky up into his arms. Lucky looked up at Evan and his tongue lolled out of his mouth. The back door of the neighbour's house opened and a head popped out.

'All right there, Evan?' the neighbour asked politely.

'Yes, thank you.'

'OK... er... Bye then.' The next-door neighbour was too polite to ask what Evan and his dog were doing.

Evan returned to the house, red cheeked and puffing with indignation rather than with the effort it had taken to catch Lucky. He did not put Lucky down until he had shut and locked all the outside doors in the house.

'He can't unlock doors, Evan,' Jayne said as she watched Evan checking the same front door that he had locked only a minute earlier.

'You never know, Jayne. It's just not worth the risk.' he replied smartly.

'Our children are out playing, they might actually want to get back in the house?'

'Get them keys and teach them how to use them.'

Jayne shook her head fearing that her husband was finally losing the plot. She watched as Evan put Lucky in his basket in the corner of the living room.

'Oh my god, Evan, look at the state of him… He must have rolled in the next-door neighbours vegetable patch or something before you caught him. He's stinking.' The colour in Evan's face turned from red to purple as he remembered the heap of dirt he had dug up for nothing. He spluttered a few failed attempts of a curse and then stormed from the room. Jayne approached Lucky and asked

'What have you been doing, you naughty dog?' Lucky met Jayne's gaze and lowered his head onto his paws, whining uneasily. He had been on his way to freedom for the first time in ages and something had gone terribly wrong. He had not only been caught but he was locked up inside the house again. Jayne sighed and decided it was time for an emergency family meeting.

It was actually the first official Davies family meeting that Jayne had called and the majority of it was spent talking about Lucky. Lucky now posed two clear problems. He was on strict instructions from the vet to rest his leg and keep his exercise limited for at least a month. If he had too much exercise there was a good chance his back leg would never heal properly and he would limp for the rest of his life. This was related to the second problem because as Jayne and Evan had witnessed earlier, they could patch up the fence as much as they liked but Lucky was still going to escape. To everyone's dismay a supervision rota was put in place so that someone was always out in the garden with him. The second problem took a little longer to resolve but it was Daniel who came up with a surprise solution.

Everyone agreed they needed a bigger and better garden fence in order to contain Lucky. But the sort of fence needed was expensive and money was tight. Evan was in between muttering about a wasted day of unnecessary labour and inappropriate vet's fees when Daniel perked up.

'We should film him and send it to the funny programme.'

Silence.

Jayne, Evan and Carys turned to stare expectantly at Daniel without any clue of what he was talking about. Daniel was always so engrossed in movies and computer games that he was usually imitating one fictional character or another. Everyone found it difficult to know when he was in touch with reality and when he was not.

'Yeah, when he rips up the newspaper' Daniel continued. 'I bet they would show that on TV and we can get the money.... And then we can go look for some more treasure guarded by the secret demon of the underworld.' Ops. Daniel had reverted back into the world of computer games but not before his idea was understood

'Oh right.'

'Of course, two hundred and fifty pounds.'

'Well done, Daniel' Jayne said. 'It's definitely worth a go.'

'You've Been Framed,' was a relatively new television program at the time showing video clips of people and animals doing daft and unintentionally funny things. Carys and Daniel were always engrossed watching footage of people tripping, animals charging and children falling. At the end of every program there was always an advert asking people to send in their funny home video clips and in return, if the video featured on the program, the senders would receive a cheque for two hundred and fifty pounds.

A simple plan was devised at the most constructive Davies family meeting ever. Jayne would film Lucky going mad and attacking the front door and newspaper and send it off to the television show 'You've Been Framed.' If the clip of Lucky were shown the two hundred and fifty pounds could be spent on a new fence to keep him in the garden.

Daniel spent a lot of his time running around the house setting booby traps and randomly screaming, pretending that his family had left him home alone. Performing was something that came naturally to him whereas it was one thing that his older sister hated, because it drew unnecessary attention to her. Since acting was a niche she had no interest in pursuing, Daniel was becoming engrossed in imaginative roles. He signed up to play the part of himself in Lucky's television debut. His role would be to try and stop Lucky from getting the newspaper. Jayne had a fleeting thought that it was probably unethical to do this to a dog that only had the use of three good legs, but then she thought about that damp smelly patch on her sofa and dismissed her reservations.

The following evening at quarter to five everyone took up his or her agreed positions. Evan was still in work because he thought it was a daft and effortless plan compared to his laborious day burying steel in the garden. Jayne sat on the stairs and pointed the camera towards the front door where Lucky would inevitably run to when the newspaper girl drew closer. Carys hid at the top of the stairs where she had perfect view of the action but was safely out of the camcorder's recording space. Daniel loitered excitedly and restlessly behind the kitchen door, ready to play his part.

Lucky saw the danger approach from his position in the bay window and he started growling menacingly. Jayne quickly switched on the camcorder while Carys stuffed her clenched fists into her mouth to stifle a giggle. Daniel was in the kitchen positioned like an Olympic runner at the start of a race, ready to leap into action. The low growl increased to a snarl then a high, manic and incessant yelp. Lucky jumped off the windowsill and hobbled to the front door. It was a decidedly less dramatic affair with only three good legs but he was pleased when his little people did not challenge him, after all, this was his job. He started to jump up repeatedly at the letterbox, barking non-stop and waiting for the newspaper.

Lucky had long torn off the internal metal flap of the letterbox and was in the process of trying to dislodge the black seal around it when something happened that even he did not expect. Lucky dug his teeth particularly hard into the rubber and became stuck. He hung there, three feet in the air, unable to fall back to the ground but not caring in the least. He continued to growl and yelp, his little body writhing with anger in mid-air. When the newspaper came it smacked him straight in his mouth. That dislodged him and he fell to the ground with the paper. Undeterred, Lucky picked up the newspaper in his mouth and the ripping and tearing started.

Daniel jumped out on cue from behind the kitchen door with one hand on his hip and the other pointing at Lucky. With his slim statue, glasses and his dark blonde hair he looked like the milky bar kid from the television adverts and he spoke deceptively like him.

'Lucky. Give me that newspaper.' He yelled with authority as he ran towards the front door. Lucky paused for one moment, realised he was being pursued so gave the newspaper a particularly rough shake and ran on his three good legs past Daniel, through the hall and out into the garden. Daniel resumed his milky bar kid posture and shouted again

'Lucky, I said give me that newspaper' and then, flailing his arms madly around his head he ran after Lucky into the garden.

Both Daniel and Lucky had done everyone proud and when Evan was shown the footage that night he chuckled not only at Lucky's antics but also Daniel's amateur dramatics. A few weeks later a letter was sent from the 'You've Been Framed' television show to say that they would be showing the clip of Lucky in three weeks time. It was also shown in nearly every introduction to the program of that same series.

Jayne and Evan ended up paying a lot more than two hundred and fifty pounds for a new fence for the middle and top parts of the garden, but the cheque from Lucky's television appearance helped considerably. By the time the high fence was erected in the garden it was the summer school holidays. It had been nearly a year since Lucky had launched an attack on the rottweiler in Margam Country Park. With such nice weather it was a while before Lucky was left alone in the garden again. When he did get out there by himself no one noticed at first so the inevitable happened and when Lucky's family searched the garden for him, Lucky had gone again.

Chapter 6

Paws, Ponies And Problems.

Sometimes one thought, one action, one innocent change will create a course that alters the trajectory of an entire family's future. It may be such a small decision in one person's life that it is taken for granted by everyone, not given any particular scrutiny or consideration of how it could affect the future. But as time progresses that one tiny decision becomes so embedded that it gradually shapes the thoughts and expectations of everyone. Like the persistent waterfall that erodes the rocks it falls on or the gradual growth of trees creating forests out of wasteland, some actions have inevitable consequences that will not be appreciated for years to come. Jayne was about to make an innocent decision that was going to have unfolding consequences for Lucky and all the family for many years.

Lucky continued to escape from the garden a couple of times a week. He rarely stayed out long and always came back in time for a walk with Carys after school. As time went on there were no more policemen knocking on the door and Lucky did not present with any more injuries.

Carys justified Lucky's walks as his time to be alone. Evan justified Lucky's walks as a naughty dog running away all the time, but he gradually stopped with his obsession for finding out how and where he escaped from the garden. Lucky's car accident had left him with more street sense. He always looked left and right before crossing a road.

Unfortunately, the supervisory rotary system organised in the one and only Davies family meeting failed to prevent Lucky from resting his leg enough and the ligaments in his back leg did not heal properly. Lucky was left with a limp. He was quite content to amble around on all four legs, but when he ran he did so mostly on three, his back left leg only touching the floor every couple of strides. Lucky earned several nicknames such as 'the Hobbling Hobo,' 'Hop Along' and 'Legless Lucky.' Undeterred by his hobbling gait, Lucky continued to tour his territory at every opportunity. Jayne was the most devastated by Lucky's limp. She felt it to be a personal failure on her behalf and was further frustrated by Evan's reaction.

'We've really let that dog down, Evan. I mean I know he's a pain sometimes but the kids love him and he is our responsibility. How would you feel if it was one of our children and they had a terminal limp because of something that we had not done?' Evan would then stare at his wife with bewilderment.

'But he's not a child, he's a dog, and it doesn't stop him from running away so it can't be that bad.'

Since Jayne was clearly not going to get any sympathy from Evan over the dog she focused on her children instead. She had recently increased her hours to become a full time crime prevention coordinator at Port Talbot police station and wanted to do something special with the extra money in her pay packet. Daniel wanted to learn the piano just like Carys so he was booked into have weekly lessons. Jayne and Evan were grateful that this was an activity that did not involve a television screen so they were enthusiastic in their support of this. Daniel found he had a natural ear for music and playing the piano came effortlessly. If he had stuck to the sheet music given to him by his teacher he might have passed Carys in the amount of exams he sat, but he much preferred to make his own compositions, absorbed in his own little world.

Carys was unsure what she wanted to do, so Jayne made the momentous decision for her. She took Carys for weekly horse riding lessons and her daughter became completely enthralled and smitten with horses and riding. Every week she bounced happily around on the back of a pony, circling an outdoor arena with views over the vast and wild sand dunes of Swansea beach. Of course, Carys hardly noticed the beautiful scenery because she was far too busy hanging on for dear life as she tried to relax and match her rhythm to the horses stride. She sustained a broken arm within her first two months of riding but the pain and inconvenience of a plaster did not deter her. Carys returned home every Sunday with dark bruises forming on whatever part of her body she had fallen on and her hair grey blonde with dust. But she would be humming to herself and her brother did not irritate her for a while. She was happy and content apart from a small ache in her stomach, which constantly reminded her that she would not feel whole unless she had a pony of her own.

She nagged her parents on a regular basis to buy her a pony. She reasoned that Lucky had been a complete success and therefore it was only natural to progress to a bigger animal.

'Carys,' Jayne sighed as she rolled her eyes. 'This philosophy of getting bigger animals when the ones you've got are a success is completely flawed, because none of your animals have ever been a success. The only ones still alive are the cat and dog and in case you haven't noticed, Lucky has a limp, has been in trouble with the law and regularly escapes to goodness knows where in the country.'

Evan remained quiet during these conversations. There was a plan unfolding in his mind that he had no intention of telling his wife about until it was absolutely necessary. He came home early from work on Carys' twelfth birthday in November. Jayne had the day off to make the necessary preparations for the evening's birthday party and Carys and Daniel had yet to arrive home from school. She was decorating her homemade cake when her husband jaunted in.

'Brilliant news, Jayne.' Evan called to his wife as he tossed his car keys lightly onto the stairs. 'Brilliant news.'

Jayne continued to concentrate on the fondant icing she was carefully cutting to size.

'I've just been given a birthday present for Carys and I know she's going to love it.' Warning bells chimed in

Jayne's head and her head snapped up to stare at her husband with nervous expectation.

'Breathe, Jayne, just keep breathing,' she muttered under her breath and then waited patiently while he proceeded to tell her about the surprise gift.

'For goodness sake, Evan.' Jayne exclaimed to him (Jayne was exclaiming a lot at Evan these days). 'Didn't you think to consult with me before you go and get her a horse?'

'No. It was offered to me, so I said yes.' Jayne groaned in response.

'What about the cost though? The money we will need for hay, food, rent for a stable and field, worming, shoeing, saddles…'

'Your working full time now and I was promoted last year, we're not struggling like we used to and this is not about money, its about Carys and she really wants this.' Evan knew it was a low blow to try and make Jayne feel guilty about her priorities, but it worked.

'Well,' Jayne reluctantly enquired 'what is this horse like…? Do you even know anything about it?'

'Course I do, Jayne. I'm not going to get Carys a horse I don't know about, am I?'

'You are too much of a soft touch with that girl, Evan. My mother was far too sensible to bring me home animals left, right and centre.' Jayne paused and Evan exhaled with relief as he thought he had been let off the hook. That was until Jayne asked

‘Well. What’s this horse like?’

‘Oh… he’s lovely Jayne, a real stunner, saw a picture of him today. Carys will love him. Better than those little ponies she’s been riding at Jersey Marine stables.’ Evan turned to go upstairs when Jayne stopped him abruptly.

‘What do you mean, better than those little ponies. She needs a little pony to start off with, she’s twelve!’

‘Don’t be stupid, she’d much rather have a bigger horse, she won’t outgrow it then will she?’

‘Evan. Exactly how big is this horse?’ Jayne’s voice was getting louder.

‘I don’t know exactly but he’s an ex-racehorse so he’s a fair size.’

‘A racehorse. Evan. Are you mad? You can’t get her a racehorse.’

‘Oh come on, Jayne, stop panicking, he’s supposed to have a lovely temperament. They are practically giving him away because he’s not fast enough to race. We just have to have him castrated, that’s all.’ Evan’s voice was getting higher and he started backing away from his wife. Jayne was approaching him menacingly pointing one perfectly manicured finger directly at his heart.

‘Are. You. Telling. Me. That. You…. Have got her a Stallion?!... Evan! You are bloody mad. You wouldn’t let her get a big dog but you’re quite happy to go and get your twelve-year-old daughter a stallion racehorse. IT’S GOING TO BE A COMPLETE NUTTER, YOU IDIOT.’

Evan attempted to splutter a completely inadequate defence but Jayne proceeded to do what he later described as his wife 'hitting the roof.' He hurriedly retreated from the house assuring Jayne that he would speak to the boys and get Carys something else instead. So it was that Carys ended up with a completely unflappable, small, dapple-grey pony whose only and primary concern was eating. He was most content when he had his head firmly wedged in a bucket of food or when he was left to his own devices, stuffing his face in a field of grass. The fastest Silver ever moved was when Evan and Carys stood at the gate to the field and rattled a bucket on it. As their cries echoed over twenty acres of rolling fields, Silver would gallop at breakneck speed from where ever he had been grazing, stopping so suddenly he would execute a sliding stop into the gate, all to get to his evening meal.

He certainly moved faster to get his food than when Carys was riding him. She spent most of her time perched in the saddle, flapping her legs against his sides as he ambled along biting into whole branches of trees. Carys constantly wished that Silver would go faster but Jayne was satisfied that he was the perfect first pony for her. He was easy to keep, safe to ride and took whatever came his way in his hoofed stride as long as he had a bucket of food at the end of it. Carys sustained another broken arm within a few months but the pony was well looked after. Jayne's only concern was that the staffs in Neath hospital were becoming suspicious about Carys' injuries and it would not be long before she had a visit from children's social services. She knew she should feel angry with Evan for bringing home another animal without discussing it with her first. But while Jayne's priorities were making sure her family were safe, loved and organised, the reason she did not really object was because she revelled in seeing her daughter so happy.

Jayne hoped for a few brief seconds that Daniel might enjoy having a pony in the family and would want to start spending more time outside. So she armed Daniel with a bag of sliced carrots and took him up the stables to greet Silver. Carys eyed her brother suspiciously as Daniel cautiously approached the stable to feed her pony. He had never shown any interest in horses the whole time Carys had been going for riding lessons and she could not understand why he conveniently wanted to develop one now.

Carys was sulking about this enough that Jayne told her to muck out the stable while she gave Daniel a ride on Silver. She was shovelling wet and rotten straw when Daniel's wail cut through her silent fuming. Jayne had confidently pushed Daniel up onto Silver and he had flown straight over his back, landing with a thud on the stony, hard ground the other side. Silver stood quietly as Jayne picked Daniel up and comforted him. Carys sniggered as she peered out from the stable. Daniel did get bunked up onto the quiet pony but the damage had been done. That was the first and the last time that Daniel ever got onto one of Carys' horses and that suited her just fine. Jayne accepted that computers, television and the piano would continue to be the main focus of Daniel's life and Carys was satisfied that her pony would remain just that, hers.

From the day that Carys' pony arrived, Lucky's world opened up before him as he never thought possible. Until this time, Lucky had been confined to the three-bedroom house of his residence, the family Ford Escort car without any seatbelts, the circular Pentwyn estate and the occasional day out to somewhere new and exciting. Now Lucky realised that there was so much more to life and he made short work of extending his territory.

Evan found a collection of old wooden stables that looked as if they had been tacked together by Bill and Ben the Flowerpot Men. They were a mile drive directly up the steep suburban hill in Baglan and another mile along an isolated, snaking mountain road that wound to the top and dropped straight over the other side of the Dinas Mountain. The stables were at the summit of the mountain and were completely surrounded by vast green fields and heather covered hills with far-reaching views of the long sandy stretch of Aberavon beach and the graceful curve of Swansea bay. There were ten stables, a couple of dented lockable metal sheds used for storing saddles and horse feed and an extremely large manure pile at the front of the yard.

Lucky was very careful to go unnoticed when he found somewhere new by the pot holed stable yard or the steep, ragwort filled fields. He rolled in as much freshly fallen horse manure as he could because that seemed to be the strongest smell to disguise him. Jayne gave him new nicknames such as 'Mucky Lucky', and 'Lucky Lips Shit face' and much to Lucky's disgust she stocked up on strawberry scented shampoo. Lucky put having a bath high on his 'danger to self' list. Jayne had to force him to stay in the muddy water by the scruff of his neck while she vigorously lathered shampoo into his coarse terrier coat, washing away the dreg smells of the Welsh countryside. But this did not deter Lucky from his excitement of going up the stables with Carys.

Lucky thought of the land surrounding the stables as his and therefore his right to act as he saw fit. He was exploring the fields at the top of the mountain when he came across a herd of dog-like creatures, but they didn't smell like dogs and they did not act like dogs. They had thick, white woollen fur instead of coarse hair like him and they each looked very much the same. Lucky immediately crouched low to the ground (even lower than he usually was) and crept around the hundred funny looking white dogs. When he got close, one animal turned around and stared at him but to Lucky's surprise he did not bark, yelp, yip, growl or whine. Instead, first one and then all of the sheep bleated so loudly it echoed down the mountain.

Lucky sprang into action. No animal was going to make this amount of noise on his territory so he chased the strange animals down the mountain. The sheep were used to being herded, albeit by larger, usually black and white dogs, but they knew what they had to do. One hundred white sheep galloped through field after field, down the side of the mountain with a tiny, brown, scruffy terrier yapping at their heels.

Carys and Evan were standing outside Silver's stables when the green fields turned white.

'What in the…' Evan started.

'It's just sheep, Dad.'

'Yes but I've never seen them move so fast.' Evan realised too late that it was Lucky herding them across the mountain.

It was Lucky's brief occupation as a renegade shepherd that made Carys and Evan decide to capitalise on his love for running and his seemingly boundless energy.

'Thing is, Carys. We can't let him chase the sheep like that again, the farmers will shoot him around here.' Evan reasoned that if they managed to tire Lucky going up to the stables and before he got back home he was less likely to chase sheep or go wandering by himself at night. It was about a mile from the start of the curving mountain road until the shabby stable yard. As soon as Evan turned off the main road and officially onto the mountain, he would stop the car, Carys would open the front door allowing Lucky out and Evan would stomp on the accelerator. Carys would hang out the side window calling to Lucky to chase them, which he did with gusto. They repeated the process on the way back home, stopping to collect him just before they emerged back under the streetlights of Baglan.

Lucky knew why he had to chase the car, this was obviously dangerous land and he was needed outside to protect his pack from any incoming hazards. He whined with adrenalin fuelled anticipation as they approached the mountain road and later, when Evan and Carys prepared to leave the stables. Often, Lucky ran to get a head start. His little legs became such a blur as he whizzed along the road that it was impossible to know if he was running on three legs or four.

Sometimes though, Lucky's exercise regime did not go to plan. If he crossed a compelling scent he had to investigate it and Carys would watch through the windows in dismay as Lucky's nose hit the floor and he veered sharply off course by diving through the thick spiky bushes and into the nearby fields. Carys and Evan would then have to stop the car in one of the few places where the narrow mountain road widened just enough for two cars to squeeze slowly past each other, get out and look for him. Carys often found herself running through fields, trying to spy a flash of coarse, brown hair bounding through the grass. If owning a dog had increased Carys' need for physical exercise it was nothing compared to owning a horse. Carys was pleased to discover that one of the side effects of meeting the needs of a pony on a daily basis and running after Lucky in the fields meant she was slimmer and fitter than the little girl who had struggled to keep up with Lucky after his arrival from the dog's home. This still did not mean that she appreciated chasing Lucky at sunset though.

Mostly, Lucky came back quickly having lost the scent trail he had started to follow. But sometimes the sun would be setting behind the Swansea coastline horizon, the jagged outline of the distant lighthouse perfectly illuminated in the gentle red glow while Lucky ran riot. Sometimes, Jayne would greet Evan and Carys with stony silence as she reheated their dinners, which had long gone cold, whilst they had searched for their dog.

In the two years that followed Silver's arrival, Lucky continued to run away to explore and mark his territory, accompany Carys up the stables and of course, protect his family from the daily dangers in their life. Silver, to Carys' increasing despair, remained the calm, safe and slow pony that Jayne wanted for her daughter. Jayne and Evan found that a good family routine required commitments not only to children, school and work but also two very demanding animals. Jayne often thought that if anyone were to take a snapshot of her family it would show committed parents with respectable jobs and reasonable incomes, providing as best they can for their children. A son who never gave her or Evan a minute's worry, never tempted by the frivolous and impish behaviour of the other boys on the estate and preferring to do his homework and compose upbeat, albeit unusual, tunes on the piano. A daughter who got good grades in school with minimum effort and delighted in the enjoyment that her pony and dog provided her. Jayne tried not to think too hard about what people thought of Lucky.

But a snapshot picture of a family would only reveal what a distant friend might observe from afar. As Carys reached her teenage years her commitment to her pony did not sway but her irritation with Daniel grew. She tired of his constant imitations of movie stars and the way he bounded tirelessly around the house. Daniel found it mildly amusing to capitalise on his new found ways of annoying his sister and continued with his childish behaviour in front of her. Carys and Daniel were less likely to be found playing together and more likely to be arguing or throwing household items around. Evan tired of shouting at them and Jayne's apparently never ending patience was tested to the limit.

Lucky's constant running away was also causing serious dissent between the two adults in the house. Jayne was still taking the fact that Lucky had a permanent limp personally and she worried that his lonesome walking would make him worse still. Evan remained baffled by this attitude, but to try and keep his wife happy he would take Lucky out of the house on a long walk somewhere. The fact that Lucky spent just as much time in the car chewing seatbelts while Evan had a quick pint in a pub only infuriated Jayne more.

The demands of keeping a pony on top of a mountain were also increasingly difficult. Evan was working longer hours as his responsibility in his job increased and so he was not able to drive Carys to look after her four-legged friend as often. Jayne struggled to do this on top of working full time and running a family home. Daniel whined constantly if he was dragged up to see Silver because Jayne could not leave him home alone and this enraged Carys as she had less quality time to spend with her pony. Carys and Daniel's grandparents were always there to help when they could but despite this, the threads that had previously wound together to form a stable family unit were being unpicked, snipped and cut away.

Carys stayed up late, tossing and turning in her bed and poking her fingers in her ears to try and drown out the muted yet seemingly heated conversations that Jayne and Evan were having at night. Daniel immersed himself further into the world of computing rather than reality and Jayne and Evan worried that one day he would wake up a robot rather than a little boy. Jayne's head was falling into her hands more than was usual and Evan yelled more than he spoke. Electric emotions poked, prodded and invaded their once comfortable sanctuary and the atmosphere teetered dangerously between frustration, anger and despair.

Lucky did not remain oblivious to the emotional turbulence of his pack and he was baffled by the growing apathy in his loved ones. He overcompensated in the only way that he knew how. If his terrible terrier antics had occurred on a regular basis before, they now reached epidemic proportions. He pursued Big Black Cat with the intensity of a swarm of bees to honey despite being beaten off every time by heavy paws with curled claws. He followed Jayne's scent around the house until he found her hairbrushes, chewing them into lumps of dangerously sharp plastic. He played tug of war with Daniel when he was wearing his dressing gown, launching himself onto the towelling cord tied around his waist and often exposing Daniel's boyhood in the process. He chased and chewed balls and plastic toys, caught most of the fish in the pond and deposited them in various places around the garden and barked at the slightest sound outside the house. When someone laughed and broke the growing tension he shook with excitement and relief and spent the next fifteen minutes chasing his tail and Big Black Cat.

His antics provided a brief release from the pressures on his family but the situation culminated the day that Carys and Evan found out that the stables where she kept Silver had been built and rented out illegally. The pony was actually living on land that belonged to the Welsh Water Board. Staff there had been complaining for seven years that the large heap of horse manure so close to a vitally managed spring source was a health and safety hazard. Then the same staff, no doubt with some considerable embarrassment, realised that the land belonged to them. They quickly initiated legal action to throw every person and horse off the land so they could bulldoze the stables to the ground.

Silver was officially declared homeless in January 1995 and there were no other suitable stables in such close proximity. Jayne and Evan were faced with travelling distances of up to an hour to get Carys backwards and forwards to visit her pony. The quiet grey pony's eviction became the catalyst for the destruction of an already shaky family life. It was a hard blow and no one in the family could find a suitable resolution. It left them only with Jayne's despair, Evan's irritation, Carys' concern, Daniel's self-induced isolation and a little scruffy terrier dog that was still escaping to goodness knows where in the country.

Chapter 7
Lucky Move

It was David's brother's wife who had a friend who knew someone that had mentioned to Charlotte the other week that her cousin, second once removed, had heard in the pub from Brian that there was a house for sale with stables, a swimming pool and a pony paddock. Lucky was taking his usual defensive position in the car and Evan was conveniently talking to the landlord of the pub when he overheard this conversation.

Evan was determined that he did not want Carys to take Silver to live on a farm in the village of Cwmafan. It was a long drive there and back and something that Evan did not want to commit to. Neither he nor Jayne had ever considered selling Silver because of their difficulties. As much as they disagreed with each other on many things they were both clear that once they made a commitment to their children they did not deviate. This was the reason they doggedly persisted with Lucky's antics. Many of Evan's friends commented that he should just get rid of the dog that always embarrassed them in public, but he always replied that it was not about the dog. It was about his kids and if having the dog made them happy then so be it. The same logic therefore applied to the pony and Evan, although he would not admit this to his friends, was so attached to Lucky that he could not bear to part with him either.

It had not occurred to Evan until this moment that there was another solution to their problems. If Silver could be kept in a pony paddock behind the house he would not have to transport Carys to see him at all. Evan left the pub convinced that his wife was wrong about the best ideas happening while having a pint…

A week later, Jayne, Evan, Carys and Daniel were visiting a house for sale. It was hidden at the top of a mountain lane and was only one of four houses in the vicinity. It was out of sight from the bustling main road but close enough that it was only a fifteen-minute drive into Port Talbot town centre. There was an added bonus of there being a small circular swimming pool, which Evan was thrilled about because none of his friends had the ability to swim in their back garden. It was actually too small to swim in properly but it was certainly bigger than the plastic fishpond, long devoid of fish, that Carys and Daniel were using through the summer months.

The house itself was smaller than Jayne would have liked, but it possessed an appealing rustic charm. The brilliant white walls contrasted with, yet complemented the dark wooden beams that lined the living and dining room ceiling. The ceilings were low and no two beams were the same, each with their own unique crevices and marks. Rich mahogany window frames were set deep into grey slate stonewalls that were two foot thick in width. The kitchen at the back of the house was a modern extension but it had been kept in tradition with the rest of the house with dark wooden beams running along an otherwise white ceiling. But the large windows on three sides of the structure made it a light and airy room with views over the whole garden. The six stables and acre paddock convincingly solved the problem of Silver's imminent eviction and the swimming pool was an added bonus for everyone.

It was going to be a straightforward part exchange deal between Jayne, Evan and the owner of their future home with no onward chain or estate agent involvement. Jayne and Evan estimated that it should take about two months and Silver had to be out of his stables by the first week of March. If everything went to plan then Silver could leave his current home and go straight to his new one.

Evan remained confident that everything would work out in timescales while Jayne hovered around the telephone and front door at key times of the day, waiting for a crucial phone call or letter from solicitors or mortgage advisors. Carys got into the habit of biting her nails whenever she thought of moving house and whether it would happen in time for Silver's eviction date. When she talked to her father about her concerns he dismissed her worries with a carefree 'It will sort itself out.'

It was a week before the first of March when Jayne and Evan received a telephone call to say that there was a minor problem with the boundaries of the land on the paperwork. They were not going to be able to move for at least another month and Silver was shortly to be made homeless and he had nowhere to go.

'You know, this would not have been such a big deal if you had just listened to me and found somewhere else for that pony, Evan.' Jayne moaned at him shortly after receiving the bad news about the house.

'Oh, come on, mun, Jayne. There was no point in worrying about something going wrong till it happened, was it? These things just usually sort themselves out.'

'No Evan, these things are sorted out by people like me while you just cross your fingers and hope. Now, I suggest you start looking for somewhere to put that poor homeless pony. I am not having him in our back garden for goodness knows how many weeks until we move.'

Silence.

'Are you going to deal with this then, Evan, or am I going to have to drive around the countryside looking for somewhere?'

'Actually, Jayne…' Evan's face brightened and he smiled a slow smile, a mischievous glint twinkling in his eye. 'I think I know somewhere, I just need to do a few things first.' Evan turned on his heels and left the house with Jayne shouting after him

'Just try and find somewhere legal this time, eh?'

Jayne was impressed when she looked out of the front window an hour later to see Evan clearing out the garage. She smiled to herself, satisfied that it was actually worth the time and effort of nagging her husband for months on end when she wanted something done. Jayne was less than impressed when a week later Evan and Carys turned up with Silver and a car full of his belongings with the intention of converting the garage into a stable.

'Evan, for goodness sake,' Jayne hissed quietly at him so Carys could not hear her. 'You cannot put a pony in a garage. Are you mad? We'll have the RSPCA around here.'

'Don't worry Jayne, it will be fine. We're moving soon anyway, it won't be for long.' Evan dismissed his wife's concerns and pointedly ended the conversation by calling Carys into earshot. 'Put him in his new home, Carys, see how he likes it.'

Jayne shuddered and she snuck quick glances over her shoulder to see if any of the neighbours were watching. She had been living in fear of social services coming to see her due to the number of broken arms Carys kept sustaining and now she was certain she would have to deal with animal welfare. Silver at least was undeterred as Carys rode him into the garage, ducking her head under the aluminium door, before dismounting inside and introducing Silver to his new home. There was a hay-net, a water bucket and a bale of straw shaken loosely out onto the floor and that was all Silver needed to fulfil his basic needs. It may not have been the most natural place for a pony to live but it was better than nothing.

Lucky was also unfazed by the new arrival in the garage. He was more concerned that he was not allowed to go in the car every day onto the mountains to continue with his explorations. Lucky had a new routine instead.

Every morning he would go to the garage with Carys who saddled Silver up and took him for a ride before school. Lucky would follow them once around the estate before they returned to the garage where Silver would be stabled for the day. Carys went to school and Lucky was locked in the house. The three of them went for the same walk in the evening and then Silver had a few hours in the back garden to munch on the grass while Lucky was left mooching around him. Evan was relieved that he did not need to use the lawn mower for a while and all the neighbours got as much fertiliser for their gardens as they wanted.

Lucky had no interest in leaving the garden while he had people or his four legged companion to protect. This did not escape Jayne's notice.

'Have you noticed, Evan, that the dog never leaves when Silver is in the garden?'

'Should have got a pony in the garden years ago then, shouldn't we?'

Of course, having a pony in the back garden was not without incident. Lucky was playing with Carys in her bedroom while Silver was having his hour in the back garden. It was peaceful until Jayne started screaming.

'Evan. Carys. Come and get this ruddy horse out of my kitchen.' Carys and Evan got there the same time to find Silver standing all four hoofs in the kitchen crunching on a stolen piece of toast, which was quickly disappearing in his long, strong jaws. Lucky ran to lick up the falling crumbs. Jayne was standing behind Silver, having followed him into the kitchen from the garden.

She was flapping her hands in despair around her head, too speechless to make any further complaint.

The kitchen was too narrow for Silver to be turned around and he refused to walk out backwards. Jayne was not impressed when Carys proceeded to lead him out of the kitchen into the carpeted hallway, straight out the front door and back to his garage. Evan thought it was probably a good job he had not got Carys that racehorse after all, or they may not have got him out of the house.

When the first week of April arrived there was still no sign of the correct paperwork for the new house so Jayne started talking, then shouting, to solicitors on a daily basis. She was assured that the correct paperwork would be sent to her imminently. All she and Evan had to do was sign and return it and they could move the following week.

When Jayne came home from work on the Tuesday, there was no letter from her solicitor. When Evan left work early on Wednesday and expectantly hurried through the front door, there was still no paperwork. By Thursday, Jayne was phoning not only the solicitors but also the post office and their head office. The solicitors were adamant that they had sent the paperwork in the post on Monday and staff from the post office were unsure whether they had it or not. Worse still, Jayne and Evan had received a message to say that if they did not return the paperwork by Friday that week, the deal was off and they would not be able to move house at all.

Jayne was drinking copious amounts of strong black coffee and Evan was stomping as well as yelling around the house. Both were under immense pressure, waiting for something that they should have received three days ago and helpless to act until they did. Jayne was hyperactive from worry and caffeine so she stayed home from work on Friday to hassle the solicitors.

She drained her fifth cup of strong percolated coffee that morning and dismissed a horrible vision of living in the same house with a pony in the garage for the next few years. She was debating whether to drive to the solicitors and demand a copy of the contract when Lucky flew past her towards the front door. For once, Jayne did not scold Lucky for trying to attack the letterbox because it signalled the postman walking up the garden path.

'Lucky…' she shouted as she ran to the front door 'Lucky come here.' Jayne grabbed Lucky by the collar and held him back as she opened the door and confronted a wary looking postman.

'Jayne,' the postman greeted her.

'Oh hi, sorry about this,' she apologised as Lucky struggled against her grip, growling ferociously with his eyes fixated on the letter in the postman's hand.

'I've tried to post this twice already this week, Jayne. Tuesday and Wednesday in fact. But your dog was attacking the letterbox and I was afraid he would rip it up. It says important on it.' The postman indicated to the large red 'IMPORTANT' stamp on the front of the brown envelope.

'Yes, thank you, it is important… Lucky. BE QUIET' Jayne shouted but Lucky continued to struggle. She gratefully took the letter from the postman and shut the front door, holding the letter out of Lucky's reach. She pulled out the contract she had been waiting to receive since the beginning of the week.

'You naughty boy.' Jayne told Lucky 'You nearly stopped us from moving house.' The blood drained from Jayne's face when she read the contract where on the first page it stated, in bold italics, that the deadline for returning it was two o' clock that afternoon. She looked at her watch and nearly swallowed her heart as it jumped into her mouth. She sprang into action, grabbed her car keys and bolted from the house clutching the contract in her hand.

For the first time in Jayne's life she deliberately exceeded the speed limit to get to the centre where Evan worked. Her husband was called to reception on the tannoy system to sign the paperwork and Jayne was at the solicitors with an hour to spare. All the way she cursed freely about 'that damn dog.'

The family finally moved to their new home in Tyddyn at the end of April. Evan, the only fluent Welsh speaker in the family, translated the Welsh street name as a small-holding. This was a very appropriate name because while Jayne and Evan packed up the contents of the house into the back of the lorry, Carys rode Silver to his new stables and paddock. Daniel sat quietly in the back of the car gripping the hamster cage on his lap tightly while Lucky and Big Black Cat sat either side of him with their eyes glued to the petrified rodent.

On arrival, the whole family took Lucky and went on a tour of their new home. Jayne and Evan were standing at the far side and highest part of their land outside three wooden stables in an L shape, painted in a rich red and with light grey slate roofs. Carys and Daniel were exploring a long block of three stone grey breezeblock stables and tack-room, with doors and a roof that had been painted in the same rich red as the wooden stables. Lucky was digging deeply in dark, soft soil outside a small livestock shed more suitable for a goat or very small pony. Silver was below in the pony paddock barely having moved from the gate, munching on thick green grass. The stable yard was higher up the mountain than their new house and the pony paddock and Evan and Jayne were really able to appreciate their new home, land and view.

The wide Afan Valley river gracefully carved through the bottom of the ice-cut valley, surrounded by a rich green wood. On the opposite side of the river from their house were the slate grey roofs of the houses in the built up village of Velindre. To the left the village of Cwmafan was just visible and in the distance it was just possible to see the start of Port Talbot town centre and the M4 motorway. Behind the stables the Dinas mountain was steep, mostly covered in moss and bracken but also scattered patches of tall, impenetrable shrubs and trees. Despite the rush of activity they knew was happening on the main road below, it was silent, a hidden crevice in the mountain where they could see out but no one could see in.

'Beautiful. Absolutely beautiful. Isn't it Jayne?'

'Yep. Couldn't have asked for a nicer spot.'

'Perfect view of the mountains'

'And so quiet up here.'

'Yet only five minutes from town.'

'Beautiful. Absolutely Beautiful.'

'Lucky… Oi. Lucky come back…' Evan shouted when he saw Lucky slink under the five bar gate leading out of the stable yard and onto the mountain road behind. Lucky had given up digging and wanted to explore further afield.

'Oh no.' Jayne sighed. 'I've just had a terrible thought.'

'What?' Evan asked as he started to walk after Lucky

'How on earth are we going to keep that dog contained in this place?'

Evan turned to look at Jayne and his eyes glazed over and his mouth fell open. He refocused and followed the sheep wire and post and rail fencing around the acre of land they now owned. His horrified eyes met Jayne's. There was no way they could ever contain Lucky in his new home. If he could escape from a garden with a brand new fence around it then leaving the boundaries of their new home would be dog's play.

'Its going to take a lot of 'You've Been Framed' television appearances to put a fence up here.'

'Carys. Daniel.' Jayne called to her children. Both Carys and Daniel stopped when they heard the panic hitch in their mother's throat. 'Now, listen to me carefully. We are not going to be able to put a fence up around this whole place, which means that you have to make sure that Lucky is with you all the time, OK?'

‘OK, Mam.’ Carys said agreeably and Daniel nodded his head.

‘Where’s Lucky now?’ Daniel asked. Evan ran and opened the five-bar gate leading out of the stable yard, only to find that Lucky had gone.

‘Well, that’s just great,’ he shouted. ‘One hour in a new home and the dog has gone already.’

Jayne sighed and Carys left the stable yard to find an overgrown mountain path leading even further away from civilisation. She found Lucky a short way up the track. He was far too engrossed in this new and exciting place to have gone far.

The whole family was on red alert to Lucky running away but their initial fears seemed unfounded. Life at Tyddyn evolved naturally for Lucky and his family. Jayne found the house harder to maintain than the previous one. Dust gathered in abundance around the wooden beams and the thickset window frames and Jayne was constantly cleaning away spiders and their webs. The thick green carpet in the living room clung to every dog and cat hair that fell onto it and Lucky and Carys were forever traipsing dirt from the stables into the kitchen and beyond. Lucky found there was more need to defend Jayne from the vacuum cleaner as she tried to keep on top of the cleaning.

There were also lots of little do-it-yourself jobs that needed to be done. The window latches all needed oiling and the door leading into the small porch at the front of the house creaked when it was opened and moaned when it was shut. There was a downstairs toilet at the back of the house by the kitchen but it was the only part of the house where the walls had not been painted with brilliant white paint. The outside back door had an upper and lower part. While the stable door was very fitting with the theme of horses and stables, the paint was peeling and the bolts cumbersome. Jayne enlisted the support of her father, Pete to undertake most of the carpentry jobs and her mother, Penelope, took charge of painting and decorating.

Evan filled and treated the swimming pool ready for the summer months and for the first time since his obsessive attempts to mend the fence in their old house in order to stop Lucky escaping, he enjoyed his chores in the garden. Jayne could not help but smile when she saw Evan mowing the lawn with Lucky in hot pursuit. Carys rarely left the stables and pony paddock during daylight hours. While her bedroom floor was littered with her clothes and belongings the stables were immaculate, constantly swept and disinfected. Daniel persuaded his parents to buy him a new computer and television for his own bedroom. This meant that he spent even more of his time hidden away. Carys sometimes forgot she had a brother until he emerged for a rare evening downstairs.

The tensions of the earlier months were forgotten but the move to the new home was accompanied by a distinct change in family dynamics. They were still a family with a mischievous dog and a placid pony but their house at Tyddyn offered each of them the freedom to follow their own individual interests. Daniel could be found in his bedroom with his computers or downstairs practising on the piano. Carys outside with her pony, Evan monitoring the chlorine levels in the swimming pool and pottering in the garden and Jayne making their new house into a home. Four distinct (human) personalities living as a family all united by love and loyalty but simultaneously ever divided by their independence.

Lucky was forced to shuffle his priorities.

Chapter 8

Homesick

Lucky was not initially pleased about moving house because he had only just got to know his previous home and territory and now he had a new one to learn to defend. Still, as he spent more time sniffing around the house, garden, paddocks and stables, rolling in anything that smelt, looked or tasted like animal excrement and chewing on as much horse dung as it was possible to digest, he begrudgingly accepted that this territory had more to offer than the previous one.

Carys was trying to combat an established mice population up the stables. Lucky, despite his terrier breeding and natural instinct to kill many, many things had no interest in chasing and killing the resident rodents. Evan and Carys had another trip over to the cats and dogs' home, this time to collect a little tortoiseshell cat. Together with Big Black Cat they slowly picked off the furry pests. Carys could never understand why Big Black Cat insisted on biting her hamsters' heads off and tearing them apart and yet left the wild mice completely intact, albeit dead, for her to find in the mornings.

Lucky found that going for a walk at the end of a lead ceased in favour of free running with Carys and her strange four legged animal. The overgrown mountain path at the back of the stables snaked steadily to the top of the Dinas mountain. Carys was riding Silver up this steep path a few weeks after they had moved to Tyddyn only to hear the bushes rustling behind as Lucky trotted happily after them. She stopped Silver, turned in the saddle and called to her dog

'Lucky, mun. Go back Lucky,' she shouted and pointed back down the mountain path but there was no way that Lucky was going to listen to her. He was going to follow them no matter how much she shouted. He eyed Carys keenly and wagged his tail wildly, lowering his head slightly as if asking for permission.

'Oh all right, you can come, but stay away from Silver's back legs,' Lucky yelped as if in acknowledgement and disappeared into the bushes only to emerge ten feet in front of Silver. He led the way to the top of the mountain, sometimes on three legs and sometimes on four.

Lucky continued to trot ahead of Silver until the snaking path joined the main track that led around the top of the Dinas Mountain. Carys took a deep breath as they reached the summit. The vast view was stunning on most days, but on this particular day the early summer sun beamed down over the town of Port Talbot. The tide on Aberavon beach was far out past the manmade stone piers and the heat waves caused the golden sand and those walking along it to shimmer. To the west, the River Neath funnelled its way through sinking sand and grass-tufted dunes before immersing with the salty seawater. Swansea Bay elegantly curved around and out to sea, the white sails of boats dotted as far out as the distant shores of Exmoor, England.

The M4 motorway twisted its way over the central town area on a concrete viaduct supported by hundreds of steel, stone covered towers. The Steelwork site dominated the village of Margam in the east, claiming kilometres along the coastal plain. Tall and narrow circular towers and blackened blast furnaces projected thick white steam and blue grey smoke that swirled together to hover menacingly in the atmosphere. Only the green Margam mountain rose higher than the smoking industry. A close encounter of the natural world and man made manufacturing both competing for coverage of the ground and skies. As Carys turned right and headed anti-clockwise around the Dinas it was a different view again. The village of Cwmafan nestled in a valley of soft green hills and dark, thick, forested mountains that extend north, deep into Afan Argoed Country Park. The powerful flow of the River Afan cascaded over weirs and waterfalls as it cut gracefully in a southwesterly direction through the rows of houses on one side and green belt land on the other.

In the distance, Carys could clearly see the top of the Foel mountain where she knew stood one of the many trig points, marking it as one of the highest points in the surrounding area. Brightly coloured paragliders soared around on thermal air pockets invisible to the naked eye.

As the three travelling companions ambled further around, Carys could stare down directly into the village of Baglan and pick out the house from which she had recently moved. Then, as the Dinas path turned to run parallel to the M4 motorway, Carys counted the number of blue swimming pools in the large back gardens of the Victorian houses along Baglan road. Further in the distance, tiny cars drove around the network of streets in the coastal districts of Sandfields and Aberavon.

By the time Carys had ridden around the Dinas Mountain and rejoined the path to take them back to Tyddyn, she once more had views of Port Talbot town centre and the Steelworks. As they descended on the narrow path back home, she noticed for the first time that there was a coarse metal footpath bridge running over a waterfall in the River Afan. Children were throwing themselves off the bridge and into a large, slow but deep river pool, their laughter echoing off the steep mountain incline. Carys smiled to herself wistfully, wishing that she were brave enough to do something as reckless as the children she was watching but knowing that all she would ever do was climb down the mud banks into the river for a swim.

Carys' musings were interrupted when she saw a hiker and a black and white sheep dog walking towards her and Silver. They had pulled over to one side of the path and were patiently waiting for her to pass. Carys desperately called to Lucky to come close to her and for a moment she considered dismounting to grab hold of him. She held her breath in anticipation of hearing the familiar growl start in

Lucky's belly, warning that he was going to attack the bigger dog.

But Lucky was less concerned about the bigger dog because he was on a far more important mission. He had to lead Carys and her strange, long legged, grey animal back home. Carys gasped as visions of Lucky attacking small dogs, medium dogs, large dogs or any dogs flashed before her. To her complete surprise though, Lucky barely paid the dog and his owner any attention as he hobbled past them in the direction of his new home. In the weeks that followed, Lucky passed dogs, cyclists, two people walking and also a large black Labrador without showing any indication of wanting to attack them. If he had been on a lead walking around the streets, the sight of any of these would have been enough to send him into frenzy, but as long as he was with a horse, free to do as he pleased, he would completely ignore anything that prior to moving to Tyddyn had been on his danger list. Of course, he never did see the newspaper girl up the mountains.

Lucky was always eager to go out and expand on his territory with Carys and Silver. He waited patiently by the tack room, watching to see if Carys collected a saddle and when she did he chased his tail in excitement until they were ready to leave. Lucky did not have any problems keeping up with Silver despite his small size. When Silver was walking (or rather dawdling), Lucky trotted out in front of him, sneaking the occasional look behind him to make sure that Silver was still keeping up. When Carys urged Silver into a rhythmic trot Lucky would fall in alongside, his head low as he ran to keep up with his larger, grey companion. If Silver was kicked into a reluctant canter Lucky would jump into action, his little legs going so fast they became a blur in his frantic attempt to keep up. It did not matter how fast Silver went, Lucky was never far behind.

Lucky stayed close to Carys and her pony as they trotted around the mountains. It was vital that he stay close to his pack while he was still exploring the lay of the land. Before long though he came to know all the paths on the Dinas Mountain, the large stony tracks and the tiny rat sized runs through the heather and moss. He knew when Carys was likely to gallop away on her pony and he learned where she usually slowed Silver to a halt. When Lucky was left behind, he just disappeared into the undergrowth and re-emerged a short while later wherever his larger, four-legged friend would be.

When Lucky was confident that Carys would be safe to continue on their usual route alone, he decided to do some exploring. He took a short cut down the mountain and found himself on Baglan road so trotted off to check on his original territory. Carys meanwhile was waiting for Lucky up the Dinas mountain with her friends on their ponies. They waited for fifteen minutes for Lucky to find them but he did not appear.

'Don't worry,' Carys said confidently 'Lucky knows these mountains better than we do, he'll probably be home before me.' But when Carys returned home and stabled Silver it was nearly dark and Lucky was not there. Noone in the house had seen him since he had left with Carys earlier that day. An uneasy feeling churned in

Carys' stomach as she waited for Lucky to arrive on their doorstep. He did not return.

The telephone rang shrilly that evening and a gruff and disgruntled man spoke harshly to Evan. Jayne, Daniel and Carys listened into the conversation.

'Oh… OK… well, I'm very sorry about that… yes of course I'll be there straight away… no don't worry it won't happen again…of course I'm very sorry but I won't be long… OK… yes, I'll be there in five.'

Evan hung up the phone and looked mischievously at his family.

'Looks like we've found Lucky,' Evan said and a slow grin spread across his face. Jayne and Carys looked at him expectantly.

'He's gone to the wrong home, his old home, and the new owner is definitely not happy.'

Jayne's hand flew to her open mouth and Carys gasped. Daniel looked unsurprised.

'I'd better go quickly' Evan said as he rushed to his feet and grabbed his car keys. 'Lucky's refusing to let the new owner out of the house and he's supposed to be going to a family party. He is fuming.'

Carys grabbed her coat and went with Evan to retrieve their renegade dog. The man who Lucky was refusing to let out of his house was over six feet tall, stocky and undoubtedly very strong. The thought of a tiny terrier defending his former territory and keeping the new owner hostage was something that both Carys and Evan during the car journey started to find very funny. Jayne stayed in the house and tried not to think about it. She was mortified and hoped that she did not bump into the new owner of their previous house in the local supermarket.

As Evan and Carys drove up to the Baglan house, the headlights of the car illuminated Lucky jumping up and down at the letterbox from the outside. Going back to the Baglan house had triggered Lucky's memory of his war against the hole in the door. Lucky heard a car stop at the bottom of the garden path and he heard Carys call to him. He ignored her and continued to scrape his teeth against the metal flap. He had to be retrieved by Evan who at the same time apologised profusely to the new owner of the house. When Evan returned to the car his previous humour had been replaced with a much sterner demeanour.

'Try and be a bit more careful when you go out with Lucky again, Carys, that man is not happy' Evan grimaced and Lucky found himself being plonked into Carys' lap. 'Just trust me when I say this should not happen again.'

The next time Lucky went back to the Baglan house the new owner was in work and when he returned he found a familiar, tiny, brown, wiry haired terrier trying to rip his letterbox off his front door. Lucky stopped jumping when the new owner approached him and his house. He started to growl a low, threatening warning and his hackles rose and fell in time with his most ferocious bark. The new owner decided not to risk a confrontation and he retreated back down the garden path and into the next-door neighbour's house to use a phone.

Evan received a telephone call in work and he left early to collect Lucky. He could not have apologised more than he had done the last time but he tried anyway. When Evan told Jayne that evening her response was a little smug.

'Well, it's about time you have to apologise on behalf of that dog, I could use a break.'

Despite Evan's assurances that they would not allow Lucky to go back to the house in Baglan, Lucky did so many times more over the next few months. Each time the new owner lectured Evan and Jayne about keeping their dog under control, Evan and Jayne apologised and made many more promises they could not keep.

'You know what, Evan.' Jayne mused one evening. 'It's so typical. All the time we lived in that house and we were trying to stop him from escaping. Now we have moved, he's spending all his time trying to get back in.'

Evan had to give his mobile number to the new owner of the Baglan house and he became a twenty-four hour call out service for Lucky. He also enlisted his parents into collecting Lucky. If Evan was too busy in work then Sherry and Owen had the onerous task of going to pick him up. The luxury of being retired backfired hugely when there was a need to collect a tiny terrier so often. They made light of excuses when they fetched him.

'Sorry, mate. Not my dog. I'm just a taxi service... But don't worry I will tell my son all about it.' Often, when Sherry and Owen dropped Lucky back home and made sure that he was safely locked inside, one would turn to the other and say,

'Better go to Halfords luv, he's had the seatbelt again.'

Carys made an effort to ensure that she did not lose Lucky while out riding but it was in vain. If she realised that Lucky had disappeared she would race home, but she was rarely fast enough and the telephone had already rung before she got into the house. Sometimes though she got back in time and Evan was able to rush out in the car and intercept Lucky on the way to the Baglan house.

Lucky did not like the fact that his original territory did not smell like his any more so he started to make greater efforts to reclaim it. His wanderings to the Baglan house came to the attention of an opportune person. Evan's sister, Davinia and her husband Cai lived in a large Georgian house facing directly onto Baglan Road. Cai was a complete whizz on computers and all things electronic and he had just purchased a new home security system. He had a twenty-four hour live streaming video camera facing directly onto the pavement outside their house so he could always see who was passing, calling at their house and most importantly, if anyone was attempting to steal or vandalise his new red car parked outside.

Cai first saw the familiar small, brown terrier dog cocking his head, then his leg and peeing over the freshly washed silver alloy wheels of his new Audi before hobbling off in the direction of Baglan. Cai got straight on the phone to Evan.

'Evan. It's Cai. I've just seen your dog walk past my house, think he's on his way to Baglan.' Evan cursed.

'Cheers for that Cai, I'll head him off before he gets to our old house.'

Evan wondered how long it would be before the new owner of the Baglan house would call the dog pound to collect Lucky, he certainly had enough cause.

The whole family tried hard to keep Lucky in the house every morning before going their separate ways to school and work. But mornings were organised chaos in the Davies household. Carys was darting up to the stables to feed the horses and Evan was clearing up the dead mice from the back door. Jayne was making sure that her children had breakfast and everything they needed for school and Daniel remained oblivious, humming one of his own compositions to himself and wondering when he would get a chance to perform it. While everyone had good intentions to keep Lucky safely under lock and key, he often took the opportunity to sneak quietly down the drive or disappear up the mountain path.

When Lucky's family returned back to the house after school and work there were often messages on the answer machine in the house concerning him. Sometimes it was Cai.

'Evan, quarter past twelve. Lucky going to Baglan. Cai. Speak soon.'

Sometimes it would be followed by an irate message from the new owner in the Baglan house.

'Evan, come get your dog… again.'

And sometimes it would be Cai again

'Evan, just gone three, Lucky coming back from Baglan. Cai.'

If Lucky was out riding with Carys up the Dinas mountain he was close enough to the Baglan house that he would disappear to resume his war against the letterbox. If he followed Carys and Silver north through Cwmafan and in the direction of Afan Argoed Park it was unfamiliar land and he stayed with them to protect them and escort them home. When Carys realised this she stopped taking Lucky up the Dinas mountain with her. Lucky could not understand why sometimes he was allowed to go out with Carys and other times he was not. The strategies that Carys used to stop him from following her had chilling repercussions for her, her friend Eryn and to a lesser extent, Lucky.

Chapter 9

A Dog's Sixth Sense

Lucky startled from a deep sleep when he heard the quiet 'tink' of the garden gate latch seep into his subconscious. He jumped up and ran to the back door, barking frantically until Jayne came to open it for him.

'All right, all right,' she exclaimed as Lucky impatiently pushed his way out into the garden. Once free, he bolted past Carys to get to the stables and stood outside the tack room waiting for her to catch him up, panting and shaking and spinning on the spot. Carys sighed, realising that her ploy to go riding up the Dinas mountain without alerting Lucky had failed dismally.

Lucky paced in circles outside Silver's stable as Carys saddled and bridled him as normal. When the stable door was opened Lucky ran inside, seeking out the freshest horse manure to roll in before he embarked on his walk. He paused in disbelief when Carys led Silver outside and shut the door behind her, locking Lucky in the ten foot by twelve-foot stable. He ran to the door and tried to jump over but he was far too tiny. His front legs only stretched half way up the stable door and no matter how much he barked Carys did not come back to let him out.

Carys tried to put aside her guilt at locking Lucky away, telling herself that it was for his own good. Any more visits back to the Baglan house and Lucky would be lucky not to end up in the dog pound. She ignored his barking, whining, yelping and mounted Silver and rode up the mountain path. Lucky listened to Silver's metal shoes clopping away into the distance until silence descended around him.

He decided to make the best of a bad situation, found a pile of fresh horse manure and spent the next ten minutes rolling on it and eating it. Then he laid his head onto his paws and began to doze. A car driving behind the back of the stables woke him a while later and his head and ears pricked up as he heard the creak of a gate opening, the slamming of the dead bolt as it was shut again and a car driving back down past the stables. He heard quiet footsteps and whined uneasily. He did not like the fact that he could not see whoever had arrived onto his territory.

A familiar face looked over the door into the stable and Lucky wagged his tail. It was Eryn, a friend of Carys' from school who also kept her pony at Tyddyn's stables. Lucky liked this girl, she spent a lot of time up the stables on her own. Eryn was fully aware of the problems that Lucky was causing by going back to the Baglan house. She was unable to ride her pony as she had found out that the mare she had recently bought was in foal. Eryn therefore spent most of her time up the stables cleaning fanatically, something that ascended into compulsive proportions while she also provided equine maternity care.

When she found Lucky lying on a bed of straw in one of the stone stables, despite his pathetic whining, she knew better than to let him out. Aside from knowing that Lucky was likely to go back to the Baglan house, Eryn had been mortified many times when Lucky had accompanied her out riding and demonstrated his loving for dogs he met en-route. She would not let him out and willingly subject anybody's dog to that type of attention.

Eryn was fascinated by supernatural stories and experiences. Port Talbot is home to many myths and legends, ghosts and mysterious activities. Margam Country Park and Margam Castle allegedly have at least five ghosts roaming the grounds. There are regular ghost hunts and séances, particularly around Halloween that take place in Margam Castle with many readings of paranormal activity. The most famous of the ghosts in Margam is the White Lady who has been sighted on the sweeping grand stone staircase where she was allegedly pushed down in a family conspiracy. In a small room tucked away in one of the irregular towers of the castle, loud and unexplained bangs have been heard through the day and night. The room used to be a children's nursery in the days where children were seen and not heard. A little boy has been sighted playing on the steep, spiralling staircase that leads to this now derelict playroom.

Margam Country Park also has strong religious links. The stone remains of Margam Abbey, which was originally built in 1147 are still well presevered in the grounds by the longest Orangery in Britain. On the mountain directly overlooking Margam Abbey is Hen Eglwys, a tiny derelict fifteenth century ruin that was used by people who did not have the right to worship in the main Abbey. Hidden in a crevice on the mountain above Margam Castle is the ancient monks' bath, an old crumbling stone building built into the mountain, its slate grey roof covered in moss and a small stream cascading underneath it. Rusty bars now prevent public access into the bath itself although if the stream flows high enough you can reach down and feel the piercing coldness of the water that many centuries ago bathed a monastery of monks.

Even Tyddyn has its own history of tragedy and ghost stories. The stone foundations of almost sixty houses on the winding mountain path from the stables can just be seen under the growth of thorny tendrils and vines. Rumours were that the houses were burnt with many people still inside them, although neither Carys nor Eryn could find any proof of this in local libraries.

The scariest ghost story was told to Carys and Eryn by an old man who randomly wandered past the stable yard one day and stopped to talk to them. He was heading up the mountain for a walk, something he claimed to have been doing for over forty years. His face was weather beaten, wrinkled and tanned and he had a twinkle in his eye as he greeted Carys and Eryn over the gate. He looked fit and active yet had a slight stoop and supported himself with a wooden walking stick.

He embellished a tragic love story about a young couple living in the 1960's. The path that starts from behind the stables is narrow but after a short while it opens up into a grassed clearing giving a perfect birds eye view of Tyddyn. On the edge of the clearing is a distinctive looking beech tree. It is a living, growing tree but with bark so dark it looks burnt and dead. The trunk is thick and straight with only a few branches reluctantly spreading at the top. Half way up the thick tree trunk is a twisted branch with no leaves that grows out horizontally.

The old man claimed this tree was where an emotional and heart broken woman hung herself when she believed her beloved had deserted her. A few days later, her lover discovered her death and he threw himself off a rock further up the mountain path. On this rock, he was supposed to have drawn the white heart that was still clearly visible as Eryn and Carys gazed up the mountain in awe. The old man seemed pleased to hear the appropriate responses of,

'Ohhh'

'Oh no'

'Really'

When Carys and Eryn tried to find out any information to verify the truth behind this story there was not a shred of evidence. Regardless, the Romeo and Juliet story intrigued them.

On the day that Lucky was locked in his stable, Eryn sat outside the tack room cleaning her saddle. Lucky had long given up whining and pawing the stable door. He was dozing in the straw bedding only barely aware of Eryn's quiet and occasional movements outside. His ears pricked when he sensed something or someone other than Carys' friend.

Eryn had become so engrossed in her tack-cleaning mission that she startled when she heard a woman's voice say,

'Aw. He's locked in there all on his own.' A male voice mumbled a reply too quiet for Eryn to hear. She did not respond immediately because it was not uncommon for people to walk up the mountain road and behind the stables to get up the Dinas mountain. Lucky leapt to his feet ready to defend his territory. He launched himself at the concrete wall backing onto the road behind and went into a frenzied spat of growling and barking at whoever or whatever he had heard. His bark became deep, something he only reserved for the newspaper girl.

At that moment, Eryn realised that if Lucky was quiet, which he had been for the last hour, there was no way any one walking past the back of the stables could have known he was in there. There were no windows facing into the stables from outside the yard. She looked around to confirm that she was definitely the only one present then rushed to the gate and looked down the mountain road. There was no one there. From the gate of the stables there was an almost perfect view to the main road. There was also good visibility up the mountain path. Whoever had spoken about Lucky only moments ago had disappeared inhumanely fast.

Lucky was still barking madly and he continued to do so for another ten minutes. When Carys returned to the stables shortly after, Eryn was sitting outside the tack room, her arms tightly wrapped around herself. With the multitude of myths, legends and ghosts surrounding the Dinas Mountain and the old village of Tyddyn, it was the Romeo and Juliet lovers that were at the forefront of Eryn's thoughts.

Eryn was adamant that Lucky had sensed the presence of a spirit. Lucky did not think about it at all. Something or someone had woken him and as far as he was concerned he had defended his territory and scared them off. Lucky was very satisfied with his day's work but he made a mental note not to allow Carys or Eryn to shut him in that stable again. Fortunately for Eryn, Carys did not have to lock Lucky in the stables many more times. He had been visiting the house in Baglan for nearly six months but as quickly as he started he stopped again.

Lucky was aware that his little people were not so little anymore and they did not require his protection as much. He had finally succeeded in scaring off the newspaper and the girl who delivered it because they did not come to his new house. Neither did the postman dare to come directly to the front door, he always stopped at the beginning of the drive where there was a strange box nailed to the front gate. With only three other houses in the near vicinity it was much quieter and he did not need to defend and protect his family from everything on his danger list. With so much more time on his paws Lucky shifted his priorities. His family were as safe as they could be since he had done such a good job protecting them. As pack leader, he made an executive decision that it was now a good time to start recruiting new people into his pack.

Chapter 10

Midnight Visitor

As well as parenting, caring for animals, housework and holding down the necessary jobs to support a family living on a small holding, Jayne and Evan also managed to fit in a lively social life. Their favourite haunt was the Forge Tavern in Port Talbot town centre, a narrow and long bar with just enough room for a pool table at the front and space for a musical band to play at the back. Every weekend, live music resonated through the wooden floors, into the hearts and heads of the people there and out onto the paved, pedestrian street. Whether it was the melodic tunes of Pink Floyd, rocking beats of Bon Jovi or contemporary pop of Take That, everyone drank, danced and sang in time to the soul of the music. In the wet and windy winter evenings the tiny pub was crammed full of people and the air thick with atmosphere. The conversation flowed as freely as the beer from the taps and everyone bopped along to the beat.

When the weather became warmer and the manager of the Forge Tavern eventually called stop on the taps,

Tyddyn provided the perfect party venue for those people who were just not ready to go to bed. Jayne, Evan and their friends often wobbled home from town to sit and lounge around the circular blue swimming pool, brightly illuminated by the dazzling floodlight and soft glow of the multicoloured fairy lights that Jayne had diligently hung around the garden.

If Carys and Daniel were at home and woken by the rabble they could sometimes be persuaded to belt out a few tunes on the piano. Or rather, Carys needed to be persuaded but Daniel was always happy to assume his stage persona and perform for the audience. Daniel still preferred to compose his own songs rather than learn the ones given to him by his piano teacher and his parent's drunken friends proved to be the ideal audience to test his new songs with. If the weather was particularly warm then Jayne and Evan made the most of being in an isolated spot and cranked up the music from their old crackling stereo system. The parties at Tyddyn became re-known for booze, good music, good company and a dip in the pool late at night. It was at these parties that Lucky met Tiny Taff. Of all the people who came back to party at Tyddyn, the man who usually stayed for the night and who Lucky decided was going to become part of his pack, only lived half a mile down the road in a small one street hamlet on Cwmafan road.

Carys often came downstairs early on a Sunday morning to find that Taff had fallen asleep the night before, usually in the dining room. There was a long comfortable three-seat sofa in the living room but Taff seemed to prefer to squash himself up onto the two-seat sofa with the uncomfortable wooden arms and no cushions. Sometimes there was an unpleasant smell where Taff had tried to turn on the gas fire without flicking the ignition switch. On such occasions, Carys would creep past him to turn the fire off completely and open the window. Taff may be cold when he woke up but at least he would still be alive.

When Taff was at Tyddyn he found that Lucky became his little shadow. One thing that appealed to Lucky was that Taff remained clear of the big, deep puddle in the middle of the garden. He had more sense than the rest of the drunken people who visited the house and refrained from jumping into the swimming pool, or getting so close that he would be pushed in. This suited Lucky because he did not like to get anywhere near to the deep round puddle in the middle of the garden. Lucky had been horrified when Evan had gently dropped him into the water one day and forgetting the doggy paddle technique, sank like a stone and had to be rescued by the man who had got him into the predicament in the first place. Lucky was content either curling up beside Taff or rolling over onto his back to have his belly tickled.

Lucky even preferred to stay in a gas-smelling dining room at the feet of a sleeping, snoring Taff than race up the stables with Carys in the mornings in order to accompany her riding. Lucky was a loyal dog but as much as he loved going out with Carys and Silver, as long as his new best friend was in the house he was going to stay by his side. Carys could not help but consider the similarities between Lucky and his new friend. Both were short and small in physical size compared to their retrospective species and both were extremely protective of those people that they loved, defending their territory to the last. Tiny Taff was re-known for taking innocent banter the wrong way and stepping up to defend himself and his friends (even if it was completely unnecessary). Fortunately, like Lucky, his temper subsided as quickly as it flared and he was a good friend and excellent company.

It did not take Lucky long to realise that when Taff stayed at Tyddyn he left the following morning on foot so he planned his escape in enough time one day to follow. It only took Taff ten minutes to walk home and Lucky was close on his heel. Taff did not realise he had his little brown shadow until he put his key in the lock of his front door and turned it. Before he could enter, Lucky rushed past him and into Taff's house only to confront the largest Alsatian dog he had ever met in such close proximity.

Lucky froze and a low growl bubbled in his stomach as Taff's large, longhaired dog stared down at the little intruder in her house.

'Lucky, quiet.' Taff sternly told him. Fortunately for Lucky, Seren was a sweet natured dog that greeted the tiny terrier with a quick sniff before running to greet Taff with a lick on his hand, she was far too good mannered to jump up on him. Lucky gracefully decided that it would be unfair to put Seren on his danger list since he was in her house. He proceeded instead through Taff's hall and into his kitchen to sniff around and claim the territory as his own. Taff dropped Lucky back at Tyddyn an hour later but the damage had been done and the precedent set.

Seren was an elderly dog and she often had to relieve herself at inconvenient times of the night. Jayne despaired when she visited Taff at his home. When Seren lost control of her continence and peed on the carpet the odour was so bad that Taff could not scrub it out. He took to cutting the stained patches out with a Stanley knife instead so the whole living room and hallway carpet was incomplete, with different size holes cut into it. Jayne tried to give Taff tips on cleaning the floor but every time she visited there was even less carpet.

Night times were a particular issue for Seren because she could not wait the entire night without a widdle. Since Taff had an enclosed garden, he would leave his back door open so Seren could let herself in and out as she needed. It was the only way Taff could get a full night's sleep. While Taff's garden fence was able to keep Seren in, he shortly discovered that it was not able to keep Lucky out.

The next time Lucky visited Taff it was gone midnight. Lucky had been out riding with Carys but when he discovered that she was only going for a short ride he disappeared into one of his hidden rabbit runs and out of sight. He followed scents all over the Dinas Mountain with little thought of where he was going and what time it was. When a light mist descended around Lucky and moisture hung in his fur like tiny diamonds in the rough, he gravitated back to Tyddyn but did not stop there. He continued on towards Taff's and entered through the back garden, into the house through the open back door and straight up the stairs.

Lucky nosed his way into Taff's bedroom and jumped up onto the end of his bed. Taff was partially aware in his subconscious state that his heart had stopped beating but before he could decide whether he needed to worry about it, a jolt of electricity that smelled like a wet dog rudely restarted his heart with a thump. By the time Taff had caught his breath and resumed normal breathing patterns after thinking he was being robbed in the middle of the night, Lucky was curled up on his duvet fast asleep besides him. Taff dropped Lucky back to Tyddyn the following morning and Evan found himself apologising again for his tiny terrier. Evan though was secretly relieved that Lucky was invading Taff's house because his friend was definitely more amicable about the tiny terrier's visit than previous people had been.

Lucky took himself to visit Taff often over the next couple of months. At first, Taff tried closing his bedroom door so Lucky would not be able to wake him up by getting into his bedroom and jumping on his bed. But Lucky was a persistent dog and if he found the bedroom door closed he would wake Taff up by scrabbling his nails against it and barking until he was allowed in. In the end, it was easier for Taff to leave his bedroom door open and get used to Lucky's midnight visits. After a while, he found that his sleep was not disturbed as often. He also found it an excellent story to entertain his friends with, claiming that he was the subject of a love crush from someone who was petite, loyal and made his heart pound in the middle of the night.

Despite Taff being mildly amused by Lucky's midnight visits to him, he did express some concerns.

'The freakiest part is, Evan, sometimes he arrives in the middle of the night and then leaves before I wake in the morning. Half the time I honestly don't know if I'm dreaming him or not. And if I am dreaming about Lucky, why am I not having better dreams?'

Taff started scouring his garden fence, not for an escape route as Evan had previously done, but for an intruder's entrance. As hard as he searched he could not work out how the tiny terrier was getting into his garden.

Taff was all but inconsolable when his beautiful Alsatian, Seren, passed away not long after Lucky started to visit. On a brighter note though, this meant he could shut and lock his back door, which effectively put an end to Lucky's midnight calls. Lucky was not impressed and Taff quickly fell out of his favour.

Jayne's parents, Penelope and Pete, lived in a large bungalow in an elevated position in Margam, overlooking the steelworks and backing onto the M4 motorway. Sunday dinner at Penelope and Pete's had been a family tradition since before Lucky had been brought from the dogs' home. Lucky enjoyed trips to Penelope and Pete's because they had a long garden with a clear stream cascading down in weirs, plenty of trees and bushes for him to explore and a guaranteed Sunday dinner. He had not intended to wake Penelope and Pete up in the middle of the night. He had been expanding on his territory one night, disguised by horse dung, when he found the winding lane leading to their house. Despite it being the early hours of the morning and pitch black, Lucky decided to take a chance and see if there was a roast dinner.

Penelope woke from a deep unconscious sleep and dozed restlessly as she struggled to fall back into unconsciousness. She was dreaming of someone knocking on the door, no, hammering on the door, how strange. Then, as she became more awake she tuned into the high-pitched yelp and had a vision of a tiny, scruffy dog. Penelope bolted upright in bed. She was not dreaming. She could hear that damn dog right outside her house. Lucky was outside barking persistently one short yelp after the other. He was hungry and his mouth was watering in anticipation of what he hoped to eat. He was still barking when the front door swung open.

'Aw, you daft dog,' Penelope greeted him as Lucky happily ran past her and straight into the kitchen. He was disappointed to find out that there was nothing in the usual dog's bowl. 'What are you doing here? You can wait till morning for some food, daft dog.' Penelope returned to bed and Lucky whined as he was locked into the living room. Pete continued to sleep on soundly through the night.

'Penelope,' Pete said to her the following morning as he slowly chewed his cereal. 'When did Jayne and Evan bring Lucky over?'

'They didn't,' she replied with a snort. 'He came here himself at two o' clock in the morning. Would you believe it?'

'Did he now,' Pete said thoughtfully. There was little that surprised Pete and he thought carefully about everything before deciding whether he should react or not. 'Well, how did he get in? Did you leave the door open again? Oh Penelope, mun! You know you shouldn't do that, you don't know who's going to be wandering around.'

'That dog is the only one wandering around and I didn't leave the door open. I got up and let him in.'

'Well I didn't hear you do that'

'Pete, you never wake up. You always sleep through the night, but I'm telling you now he barked and barked and then I got up and let him in. It's a good job we were both offered early retirement or I would be going to work tired and ratty.'

'Oh well, you'd better phone Jayne and let her know he's here.' Penelope got on the phone to her daughter and agreed to drop Lucky back home that afternoon.

Lucky had a chicken dinner for his breakfast and this was followed by a car journey to the beach and a walk over the sand dunes. He was very pleased with how his day had turned out and over the next two months he went back four more times.

Lucky also visited Evan's parents. They were much easier to find since Carys had walked him to their terraced house in Port Talbot town centre on numerous occasions. He had not intended to visit them, but he just so happened to be wandering around in town thirsty and hungry, so he sought out their house. He arrived at a far more respectable time of day than he had done at Taff's or Penelope and Pete's.

He found the familiar front door, checked that he knew the scents on the doorstep and he barked until he heard a key turn in the lock. Sherry cautiously opened the front door and peered from behind the security chain. She saw no one so jumped backwards when something pushed against the front door. She looked down and saw Lucky trying to ram his way into the house with his tiny, wet nose.

'Oh, Lucky, bach.' Sherry took the security chain off and opened the front door for Lucky to enter. Lucky ran into the kitchen, helped himself to a drink, gulped down the bacon that Sherry offered him and then flopped in front of the fire in the living room and fell asleep.

'Well, well, well. Lucky is it?' Owen chuckled as he came down the stairs. 'When did Jayne and Evan drop him around, Sherry?'

'They didn't, Owen. He just turned up now.'

'Oh well, better give them a ring and tell them we'll drop him off later.' Sherry and Owen were less surprised at Lucky's arrival than his previous hosts. They were well informed about his travels.

Despite the family's good intentions to make sure that Lucky did not run away in the morning he often wandered off unnoticed. He did not intend to run away most of the time, just as he did not intend to visit Penelope, Pete, Sherry and Owen at first. His first priority was always to protect his family by checking for danger. He just got carried away with this task, only seeking out water, food and rest from the places he knew well when his basic instincts kicked in. Every time he returned to his family he would run first to his equal to tell her about his day, then his second in command for a pat on the head.

He would see Jayne if he was hungry and Daniel if he was not holed up in his bedroom.

The speed with which Lucky disappeared always astonished Jayne, Evan and Carys. Daniel of course, was oblivious for the most part. Just like the mysterious whisperings that Eryn heard from behind the stable wall, as soon everyone realised that Lucky had gone again, no one could find him.

'He treats this place like a hotel.' Penelope complained loudly to Jayne over Sunday dinner. Jayne shrugged helplessly. She could just about cope with her own mother moaning about him.

'I just hope that he does not find anymore people to visit at unsocial hours.'

It was lucky for Lucky that the next group of people he started to visit did not moan about him at all. In fact, to Jayne and Evan's bemusement, they absolutely loved him.

Chapter 11

Alternative Company

Shortly after they had moved into Tyddyn, Jayne and Evan had been invited to meet their next-door neighbours over a supposedly quiet and innocent evening meal. Dai and his girlfriend lived in one of the other three houses at Tyddyn. The drive that led to his house was a stone's throw from the end of Jayne and Evan's front garden. They arrived armed with a bottle of wine, a few cans of cider and no particular expectations or concerns.

They had begun the evening by eating a delicious curry and drinking copious amounts of liquor and finished the night by looking at Dai's earring collection and prosthetic boobs. Dai was not just any transvestite, he was the treasurer of the South Wales Transvestite Order and he hosted a party at his house the first Saturday of every month for cross dressers living in South Wales from Carmarthen to Cardiff and beyond

Jayne broke the news to her daughter first about Dai's lifestyle choice.

'Carys,' Jayne had started hesitantly as she indicated to her daughter to sit with her at the kitchen table. 'You know how some people prefer to have the company of women and some people prefer to have the company of men, even if they are also women and men?'

'Gay people, Mum' Carys stated the obvious and shifted her weight uncomfortably. She hated any conversation with her parents about the ways of the world because she was of the opinion that she knew far more than they did.

'Yes Carys, people who are gay or lesbians. Well our new next-door neighbour, his name is Dai by the way, he isn't gay or a lesbian.'

'He can't be a lesbian if he's a man, Mum.'

'No, you're right, but he does like to dress up in women's clothes.' Jayne settled back into her chair to wait for her daughter's reaction.

'Oh, I see' Carys paused as she digested this piece of information.

'I mean there's nothing wrong with that and he and his girlfriend are really good company' Jayne continued in a hurry. 'It's just I thought I better warn you that sometimes he's a man and sometimes he's a woman.' Carys paused again and her eyebrows creased together.

'But how am I going to know? If I see him as a woman, I mean. I might not recognise him.'

'I wouldn't worry, you'll be able to tell exactly who he is regardless of what he is wearing.' Jayne said dryly and said no more on the subject. Jayne and Evan had both deliberated whether to tell Daniel but in all honesty, neither thought he would notice.

Carys discovered something else about Dai before she had the opportunity to meet him and see for herself how he would be dressed. She was proudly showing her friend, Sara, around her home, stables and garden. Sara was less interested in the horses and more fascinated by the swimming pool.

'Is it warm enough to swim in yet?'

'Don't think so, Dad's only just filled it and he said to wait a week before all the chlorine and stuff has worked properly.'

'Pool parties this summer?'

'Yeah, definitely. Won't be long, there's been loads of people swimming in the river the last week as well, we could go down there?'

'What, the Afan River?' Sara looked up at Carys in surprise?

'Yeah, you can just see it from the fence.'

Sara hurried over to the edge of the garden and tried to see how far they were from the river. She was too short to see directly over the fence so she found a gap by the wooden shed. Sara easily slipped her slim body through and returned a few seconds later stifling a laugh with her hand over her mouth.

'Carys. Quick! There's a naked man in the next-door garden,' she whispered loudly. Naturally, Carys ran over for a look. As she slid through the small gap and peered over and below into her neighbour's garden, a rather round, naked man looked up at her and waved. Carys felt a large ball of heat erupt in her stomach and spread shockingly quickly through every nerve in her body. She gasped loudly and then, realising that she was just staring at the friendly, naked man, hurriedly retreated into her garden without waving back.

'Awww, Sara,' she complained, still in a loud whisper. 'You didn't tell me he was looking up at us.'

'I know,' she giggled 'he waved at me as well.'

Carys reported to her mother the following day that she had seen the next-door neighbour naked in his garden. Jayne grimaced at the thought.

'Mum, I thought you said he liked to wear women's clothes? He wasn't wearing anything... Not even a bikini.'

'Yes... well, I might have forgotten to mention that he is also a naturist and when he's not wearing a dress he's likely to be naked.' Carys smirked and went to walk out the door when her mother added

'Oh, Carys. I forgot to tell you that when he's a woman he likes to be called Delilah.'

'What should I call him when he's naked.'

'I suggest you don't get that close.'

While Jayne, Evan and Carys accepted their next-door neighbour's ways without question, they were naturally curious. So, on the first Saturday of the month after moving into Tyddyn, Lucky and his family gathered into

Jayne and Evan's bedroom, which overlooked the front of their house. Jayne had bitten the bullet and told Daniel about their next door neighbour's covert way of life but his reaction had been as expected.

'Oh. OK.'

Lucky jumped up onto the bed to sit with his family all perched on the side of it, huddled together and peering out of the window. He was far more interested in the popcorn, crisps and drinks they all had and he managed to steal a particularly large potato snack from Daniel's hand without him noticing. As Lucky crunched his stolen treat his family sat watching and waiting, staring intently out the window as the light from the setting sun gradually faded. The blinds were drawn across the window but the slats were open so they could see out but no one could see in.

'It's nice to have some family time together,' Evan said as he threw one arm around his wife's shoulders and the other around his son.

'Yes, lets hope that Daniel doesn't feel the need to share this one in school assembly though,' Jayne sighed.

'What?' Daniel asked with a distant look in his eye.

'Never mind,' Jayne and Evan said in unison.

When the first party guests started teetering up the drive in high heels and tight, shiny dresses, everyone had difficulty believing most or all of them were male.

‘I thought you said that they were men’ Daniel whined as a particularly gorgeous person with long beautiful and glossy hair turned into Dai, or rather Delilah’s, driveway.

‘They are men, Daniel. Now hush up and keep watching.’

Carys and Jayne were both starting to feel a bit put out and self-conscious about their own body image as they watched long slender legs delicately balancing on stilettos and beautiful hair bouncing around tiny buxom waists. It was like Joan Doe meets Hollywood Hotties.

However, there quickly started to be more masculine figures strolling up the drive. Six feet in height, broad shoulders swinging tiny handbags and thick muscular thighs. Middle age women with middle-aged spread and strong jaw lines with five o clock shadow. Daniel lost interest first and hurried downstairs to watch a film on television. Lucky followed him. He did not understand why everyone had excitedly gathered into the bedroom. Jayne, Carys and Evan stayed a while longer but their interest also waned soon after.

The novelty of Delilah’s monthly parties soon wore off and transvestites became a normal part of life. The first Saturday of every month saw a string of cars being parked along Cwmafan road as people prepared to party. Testosterone-fuelled men honked their car horns as they drove by at what they thought were beautiful and well-dressed women.

Carys became friendly with her next-door neighbour but she always made the mistake of calling Delilah Dai when he was a woman and Delilah was quick to correct her. So, to avoid any confusion, she simply called him Dai Delilah however he was dressed and this was O.K. for both Dai and Delilah. While Carys saw him dressed in many different female disguises, she was fortunate not to see him in his birthday suit again. Jayne was in competition with Delilah over who had the better earring collection, something that she declared victory over on many occasions.

Daniel was so engrossed in his television programmes, computer games and music that after the first couple of months he seemed to forget altogether about his colourful neighbours. Evan also carried on mostly without noticing the multitude of women coming and going. However, whenever he arrived home from town after having a few drinks and it was the first Saturday of the month, he would sometimes dither, wondering whether to take up Dai Delilah's open invitation and go next door for a drink. Usually, Jayne had a few sharp words of warning and put him off the idea. Jayne hated it when her husband became drunk because he had a tendency to tease people, a lot. A household of cross-dressers would give him more than enough humorous material to use and that was something she was not going to permit.

Lucky discovered the friendly gatherings long before any of his family found out he was attending the parties. Carys came home from riding about a year after moving to Tyddyn to find that the party had started early. There was a group of ladies cooking food on a barbeque in Dai Delilah's front garden and there was a tiny brown scruffy terrier at their feet. Carys groaned when she recognised

Lucky chomping down a whole sausage that he had probably stolen.

She jumped off Silver and led him down Dai Delilah's drive calling to Lucky as she approached. He glanced in her direction then ignored her, his wagging tail not missing a beat as he stared up at the nice people who were feeding him. Before Carys could reach him and grab his collar to drag him home, Silver stopped dead and refused to go any further. He was eyeing the smoke coming from the barbeque with alarm and it was clear that Carys would not be able to get him to move another step.

'Don't worry about him, luv,' a gorgeous woman with long blonde hair said to Carys.

'He comes down here quite often. He's so lovely.' The other women laughed and agreed.

'Oh, is he your dog?'

'He's always here when we're havin' a party'

'I thought he belonged to Delly' (which Carys presumed was short for Delilah).

'No, he's my dog, but you'd never guess,' Carys laughed. 'I'll take my pony back and come and get him.'

'Aw, leave him here he usually comes for a walk with us later when we take Delilah's little dog,' another gorgeous woman pleaded, this one a brunette with extremely long legs, a very short skirt and rather thick thighs.

'Oh,' Carys stuttered 'That's lovely... I suppose. Where do you go for walks?' She could not imagine any of the women in their ridiculous heels tottering up the stony mountain path although she certainly would have paid to see it.

'Eh, eh, excuse me. It's only some of them that are daft enough to go prancing down the main road with a couple of dogs at two o' clock in the morning,' another woman with a particularly deep and gruff voice protested. This woman was older and was dressed as if she were about to play bingo in a conservative skirt and shirt. Everyone laughed and some started to protest their case but gave up, taking a swig of their drinks instead.

'OK,' Carys laughed again. 'I'll leave him with you, if you get sick of him send him home.'

Silver nervously began to retreat up the drive, still eyeing the thickening, barbeque smoke and snorting slightly through his flared nostrils. Even the quietest of ponies have their limits and get disturbed at some things. Carys turned around before Silver pulled her over backwards, threw his reins over his head, jumped back onto him and trotted up to the stables. Lucky did not even turn to see her go. He was enjoying the abundant attention far too much, what a nice addition these friendly people made to his pack.

Carys did go back to Delilah's party when she had settled Silver in for the night. She wanted to see if Lucky was still there but she was also a little bored on the account that her parents had recently grounded her. It was completely unfair because it had actually been her friend, Sara who had snuck the two boys into the stables late at night and not her, but it was pointless trying to tell her father that while he was yelling all red faced at her. So, she had sucked it up and was now impatiently waiting for her two-week freedom ban to be lifted. She was not breaking any rules by visiting Dai Delilah but when she wandered to his front garden she was told that Lucky was inside the house playing with Delilah's dog, a scruffy white highland terrier. She was assured that Lucky would be fine and if he was still there at the end of the night they would send him home. Whoever promised this must have forgotten because Lucky did not come back home until the following morning.

Jayne let him in and he went straight to his water bowl, lapping fervently before flopping down to sleep in front of the dining room fire for the rest of the morning.

'Dirty stop out.' Jayne grumbled at him.

'What's wrong with that dog?' Evan asked Carys as the morning turned into afternoon. 'He's slept all day and hasn't even tried to get out of the house.'

'He went to Dai Delilah's party last night and didn't get back till this morning. Mum let him in when she got up.'

'What?' Evan stopped in his tracks, his jaw agape.

'Yeah, apparently he's been there before and when some of them get drunk they walk up and down Cwmafan road with Delilah's dog and Lucky.' Evan was extremely glad that it was his dog and not his son who was going to parties where men dressed up as women.

Carys' friend, Sara, often accompanied her parents to local pubs and clubs where her father played in a popular band called 'Panic Station.' When the weather was warm and the evenings light, the band played late into the night. When Sara returned home with her family it was often the early hours of the morning.

'Carys, I'm sure I saw your dog walking up Cwmafan road last night with a bunch of women?' she said one Sunday.

'Yeah, first Saturday of the month. He was probably with Delilah's lot.'

'Oh.'

Evan became frustrated that there were parties happening next door and he had still not been to one. He did not want to go dressed as a woman but his curiosity was growing and to make matters worse, Lucky was using his open invitation. There were not many parties Evan did not go to in Port Talbot, invited or uninvited.

When Lucky saw the cars lining up on Cwmafan road or smelt the smoke from the barbeque outside Delilah's house, he would quickly and happily go running next door. Every time Evan broached the subject of going as well, Jayne put him off the idea, still convinced he would cause lots of problems by making inappropriate comments and ultimately upsetting Dai and Delilah who she had to live next door to. With the diversity of people at the parties next-door, Jayne could not second-guess what would come out of his mouth. The inevitable soon happened though.

Jayne, Evan and their friend Barri were returning from town after a good drink in the Forge Tavern. Evan and

Barri held onto each other as they wobbled unsteadily home only to be greeted with loud music coming from Delilah's house and cars parked all the way up the drive and along Cwmafan road. While Evan and Barri had been having a very, very good drink, Jayne was more sober.

'First Saturday of the month,' Evan said to Barri, pointing to all the cars parked along Cwmafan road. 'Shall we go?'

'If you want, Evan,' Barri replied evenly, he did not mind where they went as long as there was company and something to drink.

'For gawd's sake, Evan,' Jayne said, exasperated that she was going to have this conversation, again. 'You're not even dressed as a woman. Don't you think it would be a bit rude?'

'Jayne,' Evan slurred. 'We've got an open invitation whatever our dress code, come on, mun. Dai and his girlfriend are always up our house having a drink.'

'Evan, you have had far too much to drink to go to that party.'

Evan began muttering in protest but reluctantly went to pass Dai Delilah's driveway and go towards his own house. When he snuck a sideways glance at a group of women waving at him, he saw that Lucky was at their heels.

'Lucky,' Evan shouted. Lucky turned and eyed Evan and Jayne. He paused for a moment and his tail stopped wagging before he abruptly turned and bounded into Dai Delilah's house.

‘That’s it,’ Evan exclaimed. ‘If Lucky can go, then so can I’ and he marched down the drive where he was greeted by a group of ladies already offering him a drink. Barri followed amicably and Jayne sighed. She was not going to let her husband loose on these poor, unsuspecting people so she headed after him with the sole intention of keeping a close eye on him. Barri was not her responsibility so he could do what he liked.

The guests at the party greeted them warmly and when Dai Delilah realised that her neighbours had finally come to one of her gatherings, she was ecstatic. She dragged them inside to introduce them to her friends whose many exotic, pseudo names were immediately forgotten. When Jayne and Evan walked into Delilah’s living room, Lucky was sitting on a sofa in between two ladies, each with one arm over his back. His mouth was slightly parted and he had what looked like a huge grin on his face, his eyes half closed as he revelled in the attention.

‘Lucky bloody dog,’ Evan commented to no one in particular. That earned him his first dig in the ribs from Jayne.

‘Evan, they are men,’ she hissed at him but Evan was barely aware of her.

Lucky saw Jayne and Evan come into the house and his expression changed. His ears pricked forward and his tail stopped wagging, he climbed down slowly off the sofa and wandered haughtily out of the living room and into the kitchen. When midnight approached, Lucky left the house with a group of women to go on their monthly midnight walk. He strutted straight past Jayne and Evan without even acknowledging them, his tail held high in the air. When he returned half an hour later he once again walked straight passed them, blatantly ignoring Jayne's calls to him as he trotted out into Dai Delilah's back garden.

As the evening progressed, it got better for Evan and worse for Jayne. Barri was engrossed in a debate with a woman twice his size, wearing a short blond wig, even shorter metallic skirt and a white pointed cone bra with red tassels, debating the contemporary merits of Madonna. Evan could not keep his eyes off the amount of tight dresses clinging to curves and bodies. Jayne frequently had to jab him in his side to remind him of the reason this particular group of people gathered at this house for a party. Evan would snap back to reality for a little while longer until the next jab in the ribs was required.

When Jayne decided that it was time to leave she went to find Lucky. He was in the back garden where several people were taking it in turns to pet him. He warily watched Jayne approach him and cowered as she reached for his collar. Jayne dragged Lucky with one hand and Evan in the other back to their house. Neither was impressed with her. Evan moaned at his wife for ending a good night early and Lucky pissed on the sofa. It was only the following morning that they realised they had left Barri there and when Evan spoke to him about it a week later, Barri feigned memory loss. On a brighter note, Jayne and Evan were glad that Lucky had found a group of people who actually enjoyed his company and Lucky was content that he had expanded his pack. For a tiny terrier,

Lucky had a busy life but Jayne was about to make another one of those life-changing decisions.

Chapter 12

'Step It Up A Gear, Lucky'

Carys sat on the edge of one of the kitchen chairs, twiddling her fingers and every now and then catching her breath and stumbling over her words. She was reluctant to broach the subject because of the unusually tragic number of deaths over the last six months. Evan had been in the pub one night when he was offered two pigmy goats, free to a good home. He was always finding excuses not to trim back the overgrown foliage up the stables and mountain path so when he was offered the goats he realised they could be his ticket to avoiding this chore altogether. He was assured that they would eat anything and everything.

A couple of days later a man walked two goats to the front door and knocked confidently. Jayne opened it, her mouth agape with a dozen questions that she could not get past the lump in her throat.

'All right luv, where shall I put them?' the goat man asked.

'Carys... Evan...?' Jayne shouted into the house, knowing that Daniel would not have anything to do with this. Evan came to the door to greet the man and Carys found them in one of her stables a few hours later.

They were the biggest pigmy goats anyone had ever seen. Their backs were higher than Carys' waist so after a while even Evan admitted that they were not the miniature ones he had been promised. Their ages were also unknown and so it was not really a surprise what happened next. On Christmas Eve, Eryn knocked the back door and spoke to Jayne for the first time in months. Eryn was traditionally very quiet in front of Carys' family and Jayne was stunned into silence that Eryn had proactively come to the house just to speak to her. Her shock was such that Eryn's words did not initially register.

'Jayne, I think the goat's dead.'

A feeling of dread enveloped Jayne as Eryn's words hit home.

There were tears, tantrums and Evan was given the responsibility of getting rid of the goat's body. The other goat was also refusing to eat or drink anything after its mate had passed away so Evan was told by Jayne to get rid of that one as well.

'The last thing we need over Christmas is a suicidal goat. Find it a home. Today.'

Evan did not have a clue what to do with one dead and one living goat so he phoned a friend. Hugh worked in Margam Country Park and he assured Evan that he could dispose of the dead goat properly and the other goat would be given a home with his friend who lived on a farm nearby.

Shortly after the passing of the goat, Evan had come home one day carrying a small cardboard box. Lucky was sleeping in his basket under the kitchen table when he could hear something scratching around above him. He tried jumping up onto one of the chairs to have a look but Evan roughly shoved him down again. Lucky sat on the floor with his eyes glued to the box and his tail wagging wildly with expectation. He was not the only curious one as to what the box contained. Jayne and Carys were close on Evan's heels to find out what was in the box too.

Evan opened the top of the box and two tiny black kittens hissed as the bright light startled them. Carys was overjoyed but Jayne was not impressed with the scared and feisty little kittens.

'Haven't we got enough mad animals, Evan?'

'Don't worry, Jayne, they are not for in the house. They can go up the stables and live. Carys, take care of these cats.'

'Why did you have to bring them home at all though?' Jayne despaired. Evan proceeded to tell her that they had been living in the boiler room underneath the swimming pool where he worked. They were so wild that they had been terrorising anyone who went down there. They hissed and spat at whoever tried to approach them but never ran away. Staff there had started to mention the word 'drowning' so Evan had saved them from this fate and brought them home to help combat the ever increasing mice population. This however, was the extent of his involvement in rescuing these kittens and he quickly delegated the responsibility of their care to Carys.

As the weeks went on the little kittens grew into little cats and their vicious temperaments started to improve. The wild cats came to appreciate the comforts that the house offered and one day Lucky ran into the garden to find the two black cats on the lawn with Big Black Cat and tortoiseshell cat. He delighted in chasing three out of the four cats off his lawn since Big Black Cat refused to move.

The first time one of the black cats wandered into the house was the last. Jayne had filled the washing machine with clothes and left the door open while she searched for some washing powder. The black cat went inside to sleep and did not come back out alive. Penelope was the unlucky one who thought she would help out by hanging the washing on the line. She screamed when she pulled out a dressing gown and a very dead ball of matted fur. The shrill of her panic was enough to draw Daniel from his bedroom and he came to survey the damage.

'Hmmmm….' he deliberated. 'Well, Penelope. It's black, it's a cat, and its ours.' The poor cat had not been able to avoid its fate of drowning after all. Evan disposed of the body without the need to telephone Hugh and within a few days the other black cat disappeared, searching for a mate he would never find.

Carys hoped that the goat and cat incidents were stored safely away in Jayne and Evan's list of things not to remember. She had developed a need for speed that Silver, her faithful and safe pony that had carried her around for years with little protest was just not able to give her. She found herself getting frustrated with having to constantly urge him forward, always wanting to go faster and further beyond his capabilities. Silver had given her a few challenges over the years such as skidding to a stop in front of a gorse bush and catapulting Carys over his head directly into it. He had thrown Carys to the ground when he got down to roll the first time he rode on the soft sand at Aberavon beach. At some point or other he had refused to cross bridges, rivers and roads but after four years of owning and riding Silver, Carys wanted another horse and she had her heart set on the grace, beauty and highly-strung nature of an Arabian horse.

When Carys finally blurted out to her parents

'I was thinking that I would like to buy, er… get… I mean… yeah, buy another horse. A bigger one… you know, because I'm getting taller… and Silver is not… and I'm too big for him now.'

'You sure that you have enough time for another horse?' Jayne asked.

'Of course I have.' Carys' reply was instant.

'Big time at school though, Carys. You'll be doing important exams soon.' Evan said, thinking that after all the animals he and Carys had brought home over the years on impulse, it was time to start helping her think through these decisions.

'And piano lessons on a Monday and practicing every day?'

'Choir practice on a Tuesday.'

'Badminton on a Wednesday.'

'Orchestra every other Thursday.'

'And seeing your friends, family, and you have applied for that job working in the library on a Saturday morning.' Jayne and Evan ticked off all the activities their daughter was already doing on a weekly basis while Carys rolled her eyes and nodded.

'Yes, mam and dad, I know I've got a lot on but I like being busy and I will be fine with another horse as well.'

Jayne and Evan looked at each other and nodded. Carys had always been this way, always busy, rarely stopping for a quiet evening in to watch television. She was in complete contrast to Daniel, who hated having too much to do and feeling the pressure of time. Daniel preferred to be doing very little, preferably one thing at a time, but spending lots of time doing it well. Carys was always trying to cram new activities into her busy schedule. Carys jumped up from the kitchen chair, threw her arms around her parents in turn and ran to find the newspaper to scour the classified adverts. Over the next week she searched for adverts containing 'pure bred Arab horse for sale' and found two of interest. She approached her mother excitedly wanting to know when they could go and see them.

'Give the people a ring and we can go in two day's time. I said I would spend one day with you and one day with Daniel this half term, and if you want to go and look for a horse, that is what we will do.'

'Cool, thanks mum. Errrr... what are you doing with Daniel?'

'Don't ask, I've already done it.' Jayne shut her eyes and shuddered at the memory.

'Oh, come on, tell me what you did?' Carys was intrigued by her mother's apparent horrified memory of her day out with Daniel.

'Well... he wanted to enter a talent competition in the town centre, so I spent the day with him to support him.'

'Did he win?'

'Oh yes. He won all right and I should blinking well think so. I have never heard so many awful renditions of 'Twinkle twinkle little star' and why did the chicken cross the road jokes, in my life.'

'That doesn't sound like fun.'

'No, it wasn't, and all the mothers of all the children who couldn't sing a note were giving me evil looks 'coz Daniel was the best. He didn't notice of course he just got more excited as the day went on because he knew he was going to win. I couldn't wait to get out of there. So, anyway.' Jayne stood up straight and collected her thoughts. 'I'm sure a day out driving in the Welsh countryside will be a nice, refreshing change.'

The two horses that Carys wanted to see were in West Wales. A forlorn Lucky looked out of the living room window as Carys and Jayne packed themselves and a picnic lunch into Jayne's tiny Ford Fiesta car and headed out without him. Carys had wanted to take Lucky on their journey but Jayne refused for obvious reasons.

The steep incline of the mountains in Port Talbot turned into rolling, green fields and hills as Jayne drove west and headed into Ammanford. Carys thought the first horse they were going to see sounded perfect because he had been advertised as being suitable for endurance or long distance riding. With the amount of time she was spending in the saddle with Silver, he sounded ideal. Jayne was less impressed with the prospect of buying this horse because he was more expensive at seven hundred and fifty pounds.

'Oh my God. You can't pay that much money for a horse that's never been ridden' she shrieked when Carys told her the price. Carys did not bother to argue that they were going to see a pedigree horse rather than a mongrel like Silver so she had passively replied

'Well, we might as well go and see him now because I've already made the arrangements.' Jayne was more confident about the second Arab horse that was advertised as a chestnut colt for only three hundred and fifty pounds.

The first Arab was exactly what Carys had been reading and dreaming about. He was slender with long legs, a dished head arching gracefully from his ears to his flaring nostrils and he had real spirit. He pranced alongside his current owner, Ronald, as he was trotted up and down for Carys to see. When Carys jogged alongside him he pushed her to go faster and moved as if he were walking on air, his head held high and his tail kinked over his back. Carys was ecstatic and she left trying to persuade her mother that there was no need to go and see another horse. She wanted this one, Bu.

Jayne was still murmuring about the price as she drove Carys to see the next horse. By the time it had taken Jayne three hours to find the isolated farm at the end of a ten-mile pot holed and rutted lane in Mid-Wales, she also thought that buying Bu was the best option. When they finally arrived to find a skinny chestnut Arab horse locked in a stable, stamping his hooves and shaking his head, Jayne thought that buying Bu was the only option. Carys telephoned Ronald later that evening and he arranged to bring Bu to Tyddyn the following month.

Ronald and his wife, Sally brought Bu to Tyddyn where Carys settled him into his new stable next to Silver. Sally and Ronald were a friendly couple who offered practical advice and guidance to Carys and her parents about owning their new horse. The last thing that Ronald said to Carys as he said good-bye was

'Any problems give me a ring. Can't see you having any trouble though, he'll settle soon enough.'

Bu did not settle as Carys expected him to but fortunately for Ronald she did not contact him every time something happened or he would have spent a lot of time on the phone. Bu's eyes were large, bright and alert and they practically bulged out of his head as he took in his new surroundings. When he was locked in his stable he spun perfect three hundred and sixty degree circles, snorting and stamping his hooves on the concrete floor. If he was turned out in the paddock he galloped around at breakneck speed, regularly stopping and skidding into the five bar gate. He was certainly the handsome, graceful yet highly-strung and challenging horse that Carys had desired.

Most domestic horses soon realise that when they are kept in a stable and confined in small paddocks the chances of being attacked and eaten by dangerous animals are practically non-existent. Bu lived every day as if there were lions, tigers and other invisible predators hiding in the bushes, behind the paddock fence or in the top of the tall trees surrounding the paddock. He jumped at anything that moved, ran away from things he had not seen before and tore around the paddock for most of the day for no reason other than he seemed to like to go fast.

Bu had a 'fright list' that consisted of most of the things on Lucky's, admittedly dwindled, danger list. This list included cats, dogs, trees, the lawnmower even though it did not venture into the paddock, the hosepipe, the next-door neighbours (whatever clothes they were dressed in), visitors, bikes, cars, balls and everything else that he had not seen yet in his short life, so that was basically everything and anything.

Lucky was baffled by Bu. Most of the large, funny looking four legged animals that Carys kept in wooden buildings were quiet, moved slowly and did not seem to mind Lucky sniffing around their back legs or trying to catch their tails. This horse was larger and whenever Lucky got close to him he turned away and galloped to the other side of the paddock. At first, Lucky thought this was a great game and eagerly chased after Bu, growling in curiosity rather than anger.

Lucky soon learned to be careful around the hyper active horse though. Bu would be grazing quietly one minute with Lucky sniffing around his legs. Then, Bu would fling his head around before rearing up onto his back legs, jumping in the air, bucking, farting and galloping to the other side of the paddock in one of his many flights from danger. Lucky also stayed well away from Bu's stable. There were all sorts of sudden bangs and crashes from within as Bu fly bucked in his stable, kicked holes through the wooden plywood walls and threw his bucket over the stable door, clattering out into the yard.

Bu was too young for Carys to ride immediately so she settled herself with preparing him for a future of being ridden under saddle. In the meantime, Carys and Silver were given the opportunity to work for Evan's friend at Margam Country Park over the school summer holidays of 1996. Hugh was organising pony rides and naturally needed ponies to provide the service. Bu and Silver were offered free grazing in the lush grass fields in the park and Carys got a small paycheck.

Carys walked Silver around in circles every day of the summer holidays with different children on his back. He was unflappable despite the boat shows, helicopters landing, kites, motorcycle stunt shows and any other loud or colourful display during one of the many shows or fetes held in the park. Bu was kept in a field at the east end of Margam Park where it was much quieter and he could gallop around and run away from whatever monsters he thought were hiding in the bushes. Hugh, who had initially started to eye up Bu's potential for giving pony rides, quickly realised he was far safer out of everybody's way.

Carys' summer spent in Margam Country Park offered Lucky plenty of opportunities to redeem himself after the unfortunate bullmastiff episode shortly after his arrival in the Davies family. Evan took to dropping Lucky off to Carys early evening when the park shut as she usually took Silver for a ride up the gallops. It is a long steep haul from outside Margam Castle up onto the heather clad hill that runs parallel to the coastline. The official start of the horse gallops is by a stone pulpit with a tall stone boulder situated in the middle, the letters 'bro' clearly marked on it. There are five square shaped clusters of sweet chestnut, oak and beech trees planted to enhance the landscape and provide for game purposes below. From here, the gallops open up and head further up the southern slopes of Margam Mountain until they reach the northern boundary of Margam Country Park. The other side is forestry land where ancient and varied, broadleaved deciduous trees group together amongst acres of Sitka Spruce evergreens and larch forest plantations.

Lucky accepted the challenge of the gallops with his usual gusto and excitement. By the time Carys and Silver slowed from the fastest gallop Silver could manage, they would both be panting but Lucky would still only be half way up the hill, his tiny body partly concealed by the long grass he was struggling to run in. It may not have been the longest path Lucky had run along but it was steep and there was no short cut he knew of. Still, Lucky knew what was expected of him when Evan brought him to see Carys and Silver in this place and during all the times he ran up the gallops, he did not have to defend his favourite little person from one bullmastiff dog. Of course, that was partly because he did not see any there but Carys still declared him reformed from past behaviour.

Hugh proved to be an entertaining person to work for. He joked constantly and revelled in telling one comical story after another. The laughter lines around his eyes deepened when he smiled broadly and he chuckled often, mostly at Carys' expense. It was quiet one day with only Carys, Hugh and some of his friends standing around the two ponies that had not moved in an hour. It was not going to be a profitable day as the park was quiet with no children in sight.

Hugh told a story about his mate's goat that had died in his back garden and he did not know what to do with it. He had phoned Hugh because he knew Hugh was working in Margam Country Park where he thought there might have been animal disposal facilities on site.

'So anyway…' Hugh told his friends with a wide smile on his face, already struggling to contain his laughter. 'I'm driving along the motorway with a dead goat in the back of my pick up truck when I realise that the man with the key to the slaughter house in Margam Park is on holiday. I can't get rid of this goat in there. So I find these group of teenagers hanging around outside the entrance to Margam Park and offered them twenty quid to bury the animal in a nearby field.' Hugh's friends roared with laughter while Carys snorted in disgust. She dreaded to think what the owner of this goat would have said if only they had known what Hugh had done. Hugh continued with his story.

'So I give them the goat, a spade and tell them to bury it in the field next to the entrance to the park. I told them I'd be back in an hour with their money. Well, I'd been given fifty quid to get rid of the thing so I was still thirty quid up. I went back in an hour to see how these kids were getting on and, well… I nearly had a heart attack.' Hugh stopped talking and put his hand over his heart dramatically.

'What had they done, Hugh?' asked one of his mates in between guffaws. Even Carys was intrigued by what Hugh had found.

'Well. They had only buried this goat upside down but they hadn't dug the hole deep enough and all four of his hoofs were sticking out of the ground.' Hugh's friends burst into peals of laughter and even Carys could not resist a smile although she quickly worked hard to correct it back into a grimace.

'What did you do, Hugh?' one of his friends asked.

'What did I do? What could I do? I told those lazy teenagers to get on their bikes and hop it, which they did. But then I was left with four hooves sticking up from the ground. I had to rebury him with some extra soil from my own garden.'

Hugh and his friends were still laughing hysterically when some wide-eyed children wanting a pony ride appeared. Hugh had a wide grin on his face as he turned to Carys, slapped her on the back with a twinkle in his eye and asked her

'All right, Carys?'

Carys nodded suspiciously, wondering why Hugh was unusually asking about her feelings. As Hugh helped the first child up onto Silver and Carys went to lead them away, Hugh's friends left, shouting goodbye and saying

'Good story mate.'

'Story,' Hugh replied to them. 'Not a story, all this happened the day before Christmas.' Carys froze as she made the connection between Hugh's story and the tragic demise of her own goat.

'Come on Carys, let's get the pony moving,' Hugh stared at her with laugher lines etched deep around his eyes. Carys led Silver in a circle, her mind working overtime as she realised that she was the owner of the dead goat buried in some farmer's field outside Margam Park. She angrily blinked back the tears stinging her eyes, clamped her mouth shut and plodded along with Silver at her side. She turned on Hugh as soon as the children were out of sight.

'You paid some kids to bury my goat?' she accused him and Hugh roared with laughter. 'It's not funny.' She continued to cry at him.

'Oh dear… I was wondering when you were going to realise the goat was yours.' and Hugh doubled over with tears streamed down his cheeks. Carys was so annoyed that Hugh found it funny that she was considering storming off and leaving him to do the work for the rest of the day.

'Don't worry, Carys,' Hugh said in between guffaws. 'I got rid of your goat just as I promised your dad and the other one went to live on my mate's farm, I'm just having you on.'

Despite Hugh's jesting of Carys, he helped her train Bu so that by the time a glorious summer spent at Margam Park was over and Bu and Silver returned to Tyddyn, Bu was finally ready to ride. Within a month he was executing perfect circles and squares in the paddock, carrying himself proudly with Carys on his back. Lucky watched Carys ride Bu in the paddock every time. He did not want to leave in case he missed the chance of going out riding with her but at the same time he was bored watching her ride circles. He sat by the edge of the paddock and whined impatiently until the day that Carys and Bu ventured out.

Lucky leapt into action when Carys and Bu headed for the mountain. Carys was pleased when she asked Bu to go forward up the mountain path and he confidently strode ahead. She had almost forgotten about the predators that stalked her young horse until they had been out for about fifteen minutes.

Lucky was trailing closely behind Bu's back legs when Bu ducked his head, snorted and stopped before jumping into the air, all four hooves off the ground. He twisted to the left mid flight and Carys was thrown into the air. When she landed she missed the saddle and her horse and was dumped unceremoniously onto the ground, nearly crushing a very surprised Lucky. Carys saw the Dinas Mountain turn upside down and then right itself as she found herself sprawled on her back with Bu and Lucky staring down at her in shock. Carys knew that there was something seriously wrong if she was looking up at Lucky. She rose unsteadily from the ground, checked for monsters in the bushes, remounted Bu and continued up the path. Lucky ducked into the bushes and reappeared ten feet in front of Bu, which he decided was a much safer place. Surprisingly, Bu did not baulk when the bushes actually rustled with something real.

Lucky was so delighted to be back up the mountain with Carys on one of her long, four-legged friends that when they joined the main track at the top he ran on ahead, looking behind him to make sure Carys was still following. Lucky knew that the path only went downhill for a short while until they reached the back gardens of the houses along Baglan road and then it was a long run up a steep track. This was where Carys and her horses always galloped so he wanted to make sure he got a head start.

Carys was pleased that Bu seemed to have forgotten about his monsters so, despite a sore backside she decided to try a trot to keep up with Lucky who was speeding off in front of her. Bu responded immediately and Carys got just slightly distracted by the sun sparkling off the retreating tide on Aberavon beach when Bu accelerated with such speed that Carys was thrown backwards into the saddle and lost her grip on his reins.

By the time she managed to catch her breath Bu was galloping at breakneck speed around the Dinas Baglan Mountain and there was nothing she could do about it. Lucky heard Bu's pounding hooves coming up behind him and he lowered his head and started using all four, instead of just three of his legs, to propel himself faster up the mountain path. He had to jump to the side of the path to avoid being run over by Bu and realised that he needed to go a lot faster if he was going to keep up. He watched helplessly as Carys and Bu rapidly disappeared into the distance.

When Lucky reached the fork in the mountain road he was surprised not to find Carys on her horse waiting. She always stopped at this point for him. He hesitated briefly as he considered which way to go and continued up the mountain, panting heavily from the extra effort he was putting into trying to catch them. Bu had bolted to the top of the Dinas Mountain and Carys had really started to panic when she realised that they were running out of up hill and would soon be going back down hill. Her heart was beating in time to Bu's pounding hooves and there were tears streaming from her eyes as she wrestled with her horse to stop.

As Bu galloped wildly to the summit of the mountain he saw another one of his imaginary monsters and slammed on the brakes skidding to a complete halt, snorting and breathing hard. Carys was propelled forward, executed a neat forward roll somersault and found herself standing on her own two feet with shaking knees, her horse's reins still in her hand. Thankful that she had landed on her feet she shakily turned her horse around and wobbled back down the mountain. She was trembling all over but her fear was also mixed with adrenalin, a hormone that was coursing through her and fast becoming addictive. Carys had progressed from riding a pony that was the mechanical equivalent to a Ford Fiesta diesel, slow, steady and safe. Bu, on the other hand, was like a Bugatti Veyron, an eight-litre quad-turbo charged car only without any working brakes.

When Lucky found Carys and Bu he stopped dead, a look of relief on his face. He even sat on his haunches for a few minutes panting heavily while Bu made his way back down towards him. Carys was secretly surprised that Lucky had not given up and gone to the Baglan house.

From then on, Lucky had to work extra hard when he went out riding with Carys and Bu. The adrenalin rush that Carys got from the speed of her new horse clouded her sixteen years of limited common sense. She raced him around the mountains with a similar sense of mania that Bu had naturally embedded in his nature and personality. Lucky had to work harder, run faster and use his short cuts over and through the mountain more creatively to keep up, but he did keep up, just. His body became leaner, fitter and wiry and for just a little while, he did not run away and he slept soundly every night. It did not last.

Chapter 13

Krystie

Lucky yelped and plunged sideways into the spiky hedgerow. Two black, metal clad hooves stamped down onto the spot where only moments earlier he had been. Lucky cowered uncomfortably against the thorns while Bu pranced in one place and Carys wrestled with him. He licked his lips nervously as he watched two grey hind legs dance dangerously close to him but just as quickly as they had nearly landed on top of him they disappeared further along the track.

Bu had been walking quietly along the mountain track just a few yards behind him so Lucky knew that there was nothing in the bushes. The nervy, grey animal had spooked anyway and jumped from one side of the track to the other. Lucky warily emerged from the bushes and once again made a mental note to keep a safe distance from the crazy animal that Carys was bringing out these days. He took a few tentative strides and spied Carys and Bu getting smaller on the horizon. He sighed heavily before running to catch up with them, he much preferred to get a head start.

When Lucky caught up with Carys she was sitting stiffly on Bu who was snorting and shaking where he stood. His neck was beautifully arched and his wide, bright eyes bulged from his dished head. He was staring at a jet-black horse with a perfect white star on his face strolling towards him. Lucky took no notice of the stocky Welsh Cob, he always encountered other horses when out with Carys but he had never been given a reason to be interested in any of them.

A tanned woman, somewhere in her late thirties and with hair as dark as her horse, sat comfortably back in the saddle with her horses reins in one hand and a cigarette in the other. She casually waved one hand in greeting to Carys and slowed her horse as she eyed Bu with a sense of admiration and wariness.

'All right to come past?' She called to Carys as she reined her horse to a complete stop.

'It's OK,' Carys said 'come past slowly, he's just looking coz he's young.'

'Oh he's gorgeous,' the woman exclaimed as she rode her chunky horse alongside Bu, his flaring red nostrils and the steam emanating from them the only sign that he was a living, breathing animal.

'Thanks,' Carys said gratefully to the woman as she felt Bu finally exhale from underneath her. 'He has a tendency to bolt off with me if I'm not careful.'

'No problem, luv,' the woman said with a stronger Welsh accent than was usual for Port Talbot. 'He is lovely isn't he? What type of horse is he?'

Since Bu was Carys' favourite subject she stopped to boast to the friendly woman. Her name was Krystie and she lived and kept her two horses in Cwmafan. She quickly confessed that she did not like keeping her horse at her current stables because the farm was in a really bad state, rubbish littered everywhere and broken fences with barbed wired protruding in every direction.

'Poor Shadow's in a tiny stable and there's no grass up there, I'm feeding him hay all day' she moaned as she leant over to pat her mount on his strong and powerful neck. He was three times the width of Bu even though he was not as tall. Lucky sniffed around the black horse's tail. He was bored with waiting but thought he should make the most of being able to catch his breath. 'Where do you keep your horse anyway?' Carys explained about her stables at Tyddyn and Krystie was immediately impressed.

'Oh its sounds fabulous up there,' Krystie indicated in the direction of Tyddyn. 'Have you got any stables free?'

'Yes, its only my two horses up there at the moment coz all the others have gone for the summer to graze elsewhere.'

'I'll come up later and have a look then, shall I?' Krystie got directions from Carys and said she would come up that evening. Before she said farewell she looked down and caught sight of Lucky.

‘Well, hello there. You funny little looking dog, you,’ she cooed to the scruffy terrier at her horse’s feet.

Lucky looked up at the woman on the strange horse and something changed. His alpha status, his family, the importance of expanding on and defending his pack, Carys’ funny four legged animals; they became of second importance compared to knowing this woman. He wagged his tail until it blurred and listened intently as the woman spoke to him kindly, a change from the many people who shouted at him when he chased after their balls, dogs’ or children. When Carys rode off Lucky dithered, looking backwards and forwards from Carys to Krystie. He turned away from Carys and ran to catch up with the woman on the black horse.

‘Oi, excuse me, luv, you’d better call your dog. He won’t keep up with me where I’m going.’

Carys sighed at the sight of Lucky once again going in the wrong direction. Lucky reluctantly followed Carys back to their home but he snuck the occasional glance behind him at the woman who had made such an impression on him.

When Krystie arrived at Tyddyn six hours later, Carys was surprised to see that she was still on the back of her black cob. Even more surprising was Lucky’s reaction. When Lucky heard the sound of hooves clattering up the road behind the stables he ran to the entrance gate and greeted Krystie like his best friend. He jumped up at her when she dismounted from her horse, whining and yelping in excitement.

'Well, hiya there, little one. You really are a funny looking dog, aren't you?' Lucky threw himself onto the floor and rolled onto his back, his paws waving at Krystie from the ground. He demoted Carys to being second in charge and made Krystie his equivalent. In that instant he would have defended her from anything, searched miles for whatever prey she required and then contentedly followed her around for the rest of his life.

'Hi Krystie, wasn't expecting you to be still on horseback' Carys greeted her over the gate.

'Well, we rode for hours after we saw you, then we had a few hours rest outside the pub. Thought I might as well come this way while I was out.' Krystie took one look around the stables at Tyddyn and immediately declared her opinion. 'Ruddy hell, it is fabulous up here.' She led her horse into one of the stone stables and took his saddle and bridle off. She phoned her brother to pick her up and reappeared an hour later with another smaller pony that she had on loan from a local farmer.

Lucky was enamoured with Krystie and followed her around whenever she was up the stables. He amalgamated himself with her shadow while she swept the stable yard and then flopped to the floor when Krystie sat outside the tack room for a cup of tea and a cigarette, something she did often. Lucky had no interest in leaving the stables when Krystie was there.

Krystie also fascinated Carys. She lived every day as if it was the only one she had to worry about and her two horses were a central part of her daily life. On the odd occasion that Krystie was not wearing jodhpurs and riding boots she was in jeans and a t-shirt and working in one of two pubs in Cwmafan. When Krystie was not pouring pints behind the bar she was usually in any of the other six pubs in the village. Krystie smoked heavily, joked often, laughed loudly, drank alcohol freely and rode her horse nearly every day.

Krystie's carefree attitude only faltered the first time she met Evan. When Evan wandered up the stables to greet the owner of the two, black horses he had spied grazing in the paddock, Krystie was in her usual place sitting on the stone step outside the tack room, cigarette in one hand and a cup of tea in the other.

'Have I met you before?' Evan asked Krystie after they exchanged pleasantries. She paused decisively, eyeing him with suspicion as a distant memory materialised.

'Um… no I don't think so.'

'You don't drink down in the Red Lion then?'

'No… I stay in Cwmafan usually.'

'Oh well… nice to meet you anyway'

Krystie's cheeks flushed red as Evan left and her head fell into her hands. The burning embers of her cigarette end were dangerously close to singeing her hair.

'What's wrong, Krys?' Carys enquired, bemused by her reaction to Evan.

'Oh my gawd. You're not going to believe this.' she replied, starting to laugh.

'What, Krys?'

'Oh... I just can't believe that's your Dad.'

'Why... come on, tell me Krys, how do you know Dad?' Krystie was laughing now.

'Well...' she started dramatically. 'I must have met your father last year sometime. I was down in Port Talbot with some of the girls and I did meet him in the Red Lion.'

'Why did you just tell him...?'

'Wait now, you haven't heard it all yet.' Krystie stubbed out her cigarette and immediately lit another. 'Someone made a joke about me riding horses... I can't remember who it was or what they said, but they were trying to be funny. Well, anyway... your Dad was standing next to me talking to one of my friends. When he heard the joke he turned to me and said, 'Oh, my daughter's got horses as well, where do you keep yours?' Krystie paused with a smile on her face.

'Come on, get to the point.'

'Well, I thought he was chatting me up but it was the worst chat-up line I ever heard so I told him to stop talking rubbish and walked away like the snob that I like to think I am.'

Krystie's initial awkwardness at meeting Evan did not last and it certainly did not deter her from keeping her horses at Tyddyn. When Carys got home from school she would change from her decent clothes to the dirty ones chucked on her bedroom floor and race up the stables where Krystie, Lucky and two horses with saddles and bridles would be waiting. It got even better when Carys finished her secondary education exams and had four glorious summer months before she had to start college in the October. The summer sun shone surprisingly reliably and Krystie, Carys, Lucky and two horses travelled considerable distances over the picture postcard-mountains in Port Talbot.

Once Krystie got over the shock of how fast and how far Lucky could travel with the horses she stopped worrying about him when she galloped off along a track deep into the forests. If Lucky was not waiting for Carys and Krystie by the time they slowed their horses he was never far behind.

Krystie took Carys and Lucky deep into the Afan Argoed forests where hectares of rolling hills and mountains are frequently filled with hikers, Sunday strollers, mountain bikers or horse riders. Long and wide paths are flanked either side by lush, thick trees, following the curves of the mountain crevices deep into the valleys. Old disused railway lines running over narrow bridges and high-rise viaducts serving as soft cycle ways and walkways. It's quiet there, only the tinkling of mountain fresh water falling softly down stone crusted gullies, cascading into the louder rush of the Afan River meandering through the bottom of the valley. Smaller tracks weave across the larger paths creating a maze that you can feel lost in when the trees obstruct the view of the enchanting and peaceful landscape.

Carys' respect for Lucky who kept up with her and Krystie when they were out riding increased when she realised that Krystie did not know where she was going most of the time. She had a vague sense of direction of where she wanted to go without knowing how to get there, so most of the time she ended up in a completely different place than intended.

Carys quickly learnt that when Krystie was lost she began blabbing about the history of ancient stone ruins.

'Now,' Krystie would instruct Carys 'you see those large stones over there? Well, they are the remains of an old Roman village.' Or 'That old stone wall there was built during the war and all the locals used to hide behind it when they thought the Germans were about to invade.' Considering Krystie was wandering aimlessly through the forests, Lucky did well to anticipate where she and Carys would end up when they galloped off, but he always did.

Chapter 14

The Stalker

It was not just the mountains that Lucky got to know during his rides out with Carys and Krystie. Courtesy of Krystie he also got to know most of the pubs in Cwmafan. Krystie did not believe in riding a horse for more than a few hours without stopping for a refreshing drink. Sometimes Carys, Krystie and Lucky would stop at her house, which was conveniently located in the centre of Cwmafan village and relatively close to all the paths leading down from the surrounding mountains. However, Krystie's favourite refreshing drink was of the stronger variety and the sort that you could only buy from pubs. Lucky was always glad for the opportunity to rest his legs while the horses ate grass and Carys and Krystie sated their thirst. He only needed half an hour before he was ready to get going again and since Krystie only even stopped for about this length of time he accepted the habit gratefully.

Lucky got a bit agitated when Carys and Krystie stopped outside a pub late afternoon and did not move again for four hours. At first he was glad to catch his breath but when Krystie kept disappearing into the building through the front porch area he got bored and tried to follow her. He was cut off every time by one of the many male regulars inside and also the landlady who had an extremely high hair do and a quick, sharp tongue. Undeterred he continued to try and break into the building that Krystie was going into but as quick as he found his way into the pub the faster he was thrown out again. Still, Lucky was nothing if not persistent and he was still being thrown out of the pub when Krystie could barely walk and Carys could hardly talk.

When a man went to help Krystie mount her horse, Lucky got ready to head in the direction of Tyddyn. He stopped to wait while Krystie was thrown up into her saddle and then, like Daniel had done years ago, as soon as she was sat astride her horse she toppled over the other side, crashing to the floor with a thud.

'Ahhhhhhhhhh........' Lucky ran underneath Krystie's horse and jumped onto her stomach.

'Ahhhhhhhhhh........' She screamed again. Krystie was lying on the floor still holding her horse's reins while her horse stood quietly beside her. Lucky pushed his wet nose into Krystie's, whining in concern and curious as to why she was on the ground.

'Ahhhhhhhhhh... Lucky, mun... Get off meeeeeee.' Krystie's wails echoed up into the mountains surrounding the village. When Krystie was able to mount her horse successfully, it was Lucky who led the way home.

When a new day had arrived and Carys and Krystie stopped off in The Copper House pub Lucky was more settled. Unlike the previous pub that had been in the middle of a built up part of Cwmafan, The Copper House was a large detached building with beer gardens on either side of it. Carys and Krystie wasted no time taking off their horses' saddles and bridles and shutting them in the enclosed beer garden to munch on grass while they settled down on a wooden picnic bench. Lucky sniffed around and explored the enclosed, grassed area of the pub grounds and the concrete car park for four hours without getting bored. He was used to this routine now and as long as Krystie stayed, so would he.

Carys and Krystie sat out the front of the pub, enjoying the warm sun that was slowly disappearing over the Foel mountain. They were unconcerned as the sky became darker and the twinkling stars lit up the night sky. In fact, they had drunk so much that they barely noticed the time at all. Lucky's protective instinct kicked in when he saw two men in uniform step out of a car with bright blue and red flashing lights. For once, the law was not there because of Lucky but he did not know that so he reacted towards them as badly as he had always done with people in uniform. He ran past Carys and Krystie, growling threateningly and stopping just in front of the policemen, barking, baring his teeth and daring them to come closer.

'Lucky. Stop it, come here.' Krystie called to him. Even in Carys' drunken state she could not believe how quickly Lucky listened to Krystie. He stopped barking at the policemen immediately and retreated to sit by her feet but his whole posture was leant forwards as he continued with what he considered to be a low and menacing growl.

'Right then, ladies.' One of the policemen announced. 'Are those your horses?' Carys and Krystie looked at each other and then simultaneously looked down at their riding boots and jodhpurs. The temptation to say no was overwhelming but given their dress code they both shrugged in defeat. Krystie took charge and Carys, being underage, kept very quiet.

'Oh, hello there,' Krystie replied, raising one hand and waving it around in greeting, doing her best to put on her posh accent without any success whatsoever. 'Yes, these are my horses. Is there a problem, sir?'

'Well, I'm afraid that we have had a complaint to say there are two horses that have been abandoned in the beer garden and that the owners are drunk.'

'Oh, I wouldn't put my horses in danger like that, we've been drinking coca-cola, its just such a lovely night, you know?' Krystie answered slowly and Carys stifled a giggle as she heard the effort that her friend was making not to slur her words.

'Yes' Carys chirped in. 'I am 'ompletely soba.' Krystie shot a warning look at her but Carys' verbal incompetence was forgotten when the heavy wooden front door of the pub flew open and the barmen appeared with two glasses of lager that Krystie had paid for earlier and forgotten about. One policeman looked at his watch pointedly as it was past the legal time to be serving drinks. The barman faltered.

'Ha ha, forgot about these drinks didn't you girls?' he stuttered nervously as he tried to cover his tracks. 'Been on the bar for the last half hour they have. Don't worry about the empty glasses, I'll get them after I finish cleaning.'

He put the drinks onto the table and retreated quickly back into the pub, slamming the door behind him. The sound of the metal clanging of the bolts being drawn gave Krystie just enough time to think of something intelligent to say.

'We'd been on ours way in a binute, now.' That was not it. Lucky compensated for Krystie's lack of organized thought by growling just a little bit louder and baring more of his teeth to show these men in uniform how serious he was. One policeman addressed Carys and Krystie sternly,

'I think this is a good time to warn you that it is possible to be charged with being drunk and disorderly in charge of a horse. I suggest you leave those drinks and get your horses back to where they are supposed to be at this time of night… and if that's your scruffy little dog, you can take him with you as well.' Lucky pricked his ears and cocked his head to one side when he saw one of the uniformed men look down at him. He stopped growling and kept looking at Krystie for some signal that she needed him to officially send these men away. Krystie assured the policemen that they would do exactly that. There was an uncomfortable silence while Carys and Krystie hoped the policeman would leave so they could drink what looked to be their last drinks of the night but as both men stood there with their arms folded, they tacked the horses up ready to go instead.

Krystie avoided having another good look at the floor by using the picnic table to mount her horse. Lucky proudly led the way home as Carys and Krystie wobbled around, clinging to the back of their horses. Naturally, he considered his protection over them to be the only reason that the men in uniform had let them leave without any harm. Carys thought that she had got off lightly but she had not counted on an anonymous person tipping her mother off to the evening's events. She did not know who had told her mother that she had been seen drunk outside the Copper house with a horse and policeman, but Jayne was not happy and Carys earned another two weeks of house curfew. Carys was able to remain fairly cheerful about this though because it had been a good night and she was still allowed to ride her horses in the evenings.

The enjoyment that Carys was having riding with Krystie was cut short at the end of the summer when both Silver and Bu became lame and Carys was unable to ride them. Krystie may have been without human company but she still had Lucky. As soon as he heard Krystie's clapped out Ford Sierra rumbling up the mountain lane he ran to the back door and yelped until someone let him out. Without a backward glance, he would race up the stables in plenty of time to greet Krystie getting out of her car.

Carys often checked with Krystie that she was OK with Lucky going riding with her. A lot of people found him a nuisance but Krystie honestly seemed to enjoy his company.

'Of course I don't mind him coming out with me.' Krystie drawled with a smile. 'Mind you. It's a bit embarrassing when he decides to have a bit of loving with another dog when he's supposed to be following me on the horse. There's too many girls for him to play with in Cwmafan.' Carys nodded in agreement, remembering how Eryn had cringed and ridden her horse off as fast as she dared when Lucky had shown off his manhood to stray dogs in the past. 'But then again, he's so funny as well. Whenever he sees children playing with a ball he goes and joins in. He even managed to push a football into a goal the other day. Half the kids were screaming at him and the other half were cheering.' Carys chuckled. She thought it hilarious that Krystie found Lucky's antics enjoyable whereas as most other people ranted and raved about how they wished they had not been there and responsible for 'that dog.'

Krystie arrived at Tyddyn one day with a pony that barely stood higher than a Labrador dog and her tiny, six year old niece, Kary, sitting astride him. The pony was the perfect size for Kary although his large, round stomach was a bit of a problem. Kary could not quite wrap her legs around him so she sat tentatively perched on top of him with her legs sticking straight out either side. This did not deter her and she was quite capable of kicking Alf persistently until he trotted or cantered off as she hung on for dear life.

Krystie decided she was going to be a good aunt and take Kary out for a ride with her. Lucky, of course, was right behind them as they rode up and around the Dinas mountain. He trotted behind the small pony that was moving its legs as quickly as possible in order to keep up with Krystie on her longer legged horse. Lucky thought that the pace was a lot slower today but as long as he was able to be with Krystie he was content to slow down and accommodate the pace.

When Lucky started to follow his equine companions through a field he saw the herd of black and white animals straight away. He did not pay them much attention until they cautiously crept up behind him and the horses. Every time he looked over his shoulder the curious cows were encroaching a few steps closer. He began to get irritated by their presence so turned around for a better look and immediately decided that twenty black and white cows should be on his danger list. He started to emit a low warning growl, his hackles on end as the largest cow nosed its way closer.

Krystie was petrified of cats, children (that do not like horses), the supernatural, pigs and fish, particularly the massive pike that apparently lurk in the freshwater lake at Kenfig nature reserve. She was always telling Carys not to ride close to the waters edge because 'They have big gnashers.'

When Krystie heard Lucky's low growl she turned around, saw the cows starting to surround her and Kary and screamed. A herd of young and inquisitive cows was definitely more frightening than any large fish with big teeth. Krystie dug her heels into her horse's chunky sides and galloped him over to the gate leading out of the field.

'Kary, come on. Quick!'

When Krystie reached the gate she turned around and froze. She got a quick glimpse of tiny Kary sitting astride Alf, her legs flapping against his fat sides while his head was lowered to scoff at the grass. Lucky was standing defiantly in front of Kary and Alf, barking at any cow that came too close. The cows completely surrounded Lucky, Kary and Alf and Krystie lost sight of them. She screamed again but since she could not think of anything else to do, she lit a cigarette and puffed heavily on it.

Meanwhile, in the middle of a herd of cows, Lucky was defending Kary and her pony with his life. He ran around her in circles barking his deepest warning. When a cow brought its large, wet nose too close to him, Lucky lunged forward and snapped at it. Kary's little legs were still flapping against her little pony but he continued to eat the lush green grass, oblivious of his surroundings.

Alf eventually realised that he had lost his equine companion, lifted his head from the grass and trotted in the direction of the sounds of Krystie screaming. The cows quickly parted and allowed Kary, Alf and Lucky to continue on their way but Lucky did not stop barking until the cows were a safe distance behind them. Kary was undisturbed by the events but by the time she had joined her aunt at the gate, Krystie was distraught, shaking, crying and breaking wind. Her emotional state had not improved much by the time Carys found her sitting outside the tack room a few hours later, cigarette in one hand and a cup of tea in the other, her face white and drawn.

'Well, I tell you what, Carys… I have never been so frightened in my life' Krystie said after relaying the afternoons events to Carys.

'Those cows are OK, Krys, they're just heifers. They don't come that near to you and they move out of the way when you approach them.'

'Approach them? You crazy or what? I got out of there as soon as I could.'

'What about poor Kary? It was her first proper ride. How was she?'

'Oh, she was all right. She had Lucky to protect her.'

'What?'

'Oh yeah, that stupid pony of hers would not move from the middle of the field. He found a bit of grass and he stood there with his head down munching away. The cows surrounded her.'

'Krys, you didn't leave Kary where she was?'

'Yes… I know… I feel really bad. I just… panicked. By the time I had shouted for her to follow me I was nearly back on the mountain track and she was left kicking a pony that would not move.'

'Oh, Krys…'

'Yeah but don't worry, Lucky was there. He would not let any of those cows near to her. He was brilliant. That dog can come riding with me any time he wants. My protector.'

Lucky had already forgotten about the cows by that evening. He lived in the moment and did not lie in front of the fire thinking about his day and what he had accomplished. He both wondered at, and enjoyed, the extra attention he got from Jayne and Evan though. Carys had been proud to announce that Lucky had not only been good, he had been heroic.

After the cow incident, Krystie was even happier to have Lucky accompany her when she rode. This arrangement was perfect for everyone because as long as Lucky was riding regularly with Krystie, he was not running away, making midnight calls or fraternising at parties. But, as history might have helped to predict, the good behaviour and the high esteem that Krystie held in Lucky did not last.

What started as a hangover and a headache for Krystie turned into a cold and then full-blown flu. She asked Carys to look after her horses for a few days while she nursed herself back to health. She did not come up the stables again for a week and it was the longest week of Lucky's life. He took to moping around outside the tack room where she usually sat smoking, or whining by the back door, waiting for the sound of her car. Every morning he would run up to the stables, straight to the spot where she usually sat. Then, when he found that she was not there he slumped back down to the house.

'That dog is a shadow of himself.' Evan commented one morning.

'Yeah well, at least he's behaving himself for once.' Jayne muttered although even she was concerned over Lucky's apathetic demeanour.

When at last Lucky heard the exhaust on Krystie's car blowing as she drove up the mountain lane he was beside himself. He was up the stables before Krystie could get out of her car and as soon as she opened the door he tried to jump up onto her lap. Krystie had to grab his collar just to stop him from clambering into the car.

'Aw all right mun,' she greeted him with her hand still on his collar. 'All right, I've missed you as well.' As Lucky wildly spun in small tight circles and continued to try and jump up on her, Krystie became less tolerant.

'For gawd's sake mun, dog, get down. NO. GET DOWN.' Undeterred by being physically pushed away Lucky continued to spin around in circles as Krystie walked through the stable gate and sat in her usual place to light a cigarette.

'All right Krys?' Carys asked, amused with Lucky's antics.

'Oh I feel awful.'

'Not going for a ride then?'

'You must be joking, I only come up for a bit of peace and quiet.'

'Fat chance you're going to get that with Lucky around.' Lucky was now sat on his haunches, as still as a statue, watching Krystie's every move with bright attentive eyes and pricked ears.

'Nice that someone wants me, I suppose.'

'Horses are all done anyway.'

'Oh ta luv.'

'I'm off now. You coming up tomorrow? I think Silver might be ready to ride at last.'

'Yeah, see you tomorrow, not early.'

'Yeah, yeah, cool. Send the dog back down the house when you go will you?'

Krystie nodded and patted Lucky on the head, which sent him spinning wildly in circles again.

Krystie smoked a few more cigarettes and fetched some carrots from the back of her car to feed the horses. When she was ready to go she looked around to find Lucky to send him down the house but he was nowhere in sight.

'So much for the daft dog being excited to see me' she muttered as she grabbed her keys and got in her car to drive home. Lucky waited for ten minutes to make sure that Krystie had actually left the stables then he jumped from his hiding place in the backseat into the front passenger one. Krystie screamed, swerved, mounted the curb and narrowly missed a lamppost.

'Ahhhhh... Lucky, Mun.' Lucky jumped up and put his front paws on the dashboard, looking at Krystie expectantly and wagging his long tail wildly.

Carys had been sitting in the living room when she saw Krystie drive her car from the stables. She was still sitting in the living room when Krystie drove back and pulled into the driveway. When Carys opened the front door, it was Lucky who was the first one in the house. He was content that he had spent some more time with Krystie on his own terms so it was acceptable to return to his own place of residence. He made a mental note to hide in her car again tomorrow.

'That ruddy dog' Krystie exclaimed. 'Typical man. I only wanted a quiet night in and I end up carting him around like a taxi driver.'

'What happened?'

'He caught a lift with me.'

Krystie could see the confusion etched on Carys' face so she tried to explain.

'He must have jumped in the back of the car before I left the yard, I didn't know he was there till I got half way home. He frightened the life out of me.'

'You'd better check your car next time then, hadn't you?' Carys laughed.

'Don't worry, I will be.'

Krystie was as good as her word and checked the car thoroughly before leaving the stables again. She did not however think of checking the boot and one day, after she had carelessly thrown her bag in the back, caught a flash of brown hair.

'Ahhhhhhh' she screamed jumping back. 'Carys, there's a rat in my car.'

The rat turned out to be Lucky's tail, the only visible part of him because he had dug his way underneath a couple of black bin bags full of clothes. After this incident Krystie had to check the front seats, back seats and the boot of her car thoroughly before leaving the stables, just in case.

Krystie had been riding for nearly every day since she had brought her horses to Tyddyn. When the weather turned wintery and the amount of daylight hours became shorter, Krystie rode her horses less. Carys started studying in Afan College so she also had less time to take Lucky riding. Lucky began skulking around the back and front door of the house, listening for Krystie's car but flopping in front of the fire to sleep when he did not. Jayne gave him nicknames of 'Lifeless Lucky' and 'Lucky in Love' but the tiny terrier was oblivious to anything but his painful pining for Krystie.

Lucky's love-struck induced depression lifted the day that he remembered he knew where Krystie lived as he had been there many times before over the summer. It did not take him long to find his own way to Krystie's house and he started to establish a regular routine. If Lucky were not able to persuade Krystie to take him home with her and if he could not break into her car, he would walk the five miles to her house instead. Five miles was a comparatively short distance compared to the long rides he had been accompanying her on.

When Lucky arrived at Krystie's house he would bark until she came out. Krystie could not let Lucky into her house because she owned a staffordshire bull terrier and Boxer dog. That was actually her saving grace because if she had let him in her house he probably would not have left. Instead, Krystie would either bring a disgraced Lucky back to Tyddyn or she would phone Carys and Jayne or Evan would have to drive to Cwmafan to get him. It got to the point where Jayne and Evan were using as much petrol fetching Lucky as Krystie was paying in rent for the hire of the stables.

When Carys tired of hearing her parents moan about her fickle dog, she and Krystie came up with a strategy. It was based on the principles that if Lucky could walk to Krystie's house he could certainly walk back again. Krystie had tried ignoring him when he barked outside her house but Lucky was persistent if nothing else. He knew when she was at home because her car was parked outside so he would just continue barking until she came out. Krystie and Carys made a plan so that when Lucky arrived outside Krystie's house she would go outside and make a fuss of him and then attempt to shoo him away.

The next time Lucky went to see Krystie and her car was outside, he began to yelp relentlessly. When Krystie opened her front door he spun wildly in circles, his traditional greeting reserved for her. Krystie ruffled the scruff of his neck and Lucky threw himself on his back with his legs in the air. He was disappointed when Krystie did not scratch his belly as she usually did.

Instead, Krystie drew herself up to her full height, pointed in the direction of Tyddyn and gave her instructions.

'No, Lucky, go home.' Lucky jumped to his feet and stared at her intently, his head cocked to one side and his ears pricked. He stopped barking but when Krystie locked herself into her house he did not leave. Instead he flopped onto the pavement outside and settled down to wait for her to re-emerge. It was a long time before he fell asleep and this was when Krystie telephoned Carys.

'Carys,' she said whispering down the phone. 'He's gone to sleep by my ruddy front gate.' Carys laughed and asked her why she was whispering.

'He can't hear you from outside Krystie,' she scoffed at her friend.

'You don't know that with Lucky though, do you?' Krystie whispered back, half joking and half serious.

'Look Krystie, don't worry about Lucky. He's not going to stay there all night. He'll come home when he's had enough.'

By the time Krystie had to leave for work that evening Lucky was still sleeping outside her front gate. He did not hear Krystie sneak out her back door and tiptoe down her garden. He did not see her climb over her garden fence and into an adjoining field. By the time Krystie had taken a sizeable detour to her place of work, Lucky was none the wiser. He woke up cold and hungry and with one last longing look at Krystie's house, returned to Tyddyn about nine o' clock that night.

'We've cracked it, Krystie,' Carys told her confidently the following day. 'He was back well before we all went to bed.' Krystie was not very impressed. Taking a detour through a field to get to work was not something she wanted to do all the time.

Chapter 15

Banned.

Once Lucky was confident that he knew where Krystie lived, there was nothing to stop him from visiting her whenever he wanted. The morning chaos in the Davies house was not getting any less despite Carys and Daniel being older and Jayne and Evan having less responsibility for them. Lucky still had a lot of opportunities to leave without being noticed.

Krystie continued with the strategy that she and Carys had devised but it did little good. Lucky did at least stop barking once Krystie had come out and seen him. There was no point wasting his yelp when he knew she knew he was outside, Lucky was always content to wait for her. When Lucky settled outside Krystie's house and time wore on, he often got bored and hobbled off on his lonely explorations. Or, with Cwmafan being filled with people, animals and things on his danger list, he also often abandoned his post with a low growl and a few sharp yelps to chase something or another. Krystie would watch him go from her upstairs bedroom window with a mixed sense of relief and guilt.

Krystie began to get concerned about what her neighbours must be thinking about the strange dog on her doorstep.

'Thing is, Carys,' she moaned one day. 'Cwmafan is the land of the moving curtains if you know what I mean. Everyone and anyone is waiting and watching for something to gossip about.'

'What are you worried about now?'

'Well… I mean… what must they all think, strange dog on my doorstep?'

'Better than a strange man on your doorstep.'

'I only wish I could get a strange man on my doorstep!'

Krystie's worst fears about people gossiping about her were confirmed only a short while after this conversation with Carys. Lucky was outside dozing on the pavement. Krystie was reluctant to go out when Lucky was laying in wait for her but she was in desperate need for her much-needed cigarettes, tea bags and milk. She certainly was not going to walk to the shops via her escape through the field so she took a deep breath and grabbed her car keys. Lucky span wildly in circles as Krystie walked reluctantly out of her front door and into her car. She only just stopped him from jumping in with her. Lucky continued to spin wildly in circles as Krystie turned the ignition switch and prepared to drive off.

Lucky knew exactly what was going to happen next. He had spent over a year chasing after Evan and Carys in their car as they went to and from the stables. He prepared himself and as Krystie drove off in her car, he ran after her. His usually perfect road sense was abandoned as he sped after Krystie driving along the main road running through Cwmafan. Krystie looked in her rear view mirror and her hands tightened on the steering wheel. She swore as she hit the thirty-mile an hour speed limit and Lucky was still not far behind her. She reached the turning for the shops but envisaged herself pulling up outside the café where everyone would watch a tiny, scruffy brown terrier chasing after her exhaust blowing Ford Sierra. They would all be talking about the cruel woman who drove off without her dog. With sweating hands she did not make the turn and continued on towards Port Talbot town centre.

Krystie startled when she heard the sound of car horns blowing behind her. As she stole another look in the rear view mirror she saw Lucky, still not too far behind her car. He was running along the middle of the road with three or four cars backed up behind him. His head was lowered and his eyes were fixed on the back of her Sierra. Krystie put her foot on the accelerator and headed into Port Talbot town centre. She saw Lucky dive from the middle of the road onto the pavement and exhaled slowly.

'I drove all the way to ruddy town to get fags, tea bags and some poxy milk and I also ended up buying four cans of lager for goodness sake,' Krystie exclaimed to Carys the following day. 'That dog is driving me to drink.' Carys laughed, secretly wondering what had been driving

Krystie to drink before Lucky had developed his obsession with her.

'You know you could have just picked him up and dropped him off here if you were going to town anyway?' Carys said reproachfully.

'I wasn't supposed to be going into town, I just couldn't stop driving.'

Lucky was getting frustrated with the amount of time that he was sitting outside Krystie's house so he tried another strategy. Carys and Krystie were having a quiet drink (inside the pub and without any horses) at the Copper House. They were sat on high stools leaning against the bar when a familiar face turned to Krystie amicably and said

'Your dog was here last night again, you know. You shouldn't let him roam around like that. Goodness knows what'll happen to him.'

'My dog?' Krystie yelled, instantly knowing who the man was referring to. 'Her dog!' and she pointed at Carys dramatically.

'Your dog is it, luv?' the man enquired kindly, peering over Krystie to Carys. Carys nodded sheepishly waiting for a lecture on the responsibilities of keeping dogs, however, for once she was excused.

'Oh right,' he continued. 'Funny that. He's been around here a few times recently, been thrown out a couple of times, but he never comes back twice in one night.'

'Oh well,' Carys turned to Krystie when the man had run out of conversation. 'Once again my parents should be thankful it's my dog getting thrown out of pubs and not their children.'

When Carys and Krystie visited other pubs they had frequented with Lucky it was the same story.

'Your dog was here. Yeah. Just a few nights ago… or last week… or was it the week before?' A heated debate would begin about the last time that the scruffy little terrier had been spotted. Everyone knew him by sight so it was always an energetic discussion.

'That funny looking brown terrier of sorts… bit of a limp like, you know who I mean?' Carys and Krystie always knew exactly which dog the locals were talking about. Lucky, bereft of Krystie's company, pub-crawling in Cwmafan looking for her.

Lucky spent a lot of time and effort looking for Krystie in Cwmafan. He did not mind though, he was so used to being out all day that wandering around Cwmafan and visiting the places where he had been with her seemed to make sense. He was understandably very excited when he found her in the Riverside pub. Krystie was working there several shifts a week and she was there the evening that Lucky came running into the pub through the legs of a short and stocky man, struggling to hold the door open with a pint in each hand.

The only room in the pub to open to customers was no bigger than someone's living room and the dark wooden floor, bar and window frames made the room look even smaller than it actually was. Apart from Krystie there were only men inside having a drink but every one had a cigarette between their lips and a thick haze of smoke swirled above their heads. Lucky found Krystie easily, she was sitting at the end of the bar with a cigarette in one hand and a glass of lager in the other.

'Lucky!' Krystie yelled as she jumped off the barstool. 'Come on, out. Out. OUT!' and she shooed an ecstatic Lucky from the pub.

'Hey Krys....' One of the regulars yelled from across the smoky room. 'That your dog?'

'No he is not. He's just... he's not... well... he's got a bit of a crush on me all right. He won't leave me alone.'

'Duw, duw, Krys. You can do better than that, surely?'

'Hey Krys,' another man shouted 'why is it that women always fall for the wrong dogs?' and the room burst into peals of deep laughter.

'All right, all right.' Krystie turned her back on the small crowd, 'Whatever, you're all very funny, making jokes about the sort of company I attract.' A bemused and exasperated Krystie sat back on the high bar stool with a huff as the distasteful dog jokes continued well into the night.

Lucky sat outside with his head cocked to one side. He heard Krystie cackle with laughter and he heard her being drowned out by the louder and deeper laughter of the other men inside. He jumped up onto the stone windowsill and waited for Krystie to join him.

When Krystie locked up and left that night she was surprised to see Lucky still outside waiting for her.

'Ruddy hell, dog,' she laughed 'if only I could find a man as loyal as you, eh. But will you leave me alone. Oh no, don't follow me home. Go home, GO HOME!' But Lucky did not go home. He walked Krystie back to her house and when he was refused entry he turned around and arrived back at Tyddyn, waking Jayne and Evan up well after midnight.

Now that Lucky had found a pub where Krystie had also been, he visited frequently. To make matters worse for Krystie the Riverside pub was only a mile's walk from Tyddyn. Lucky only had to leave his house, cross Cwmafan road and trot onto the cycle path that runs alongside the Afan Valley River. The Riverside was a small pub nestled discreetly on the riverbank.

When Krystie had told the locals in the pub that Lucky had a crush on her, it was a spur of the moment defence. But this explanation certainly suited Lucky's behaviour so everyone knew Lucky as Krystie's crush. Lucky was like an amorous boyfriend who waited for Krystie to finish work, escorted her home but was denied entry every time. It was only really a problem for Krystie and she was so laid back that it did not really bother her. However, it soon began to affect other people. Krystie was finishing her evening shift one night when the landlady came in and said.

'Krystie, your dog is outside waiting for you. Don't you think you'd better lock him in the house next time?' Krystie sighed and did not have the energy to explain the situation to her boss. Rather than go through the ritual of having Lucky escort her home, she sneaked out of the back entrance.

When Krystie went in to start work the following evening, the landlady greeted her sternly,

'Now, you listen to me Chris,' she began. 'I know you say that little mongrel is not your dog but he seems to think you are his owner. I would therefore appreciate it if you didn't leave him sleeping on the windowsill again. He woke me and my husband up at three in the morning and the whole street was awake by the time we shooed him away.'

'Oh no. I am so sorry,' Krystie said closing her eyes and blushing.

'It's all right, because it ain't going to happen again. I don't want to see that dog in or outside this pub. Make sure you tell that little girl who comes here with you as well.' Krystie was right in presuming that the little girl the landlady was referring to was Carys. Indeed, when Carys went to meet Krystie a few days later in the Riverside, she had the same warning from the landlady, just in case Krystie had forgotten any of the details.

Unfortunately, even if Lucky did understand Carys telling him not to wait outside the pub for Krystie, he would not have listened. Lucky fell asleep waiting for Krystie outside the Riverside on another occasion. When he woke up he was cold, hungry and too impatient to wait for Krystie any longer. He started barking and did not stop, one sharp yelp after another. When the pub front door was thrown open Lucky did not see the person he had been waiting for. A man as wide as he was tall came running out of the pub shouting, screaming and with two closed fists raised and ready. Lucky turned on his tail and ran onto the cycle path. He did not stop running again until he got back to Tyddyn. Lucky consoled himself with the knowledge that he could at least get into his own house at four o clock in the morning.

Krystie was the first person to find out about Lucky waking her employers up again.

'Right then, Krys. I warned you before but now I am telling you. That dog is not. To. COME. HERE. AGAIN. He is banned from here and the surrounding area.'

The message was very clear. Lucky was banished from the pub, the gardens and the street. If he so much as uttered a whine after eleven o' clock at night she would call the dog pound. When Carys reported this back to her parents there was not a lot either of them could say.

'How long do you reckon he's got? Evan asked

'What do you mean, Dad?'

'I mean how long is he banned for?'

'Ummm, she didn't exactly say but from the way she said it I think its safe to assume that it's a lifetime ban.'

Krystie stopped working in the Riverside shortly after Lucky's sentence. She decided that drinking in pubs was more productive than working in them. Evan and Jayne were glad that it was the dog and not their children who were in trouble. Lucky was re-writing all the rules and expectations of tiny terriers all over the world and he was doing it in style.

Chapter 16

Pawing A Lift

It took most of the winter and early months of spring for Bu's leg to heal. When the vet declared him to have a clean bill of health, Carys resumed galloping around the mountains at breakneck speed. Lucky had not forgotten the amount of times the large, grey animal had nearly landed on him so he kept a wary distance when he went out with Carys and Bu for the first time in many months.

The ride started as well as it could have. Bu pranced and danced along Cwmafan road, occasionally jumping into the air and giving a gleeful buck. Lucky trotted along the pavement a safe distance from the grey animal that had not calmed in his six months off work. Passing cars were steered carefully around Bu as he regularly leapt into the air and kicked his hind legs outwards, but both Carys and Lucky were oblivious to the sceptical drivers. They were all glad to be back out again. Due to Lucky's ban from the Riverside, Carys avoided riding alongside the Afan River, as the cycle track emerged right outside the front door of the pub. Instead, she waited until she had ridden into the heart of Cwmafan on the main road before leaving the paved streets and crossing over the Afan River onto green belt land.

Bu was walking quietly and Lucky was being lulled into a false sense of security when two cyclists rode up behind them. Bu's ears flattened onto the back of his head and his whole body tensed. Carys recognised the signs but her reactions were too slow to stop what happened next. Lucky yelped and sprung into action, running after a bolting Bu and helpless Carys.

While Bu's brakes left a lot to be desired, his steering was perfect. As he pounded his way towards the end of the green belt land, Carys at least had the luxury of deciding which way she wanted to go since stopping was not an available option. She knew that the path forked and if they turned left they would ride over an old red brick railway bridge viaduct, fifty feet from the road below and this terrified her. Go right and there was a field before a small housing estate, an option that, given the circumstances, she much preferred. She formulated a quick plan to direct Bu onto the field and circle him until she was able to stop.

When Bu was bolting out of control the surge of adrenalin paralysed Carys' senses. She did not hear the screaming and shouting or see the scattered crowd of people until it was too late. Carys had not known that the field they were heading towards was actually a rugby pitch and to make matters worse, it was Saturday and Pontrhydyfen were playing Tonna. Bu galloped onto the pitch without any thought of where he was. When he saw a large, flapping banner directly ahead of him he skidded to a stop, deep hoof furrows marking into the pitch as bits of mud and grass flicked into the air. He reared up, his eyes white and wild, spun on his hind legs and galloped off the pitch just as fast as he had entered. The majority of rugby players were bent over and huddled together in a scrum at the far end of the field but there were still some players and most of the supporters who screamed at Carys to get out of the game, some angry and others horrified to see the out of control horse.

As Bu raced away from the rugby field, Carys just registered Lucky running onto the pitch. His debut rugby match was longer than Bu's as when he saw the rugby ball being kicked from out of the scrum he eagerly raced after it. The second row of the Tonna rugby side carried the ball towards their scoring line. It was passed sideways from one player to another and then thrown again and... intercepted by Lucky. The whistle blew not because of the forward pass but because Tonna had gained an extra player.

'Sorry... so sorry,' Carys yelled behind her.

Between her, Bu and Lucky they had successfully created mayhem within the national sport of Wales. Thankfully it was a third division match. Thirty rugby players chased Lucky off the rugby pitch. He was disappointed that he had not been able to sink his teeth into the ball but at least he caught up with Carys as she finally managed to wrestle Bu to a stop. Carys' mouth was dry and her heart was beating hard and fast from the embarrassment at what had just happened. She hoped that no one had recognised her or Bu as she crossed the river and headed towards Krystie's house for a much-needed drink and debrief.

Lucky ran ahead of Carys when he realised where they were headed. He was thoroughly enjoying himself. He had forgotten the challenge that running with Bu posed to him but he thrived on it and the opportunity to chase a ball was an added bonus. Going to see Krystie made this one of his favourite rides with Carys and the mad grey animal so far.

When Lucky ran up to Krystie's front gate it was closed with a Boxer dog and staffordshire bull terrier running freely around in the front garden. Lucky saw the dogs in what he considered to be his garden and halted abruptly. Krystie emerged from her house and strolled to the front gate.

'Hiya, Krys,' Carys called to her as she rode Bu up onto the pavement. 'You haven't got a drink have you? I'm parched.'

'Yeah, no worries, hang on there a minute.' Krystie disappeared into her house and reappeared with a glass of water. 'Sorry it's nothing stronger. Nice to be back out riding again?'

'Wish you did have something stronger, he just bolted with me.'

'Oh well, nothing new there.'

Carys swigged back the water and looked around for Lucky.

'Where's my dog gone?'

'Didn't see him with you?'

'Strange. Thought I'd have trouble getting him away from your house.'

'He's fickle.'

'Yeah, fickle is about right, but... oh there he is down the street. I'd better go after him. See you up the stables later?'

'Yeah, nice one, ta-ta.'

Carys trotted Bu around the corner and caught up with Lucky. For the first time since Krystie had come into his life, Lucky actually listened to Carys when she called him. He walked away from Krystie's house without a backward glance, his recent obsession with his guard dog duties forgotten. His attempts to get Krystie to join his pack were useless because all this time she had her own. From that day on he stopped going to sit outside her house and neither Carys nor Krystie heard anything more about him trawling the pubs in Cwmafan.

When Lucky saw Krystie after that momentous day he still greeted her by spinning wildly in circles and jumping up on her if given the chance. He also accompanied her riding as often as he could. But his beloved had rejected him in favour of those other strange dogs and Lucky had lost his incentive to want to be with her. Like Tiny Taff before her, Krystie fell out of his favour.

Krystie found that there were considerable benefits of not having a tiny, scruffy terrier as a stalker. She was able to leave her house through her own front door and she did not have to worry about looking into the rear view mirror of her car and see a dog chasing after her. Despite all this, Krystie did admit to missing his company. It would have been hard for any one not to appreciate the efforts Lucky had made in order to be with her, even if he was just a small, brown, wiry haired mongrel.

It had been Jayne's bright idea in the early days of Lucky's life to give him as much exercise as possible to try and combat the way he wanted to take on the world. This had backfired though because Lucky considered it his job to roam and expand on his territory. First, by waking endless circles around the Pentwyn estate, then having free rein of the Dinas mountain following Carys on her horse. Moving to Tyddyn had just given him endless opportunities to explore his surroundings.

Despite the recent setback with Krystie, Lucky was still looking to increase his pack numbers and so he continued with his explorations around Port Talbot. Sightings of Lucky began to increase amongst those who knew him. Evan, Jayne, Carys and Daniel often got telephone calls from their friends and family to say that Lucky had been seen on a lonely and deserted road leading over one of the nearby mountains. Lucky was always pleased when someone stopped and offered him a ride in a car. He only got into the cars of those that he recognised but he had been raised in a family with a lively social life so he knew a lot of people.

There were times when he did not remember the person so well and he became indignant when they got out of their cars to pick him up and drive him to his home against his will. Lucky always attacked the seat belts with extra vigour when this happened. Of all the numerous people who came across Lucky only one ever had the decency to ask Lucky what he wanted.

Bob and Jenny were Jayne and Evan's friends from across the valley. They did not live anywhere close to Tyddyn, but their house was clearly visible half way up the opposite mountain. Jenny had taught in the same comprehensive school with Penelope but while Penelope had retired years ago, Jenny was still there. They had remained firm friends and Bob and Jenny were godparents to Daniel.

Lucky had known Jenny and Bob since he had been living with his family. Penelope often took Carys and Daniel up to see her friends and Lucky was naturally with them. He always revelled in the attention and titbits he received from Bob in particular. Lucky liked Bob so much that if he was in a good mood, he may have grudgingly admitted, if he could talk as well, that Bob was just a little bit taller than him. At six foot four, Bob actually towered over Lucky but his gentle giant demeanour always endeared the tiny terrier to him.

In his lonesome wanderings, Lucky was starting to explore further up the Afan Valley countryside. Bob was a technician working for a Telecom Company and he spent much of his time driving from one location to another in South and Mid Wales. Bob had spent the day working in the Rhondda, an old coal-mining valley with villages centred on and around the Rhondda River. He was starting to mentally unwind as he drove slowly along a snaking country road heading back to Port Talbot and his dinner, which he hoped would be on the table waiting.

Bob always enjoyed the peaceful drive through valleys with forests as vast as the eye could see. He drove carefully along the road as it dipped up, down and around the crevices of the rolling hills. As Bob drove into the tiny valley village of Blaengwynfi, he rounded a corner and braked heavily to avoid driving into a tiny, brown dog that was sniffing his way along the steep embankment by the side of the road.

As Bob swerved around the dog he did a double take in the side mirror of his van. He was sure that he recognised the terrier. The light was fading quickly though and it was too dark for Bob to fully see the little brown dog's face.

'Can't be,' he sternly told himself as he continued to drive along the road. 'He's miles away from home.'

The following week Bob was driving from the town of Neath and up towards Seven Sisters, another small village in the heart of the Welsh countryside. Once again, Bob did a double take as this time he drove passed what looked like the same tiny, brown dog hobbling his way along the pavement. This time, in the bright light of day, Bob saw the dog far more clearly and recognition began to dawn. He was just about to pull over, but the distance that he was from Tyddyn caused doubt in his mind. With a string of traffic behind Bob's van and a row of cars parked on the side of the road, he could not safely stop and check out what he thought he was seeing, again.

'Can't be, it just can't' he muttered to himself as he continued to drive along the road with one eye glued to his van's rear mirror. The little dog had disappeared from his sight. A few hours later when Bob was driving back towards Neath he kept his eyes peeled for the same dog. He was nowhere to be seen.

The next time Bob was driving back from the Rhondda he saw the tiny brown dog hobbling along the embankment of the same road. This time he was determined to identify him properly. Since he could not stop on such a winding country road, Bob continued to drive and parked his van in the next lay-by. He turned off the engine and waited, his fingers tapping against the steering wheel. With no sign of the dog coming around the corner he started muttering to himself.

'I must be mad… seeing things now. Waiting for a dog I don't even know if I know. Ridiculous!'

Lucky was getting hungry. He had left Tyddyn before his family this morning and had been walking ever since. He had found a bowl of food outside someone's house a few hours ago and gobbled it down before a door had flung open and he had been chased from the garden. He always found plenty to drink with the abundance of rivers flowing freeing through his town but food was more difficult.

As Lucky's stomach rumbled he stopped by a van parked on the side of the road. He carefully sniffed the rear tyre, cocked his head and then his leg. At least that was one instinct he could always take care of when needed. He prepared to run when he heard the van door open and heavy footsteps come towards him. Lucky was always ready to run off after relieving himself because it seemed to get him in the most trouble with people. He was surprised when a soft, kind voice spoke to him instead.

'Lucky?' Bob called to him questioningly. Lucky stared up at the tall man in his dark blue uniform and wagged his tail, he recognised Bob immediately from his kind voice.

'Hiya boy,' Bob bent down and welcomed Lucky by ruffling the fur on his neck. 'What you doing all the way up here then...? You want a lift home, butt? Eh, you want me to take you home?' Lucky continued to wag his tail as Bob spoke to him.

When Lucky had the passenger door of the van opened for him he did not hesitate to jump straight in. By the time Bob had settled himself back in the driver's seat, Lucky was standing with his back legs on the front seat and his front legs on the dashboard. He was only just long enough to reach in such a large van but he yelped in delight at this surprising turn of events.

'Right then, Lucky. Home it is.' Bob said to him. Lucky yowled and Bob took that as a yes.

As he continued to drive Bob found the silence uncomfortable with clearly such an intelligent presence in his company.

'So, Lucky my boy. Where were you going the other day when I saw you coming?' Lucky looked Bob directly in the eyes before turning his attention back to the window. Bob hesitated, he would not have been surprised if Lucky had answered him back but he was glad that he did not. He chuckled at himself for trying to have a conversation with a dog, turned up the radio and continued driving.

When Bob drove up Cwmafan road and reached the sharp turning for Tyddyn he did not want to drive up the steep mountain lane and have to turn his van around up there. He pulled over to the left side of the road and feeling slightly foolish turned to his hitchhiker and said

'Right Lucky. I'll have to drop you off here mate, I can't turn the van around outside your house.' Bob leaned across and opened the passenger door. With a last look at Bob and a small yelp, Lucky jumped out onto the pavement and ran around to the front of the van. Bob closed the passenger door and waited to make sure Lucky was actually going to head up to his house. He watched the tiny terrier look both ways on Cwmafan road and when he was satisfied there were no cars coming, he ran across and disappeared up the mountain lane.

'I must be mad' Bob muttered to himself as he drove off.

Lucky ran straight into the kitchen and found Jayne there. He barked and nudged his food bowl with his nose.

'Home are you?' Jayne addressed him with her hands on her hips. 'Where have you been today then, I hope you've been a good boy?' Lucky looked up at her. He did not know what she was asking him but he hoped it was something to do with her getting him some food. He was very pleased with the way his day had turned out.

The next time Bob pulled over to offer Lucky a lift, Lucky gladly jumped into the van with him. This time

Bob did not have to get out, he just leaned over to open the passenger door so Lucky could scramble up onto the high backed seats. Lucky assumed his position with his paws on the dashboard and his eager eyes looking out the window.

'I can't take you home yet, Lucky.' Bob said to him. 'It's only one in the afternoon and I don't finish till five. You'll have to come with me.'

Lucky was more than happy to accompany Bob on his daily rounds. When Bob stopped to get a job done, Lucky got out of the van and explored the surrounding area, jumping back into the van when it was time to go. Bob took Lucky home at the end of his shift and when the tiny terrier jumped out of the van, looked both ways before crossing the road and headed to his house, Bob shook his head in disbelief.

'I am going mad, taking a dog to work indeed. He's not even mine.' A few months later, Bob gratefully accepted the offer of an office job.

Chapter 17

Lucky Hotel

When Lucky did not come home one night, Jayne and Evan assumed that he would either be brought home by whomever he was staying with or he would wander up the drive in the morning. When Lucky had not arrived home the following evening, Carys began to worry so she made some telephone calls to the usual suspects. Cai checked his home security system but Lucky had not walked to Baglan or come back from that direction, at least not along the main road. Penelope, Pete, Sherry and Owen had all been sleeping through the night for many weeks without being woken and neither Krystie nor Tiny Taff had seen or heard him. It was the first time Lucky had stayed away for so long and no one appeared to know where he was.

Carys took to horseback and rode up onto the Dinas mountain, calling Lucky as she travelled. She felt a bit stupid as she stared from great heights down into the hustle and bustle of the town centre where the people scurrying around were unrecognisable. There was no way she could have seen Lucky but it did not stop her from looking anyway. She returned home with a hoarse voice from calling to her tiny terrier and weary from worry. Jayne and Evan both tried to assure their daughter that wherever Lucky was he would be fine but as the evening wore on, Carys became more despondent, switching from playing the piano to doing her homework to watching the television with no real effort. Jayne promised her that if Lucky did not come home by tomorrow, Evan would take her out in the car to look for him.

True to his wife's word, Evan and Carys drove around looking for Lucky on the third day he had been missing. The first place they drove to was Cwmafan, the place that seemed to be Lucky's favourite haunt. They trawled the pubs, shops and along the river, all places where he was likely to be, but there was no sign of him.

When they reached the far end of Cwmafan by the main road, Evan doubled back by driving under the large nineteenth century railway viaduct bridge and along a desolate road overlooking Cwmafan. Eventually they reached Port Talbot town and drove around the streets close to Carys' grandparents' houses. There was still no sign or clue.

As a last resort Evan drove through Sandfields estate and into Aberavon, driving alongside the beach until they reached the M4 motorway at Baglan. Lucky had never shown a fascination for the beach but with his habit of seeking out new places, Evan and Carys did not want to leave anything to chance. The stormy sea pounded against the grey, man made seaside shore, reflecting the dark mood in the car.

They drove past the Baglan house but Lucky was not on guard, so they admitted defeat and headed home. Evan was quiet as he drove and Carys could no longer cope with the contemplative silence.

'Where do you think he is, Dad?' she asked again, her eyes brimming with tears and a deep crease in her forehead. Evan sighed as he stole a sideways glance at his sorrowful daughter but he was lost for words. 'It's my fault' Carys declared as she wrung her hands and a tear finally slid down her cheek.

'How come?' Evan asked confused.

'I should have taken better care of him, he's my dog. He came up the stables and I forgot all about him until it was too late and then he was gone.'

'Don't be…' Evan tried to comfort his daughter but her guilt continued to pour out.

'He comes up the stables every day and I never put him on a lead… and I gallop off and leave him when I'm out riding… and I never even thought that taking him to the pub would get him into so much trouble… and he's been gone for three days and we are only now looking for him properly.' A sob hitched in Carys' throat and her head fell into her hands. Evan was momentarily distracted by how much his daughter resembled her mother in that moment.

'It's not your fault, Carys' he said softly. 'He belongs to all of us and we all take him out without a lead. But Lucky has always gone out by himself; he's not going to change now.'

'But why does he go out by himself? He is our dog and we all love him. Why is that not enough?'

An uncomfortable hush descended on the car again as Carys and Evan thought about the reasons for Lucky's constant wanderings. Evan could not think of a logical answer so he improvised, desperate to comfort his distraught daughter.

'Well, think about it Carys, in a way Lucky is just like us. I mean, when we got him he was just a puppy and he needed us to do everything for him, like feed him, walk him, clean him. And you and Daniel also needed looking after. But now you are all older and you can look after yourself, with mine and mammy's help of course. And Daniel is doing what he likes doing. You're both growing up and so is Lucky, he's just doing what he likes to do.'

Evan was quite impressed by his explanation and the more he thought about it the more appropriate it seemed. It made sense that Lucky was just growing up like the rest of them. He did not tell Carys actually how independent he and Jayne were from each other at the moment. That was a conversation for another time. But he could not secretly wonder if Lucky sensed the different vibes from him and Jayne these days and whether that had anything to do with the way he left them so often to go wandering far afield.

'But Dad, little dogs are not supposed to get older and do stuff themselves. That's why dogs are called man's best friend. What are we doing that he doesn't like and which makes him run away all the time?' Evan sighed, acknowledging the flaw in his reasoning.

'He's not running away, Carys. He's just a wanderer, an explorer or an adventurer if you like. He will come back.' Carys smiled shyly, she liked this explanation and considering that she also was always exploring Port Talbot by horseback and Lucky was her dog, it seemed appropriate. Still, an eerily quiet atmosphere descended on the house that night. Even Daniel noticed that Lucky was absent. Of course, since the only time Daniel emerged from his bedroom was to go to school, three days was relatively observant for him.

Meanwhile, stuck in his enclosed space, Lucky was starting to get impatient. He had been ready to go for a walk again for over a day but he was confined too tightly to rid his excess energy. He enjoyed the food and he spent time with the lovely girl who had enticed him into the place to begin with. There were also lots of horses on the yard so Lucky felt very much at home with such familiar scents and noises. He was hoping to make this new land his family's territory but he had been unable to get back to them. And a ten-minute walk outside twice a day was not what he was used to. It reminded him of a very distant past long, long ago…

On his fourth day sitting in a small but comfortable kennel he became excited when he heard two familiar voices. They were the voices of the people he had lived with for as long as he could remember. Carys was talking quickly and Evan was making the occasional comment in a low, gruff voice. Their voices grew louder and Lucky started to spin in circles. He was glad that his family were safe and excited that they had come to help him mark this new territory as their own.

Lucky stopped spinning in circles and jumped up onto the front of the kennel as Carys rounded the corner and raced over to him, stumbling as she crouched down by his cage.

'Dad. Quick. It's him, it's Lucky.' The light in her sparking blue eyes danced with childish excitement as she smiled at Lucky in wonder. Evan bent over and stared down at Lucky over Carys' shoulder.

'All right, mush.' He greeted him. Lucky became so excited that he tried to climb up the caged door of the kennel but fell over backwards, executing a very wobbly back flip. Carys giggled and Evan grinned. This was the second time that they had found a tiny, scruffy, brown-haired terrier doing somersaults off the side of a kennel, although neither of them had thought that they would bring Lucky from a dogs' home twice.

The girl that Lucky liked so much let him out of his kennel and Carys quickly slipped a lead over his head.

'You know he did not have a collar on when he arrived,' Lucky's friend explained to Carys and Evan. 'Otherwise we would have called you, that's presuming he has a collar of course?' Evan assured the girl that Lucky did have a collar and a name tag with a contact number but since Lucky had demolished it somewhere he would get him a new one immediately.

Carys knew the horse-riding centre in Goytre because her parents had often brought her and Daniel to the barn dances on Bonfire nights. She had also brought Silver to lots of pony club events and shows held on the grounds over the years. She was not aware until she was walking out with Lucky tucked under her arm that it was also a dog pound. Evan went into the office to pay for the accommodation costs of Lucky's four-day stay and Carys took Lucky straight back to the car. Lucky wasted no time in launching himself onto the seat belt and Carys could do little to deter him. When Evan returned from the office his face was like thunder and he wasted no time in shouting at Lucky to leave the seat belt alone. A four-day visit to the dog pound had been charged at just over one hundred pound, a new collar and nametag cost another ten pound and the usual costs for a seatbelt. Lucky was oblivious to the fact that his accommodation over the past few days had been an expensive time.

On his return home he wasted no time in doing all the things that he had missed whilst cooped up in his kennel. He chased the cat, nipped at Daniel and threw himself into a barking frenzy at the lawnmower even though it was stationary in the garden. Jayne had mixed feelings about Lucky's return.

'That dog stinks, Carys. He stinks of dog, even worse than he normally does. Put him in the bath.' Not even strawberry smelling shampoo could dampen Lucky's spirits though, he splashed around in the bath getting Carys and the floor as wet as he was.

Lucky was back at Goytre dog pound within the week. He was disappointed that Carys had not gone back with him to their latest territorial acquisition and he wanted to make sure that no one else had claimed it in their absence. He also remembered the nice girls who spent all their time at the stables hidden at the bottom of Goytre Valley.

When Lucky did not arrive home by the following morning Jayne and Evan telephoned Goytre riding stables and dog pound first. They confirmed that there was a tiny, scruffy terrier in custody so Evan and Carys left to pick him up. While Carys took Lucky back to the car Evan had a tense conversation with the receptionist.

'You want to charge me how much?'

'It's a thirty pound pick-up fee plus the accommodation and feeding costs for one night.'

'What do you mean pick-up costs? The girl out there told me he came here voluntarily. You just detained him!'

'It's policy that…'

'Hang on a minute now. You still have my contact details from last week,' Evan argued with the woman. 'So don't tell me you couldn't tell that this was the same little dog that stayed with you before. You should have phoned me.'

'I'm sorry sir,' the receptionist replied haughtily. 'We have a lot of dogs passing through here.' Evan's voice began to echo out the office and down the stable yard.

'You told me you found him on your yard a few hours after we lost him yesterday. You think he took his collar off himself before he got here? You took his collar off and now you're trying to charge me money when you should have phoned me yesterday.'

'I'm not sure what you are suggesting sir...'

'I'm not suggesting anything. I'm telling you, you are ripping me off and I'm not having it!' Evan stormed from the office without paying and Carys was glad she had collected Lucky from the kennel before her father had started to discuss accommodation costs. When Evan got home he telephoned the manager of the riding stables and dog pound and wasted no time passing on how unhappy he was with the way he had been treated and the amount they had tried to charge him.

'I didn't mind paying the first time,' Evan lied down the phone. 'But the second time they knew it was our dog, they had my number and they never even phoned me.'

Evan was satisfied when he got reassurances from the manager that if Lucky returned to the pound or they picked him up again they would phone immediately. He took a photo of Lucky to the riding centre and dog pound the following day with his address and telephone number on the back. Lucky got another new collar and nametag as well as a stern warning from Jayne about finding cheaper places to stay. Lucky did not heed any of Jayne's warnings. He had been to Goytre dog pound twice and both times he had been fed, satisfied his thirst and had a fuss from the girls on the yard there. He was determined to stamp his authority on this land and mark it as his own.

An hour after Lucky had arrived at Goytre dog pound, the telephone rang in Tyddyn. Evan answered.

'Hello. Yes… Yes… Yes… Well, thank you for phoning this time, my wife will be over shortly. Thank you. Goodbye.'

'Where exactly is your wife going?' Jayne asked Evan sceptically.

'Do us a favour and go and pick the dog up. I can't be bothered with that woman again, no matter how nice she's being now. He's up the dog pound again, hurry now before they start charging.'

Jayne only agreed because she considered herself to be far more diplomatic than her husband. She intended to smooth over any past aggravation between Evan and the staff while she picked up their dog. When Jayne walked into the reception area of Goytre dog pound she was immediately struck by an advert on the notice board about the Terriers Trust, an organisation that made a commitment to prevent terriers from being put down. If a terrier was left unclaimed they would re-home it after one month.

Jayne hesitated when she read this advert and deliberated whether she should turn around and go home without him. After all… was Lucky really that happy if he was running away all the time? Perhaps another family might have more luck with him than hers had? Jayne's musings were interrupted when a friendly woman approached her asking if she could help. She did not have the time to really think about the consequences of the Terrier's Trust advert and answered automatically

'Oh... yes... um, I'm here to pick up my little terrier dog, you just phoned.'

'Hmmmm.' The friendly smile disappeared and it was replaced with a frown. Jayne was led to the kennels where Lucky greeted her hesitantly. Jayne thanked the women profusely but the damage had been done and her gratitude was wasted.

'I've been told there is no charge if he comes here of his own accord, but if he's picked up there will be a transportation cost.' The woman told Jayne sharply.

'Yes, thank you.'

'Perhaps you should invest in a new garden fence' the receptionist called after Jayne as she left with her dog. Jayne gritted her teeth, knowing full well that the tallest and thickest of fences were incapable of keeping Lucky in or out of gardens.

Lucky's return home was far less triumphant than the previous times because he had not got anything of what he had wanted from today's wanderings. No food, no attention and no walk with the nice friendly girls. He raced over to Carys lying on the sofa and jumped up onto her stomach, pushing his wet nose into the side of her face until she giggled helplessly. When he finally left her alone in search of food, Jayne confessed to Carys her hesitation to bring him home after seeing the Terrier's Trust advertisement.

'Mum!' Carys immediately protested. 'How could you? He's our dog.'

'Oh come on Carys, he seems to think he'd be happier elsewhere, he's always running away.'

'Yeah but he always comes back, he's just...' Carys hesitated and stumbled to find the right words.

'Exactly.' Jayne declared. 'He's just... looking for something that doesn't seem to involve us. That dog would leave home tomorrow without a minute's thought if he found somewhere better. I bet he wouldn't even look back at us.' Carys immediately launched into a complicated explanation of why Lucky left home so much, defending him as vehemently as Lucky had tried to protect her over the years. Jayne lapsed into unconvinced silence, her lips pursed and her eyebrows raised.

Lucky was not thinking too much about the future, or whether he was actually looking for something different or not, he only cared about the present. But the next time he escaped it was in the evening and he knew exactly where he was going. On arrival though the yard was deserted. He found an enticing and mouth-watering scent, something he had not come across before and it was strong… so he tracked it.

Jayne got a telephone call the following morning from the now openly hostile receptionist.

'He came to us last night. You know most times we send him away and he doesn't come back but yesterday he really made a nuisance of himself. He woke up all the holidaymakers in the log cabins, barking at goodness knows what. He's lucky that he hasn't been shot. Anyway, one of the girls was working late last night so she just locked him away just to shut him up. I would appreciate it if you could come and get him now.' Jayne apologised profusely again, and agreed to come and get Lucky straight away.

She telephoned work and told them that she would be late for her morning meeting and drove over to the Goytre dog pound to pick up Lucky. He was less reluctant to stay there this time and was already pacing when Jayne arrived. He had been chasing one of the most enticing smells he had encountered in a while last night when a not so friendly girl had picked him up and put him in his usual kennel with no food, only water. This was not how Lucky remembered it. Still, he was not quite ready to give up on the place yet. After all, he had been looked after very well the first few times.

When Jayne brought Lucky back home the telephone rang as she opened the front door. It was someone trying to sell her house insurance. Jayne was too polite to hang up on them and it took her a few minutes to persuade them, as tactfully as she dared, that she did not want to buy anything. By the time Jayne had hung up the phone, Lucky had gone again. She checked the garden, the stables and called to him at the bottom of the mountain path but he had disappeared.

'Damn dog.' Jayne cursed as she locked the house up and jumped back into her car. She had to get to that meeting before it finished, the Chief Inspector of Police and the Sergeant were both expecting her to update them on the latest crime prevention initiatives within the borough. Meanwhile, Lucky was heading back to find that scent and the prey that had eluded him.

Jayne cursed Lucky again when she got into work and found out that her meeting had finished ten minutes earlier. She settled in front of her computer and proceeded to email some apologies for failing to give her contribution that morning. Jayne tried to concentrate on the task at hand but she could not shake Lucky from her thoughts. She had an uncomfortable feeling deep in her stomach whenever she thought of how quickly Lucky had disappeared. She dreaded to think where he could be at this very moment. At half past eleven the queasy feeling in Jayne's stomach turned to hunger pangs when she realised she had left her lunch at home. Sighing, Jayne decided it was quicker to drive home and eat rather than walk up into town and be confronted with the lunchtime rush.

The light on the answer machine was flashing as she walked in and the very voice she did not want to hear spoke clearly when she pressed the play button.

'Jayne. Come and get your dog, he's been chasing the chickens and if this continues there will be a hefty fine.' The hunger pangs in Jayne's stomach were replaced with uncomfortable flutters and she was also concerned to realise that she was now on a first name basis with the dog pound.

When Jayne arrived at the dog's home for a second time that day, hanging her head in shame, she decided to explore the other option.

'Excuse me,' she asked the receptionist tentatively. 'This advert for the Terriers Trust, can you tell me how it works please?'

'Once a dog has been here for a month we contact them to come and collect it. But your dog is not going to stay with us for a month, you can go and pick him up from the girls right now' the receptionist said without meeting Jayne's eye. Jayne ducked her head even further and Lucky was returned and locked into his house. When Jayne returned to work the butterflies once more turned into hunger pangs and she realised that her lunch was still sitting on the kitchen counter.

'Damn dog,' she cursed again. 'I've got the only dog in Port Talbot and probably South Wales who cannot get into a dog pound.'

Chapter 18

Bus Pass

Lucky was in unfamiliar territory when he met his new potential pack members. He had not been to this place before and he did not know where he was in relation to his home but he was content to continue exploring anyway. He saw a woman and a man standing outside a car with the front doors open. Lucky also liked cars so he walked up to the couple and greeted them with a quiet yelp.

'Well, hello there, little one' the woman said quietly to him as she bent over to pat him on the head. Lucky's tail wagged wildly as he recognised the friendly tone in her voice and the smile on her face.

'Who does he belong to, then?' the man asked the woman as he also came around to greet Lucky.

'Don't know, he seems to be by himself. He has a collar on though and a name tag.'

Lucky listened to the two people talking and he liked the way they spoke. He decided that he would like to stay with them longer so he jumped into the passenger seat of their car and over the headrest into the back seat where he assumed his usual driving position. His tongue lolled out of his mouth and he panted happily. Wherever these people were going, he was going with them.

Carys was sitting in the living room revising for her mock exams in college. She had long bored of learning about psychological theories and she wished she could go for a ride on Bu instead. Unfortunately, even if she could have spared the time away from her revision, it was raining hard and Bu was difficult to ride when it was wet. He spooked even more than usual and insisted on walking sideways with his head tucked as far between his front legs as possible. The phone rang just after eleven in the morning and a polite and eloquent woman's voice spoke down the phone.

'Oh hello, excuse me for calling but have you got a tiny, brown terrier dog called Lucky?' Carys glanced around the living room and peeked through the door into the dining room and kitchen, realising that Lucky was not with her in the house.

'Yes, that is my dog. Is there a problem?' Carys asked hesitantly, knowing that there would be. There always was when someone telephoned the house to speak about her little dog.

'Oh, don't worry. It's OK. I like dogs and I'm not in any rush. It's just your dog has jumped into my car and he's sitting in the back seat and won't come out again. He's very friendly. He let me get the number from his nametag. But when I try and grab his collar he growls and I don't want to push him, you know?'

'Oh my gosh,' Carys replied, genuinely shocked that Lucky would do such a thing. Still, she was glad that he was in the car as opposed to attacking it. 'I'm really very sorry' she apologised to the woman.

'Oh, it's OK,' she replied, 'I do really like dogs and he's not being nasty, I think he'd be quite happy if I got in and drove home but I don't really want to do that. Can you come and get him?'

'Yes of course, where are you?' Carys was already planning on using either her horse or her mountain bike to get Lucky, even though it was raining and Bu would no doubt buck and bolt all the way.

'I'm outside B&Q.'

'Oh.' Carys hesitated as she tried to remember where B&Q was in Port Talbot. 'Where exactly is that again?'

'It's the hardware store next to the canal?'

Silence.

'I didn't even know there was a canal in Port Talbot?' Carys said as she concentrated on picturing all the running water sources in Port Talbot.

'I'm not in Port Talbot, I'm in the next town over, Neath,' the woman replied patiently

'Neath?' Carys asked sharply.

'Yes, why? Where do you live?'

'I live in Port Talbot.'

'Oh...' the woman paused. 'What is your dog doing all the way over in Neath then?'

'I don't know,' Carys said and hesitated as she thought of what to do next. The bus station was quite close to B&Q but it would take ages to get there on a bus and they probably would not let Lucky catch it back with her. Carys did not even know anyone who lived in that area… but she was sure that she remembered her mother saying she was working in Neath police station for a while.

Carys assured the woman that she would telephone her mother who was in Neath at that time and ask her to come and pick up Lucky.

'OK' the woman replied cheerily. 'Do you think she will be long? It's just my husband and I need to get home.' The woman gave Carys the details of her car and her location in the car park.

Jayne spotted the car immediately when she pulled up outside the hardware store. A woman and a man were standing by the passenger door of a car and she could just see a tiny brown dog in the back seat. Lucky's tail wagged furiously as he watched Jayne approach him but he did not move.

Jayne apologised unreservedly to the woman and her husband, both of whom were bemused but surprisingly friendly given that Lucky had been holding their car hostage for at least half an hour.

'Lucky,' Jayne yelled into the back of the car at him. 'For goodness sake, what do you think you're doing? Get out.' Lucky did not move an inch but his tail stopped wagging and he stared at Jayne with bright alert eyes, he was not going to answer to someone so low down in his pack. He was actually giving serious consideration over whether he should demote her in favour of the nice friendly couple with the completely intact seatbelts. He refused to move until he was grabbed by the collar and pulled out. He struggled as Jayne tucked him under her arm and apologised again to the couple.

'I really am very sorry, I don't know what else to say…'

'It's O.K. If we see him again, we won't open the car door.'

'Well, hopefully you won't see him again.' Jayne snorted. Lucky went limp as Jayne carried him into her own car. He watched the couple from behind the safety of Jayne's car windows as she drove him out of the car park and headed for home. When the couple disappeared from his sight he resumed his usual position in the car and resigned himself to the fact that those friendly people would probably not be joining his pack after all.

Lucky had found a place where there were plenty of friendly people. It was only a short walk away from his home and he had been there a lot recently. It had everything that he liked best and on another day after his disastrous attempt to get the B&Q couple to join his pack, it was no exception. He strolled to his newest favourite place and found some mushy food on the floor, which he quickly gobbled. He was drawn to a lovely lady with white hair and she spoke softly to him and laughed when he threw himself onto his back for her to stroke his tummy with her walking stick. He would have been content to stay a little longer and try and go wherever the lady was going but he jumped up when he heard a familiar voice.

He watched as Carys entered the short, enclosed bus station with her friend. Lucky knew that seeing Carys when he was out usually ended with her taking him back home again and he was not ready to do that yet, so he quickly left the bus station by the opposite entrance to the one that Carys had entered from. He heard her and her friend chat until he was out of hearing range.

'How you feeling bout the exam today then?'

'Nervous.'

'Yeah, me too. I…'

'What?'

'I thought I saw something…'

'Yeah, what?'

'My dog. Or at least I thought I saw his tail…'

'Don't be …' Lucky was too far away to hear the rest.

Lucky did not stay out long that day. He had not achieved what he had set out to do so Jayne found him waiting on the doorstep when she arrived home.

'Oh, back are you?' she greeted him as she opened the front door. Lucky raced into the kitchen, he was starving. He was gulping down his food when Carys arrived home from college.

'Hiya, luv,' Jayne greeted her. 'How was the exam?'

'Yeah, it was all right, only one left now, thank goodness.' Carys sat down at the table and watched Lucky eat. She was starting to make a connection between some random thoughts and events but it did not make sense yet. Still, having had much stranger conversations with her mother in the past she decided to share her idea.

'I think I saw Lucky this morning, Mam. On my way to college.'

'Where?'

'Well, I think I saw him anyway. In the bus station in town.'

'OK..?' Jayne prompted Carys.

'Mam, B&Q really is not that far from the bus station in Neath.'

'Yes.'

'And I saw him in Port Talbot Bus Station today.'

'Yes.'

'Are you really not seeing where this is going?' Carys threw her hands into the air as she stared expectantly at her mother.

Jayne gazed at her daughter intently, trying to figure out what Carys was implying. Then she remembered a very small detail that at the time had not seemed significant but now that she was really thinking about it... Jayne gasped and her hands flew to her open mouth.

'Oh no! I have just thought of something else.'

'What?'

'The day that I picked Lucky up from B&Q...'

'Yes…'

'Well. I remember thinking how strange it was that Lucky was completely dry. It had been hammering down with rain all day and if he had walked to Neath he would have been soaking wet, but he was as dry as a bone.'

Carys and Jayne both stared at Lucky who was licking his food bowl. They spoke the same time

'Do you really think…'

'He never is…'

'Catching a bus everywhere?' Carys finished cautiously. Lucky licked his bowl clean and stopped to stare up at Jayne and Carys. He was blissfully unaware that his latest favourite thing to do had been discovered.

Lucky stretched out in front of the radiator in the living room that evening while Jayne, Evan and Carys settled down to discuss their latest idea. Daniel was silently engrossed in playing a computer game in the corner of the room and did not appear to be listening to the conversation. Lucky listened to his family talk for a while but not being able to understand anything he fell asleep. Evan was laughing at his wife and daughter's latest brainwave.

'He's not catching buses everywhere, I mean that's just ridiculous.' He took his glasses off so he could wipe the laughter tears from his eyes.

'Well how else would he have got to Neath in such a short period of time then, Evan?' Jayne asked.

'He probably walked through Baglan and Briton Ferry, that's the only direct route unless he went on the motorway.' Evan said but Carys shook her head and disagreed.

'No he's never been on the motorway before, I bet he was in Cwmafan and walked to Neath over the mountain. I mean, he's always in Cwmafan so that's more likely.'

'Well, whatever way Lucky went to B&Q, it's a good ten miles as the crow flies and for a little dog that only uses three legs, he couldn't have got there in just over an hour.'

Then, to everyone's surprise, Daniel chirped up. Even Lucky startled awake at the sound of his voice.

'B&Q is not as far as Swansea. He could have done it,' Lucky and the rest of the family all turned to stare at Daniel. He was so engrossed on his computer that they had forgotten he was even there.

'What has Swansea got to do with it? That's nearly twice as far as Neath' Jayne asked, puzzled.

'Oh Neath is nothing,' Daniel explained. 'I got a phone call from the controller of Swansea bus station last week to say Lucky was running around with the buses in the station. They had already thrown him off one bus and wanted to know if we could go and get him.'

Silence.

'Well...' Jayne stammered, 'What did you tell him?'

'I told him not to worry, he'd be back by dinner-time.'

'You didn't say that, did you?'

'Yeah... and he was back... by dinnertime, I mean. He got back about four hours later.'

'Daniel,' Carys demanded. 'Why didn't you say anything?' Daniel shrugged and replied nonchalantly as he turned back to his computer. 'I didn't say about college phoning to see why you weren't in lessons last week either. They want you to contact them ASAP by the way.'

Carys glared at Daniel, her ears burning as she felt her parents eyes boring into the back of her head. Could her brother even be human? She could not remember even one time that he had been in trouble with their parents whereas she had been grounded several times over the years. Surely he had by-passed his teenage years and was middle aged by now. Maybe he was not a real boy? A robot? Perhaps he was sedated? Either way he did not ever seem to get into trouble and his last remark had caused the need for some serious deflection tactics.

'But why didn't you tell us about Lucky being in the bus station?'

'Didn't think it was that big a deal, he's always going places he shouldn't but he still comes back.' There was a tense pause while Jayne and Evan decided whether to continue with the Lucky conversation or ask Carys about college, but by silent agreement they decided to corner her when Daniel was not around.

'How old is Lucky now, Jayne?' Evan asked her and Carys breathed a quick sigh of relief.

‘Well. We had him in 1989 and he was a young pup. So he’s got to be ten years old now. You can tell he’s getting older, look at all his grey hair.’

Carys and Evan turned and stared at Lucky who appeared to be sleeping again. They saw him for the dog he was and realised that he was indeed ageing. He had as many grey body hairs as brown and the soft fine hair around his muzzle was completely silver. He was the biggest he was going to be and yet still tiny even for a terrier dog. His body was lean and muscular but even as he laid spread out on the floor, his left leg was positioned awkwardly underneath him.

‘How did that happen?’ Evan asked.

‘How did what happen, luv?’ she replied patiently

‘Well he must be middle aged now for a dog and I never noticed before but… he’s gone grey.’

‘None of us are getting any younger, Evan,’ Jayne said as she rolled her eyes. ‘And I’ve been grey for years.’

‘Have you?’ Evan asked, his eyes wide. ‘You don’t look grey.’

‘That’s because I use hair dye or haven’t you noticed that you married a dark brunette and now I’m mahogany gold?’

Evan shot his wife the ‘I’m right she has gone completely mad’ gawp and Jayne glared back with her ‘your completely useless’ look.

‘Anyway,’ Evan said, coming back to the topic at hand. ‘I was just saying that I didn’t realise how much older Lucky was getting.’

‘Our children are growing up too, Evan,’ Jayne said softer now. ‘Carys is eighteen and Daniel has just turned fifteen. It’s not just the dog that’s getting older, changing.’ Evan and Jayne locked eyes and exchanged a meaningful stare. The unspoken words between them resonated hard with implications. Lucky was getting older as were they all. Carys was already technically an adult although she did not seem to be interested in the responsibility that accompanies that. A childhood lived is a childhood lost, never to be forgotten but forever forbidden to experience it twice. Daniel still had a few years but soon he too would be making momentous decisions about his adult life.

Ageing meant different things to all of them, a changing identity for the parents whose children needed them less. Children who are no longer childlike, but young adults pushing against the confines of their safe and comfortable world as they start to carve out their own individual path in life. Jayne and Evan felt an overwhelming sense of gratitude for the closeness of their family, the love and loyalty that bound them and for the years they had spent together. This though was marred by the knowledge of the inevitable, a widening black hole in an otherwise infinite blue sky shining with the brightness of summer. They were unable to stop what was coming, what their children were completely oblivious to and what made them even more grateful for the time they had together now.

Then, panic hit them both like a steel spiked wrecking ball ripping into their chests and leaving them breathless. Where had the time gone with their children? They had planned on having plenty of time to prepare for them being all grown up and to plan on how to tell them. Now they did not know how to approach the subject, how to tell them, how to find the comforting words to buffet them against the harsh realities of the future?

Jayne and Evan shuddered, they had not been on the same mental and emotional wavelength for a long time and they were both shaken to feel how interconnected their minds were at that point in time.

'Well.' Evan said when he finally broke eye contact with Jayne. 'I suppose he is getting on a bit now. Maybe he doesn't like walking as much as we think he does. Maybe catching a bus is a lot easier for him.'

'He's turned out to be a right scoundrel, always searching for something or other.' Jayne agreed, relieved for the lighter conversation.

'He's a lovable rogue, Mam.' Carys said with an uncertain smile. She was confused by the intensity of her parent's silent exchange.

'Hmmmm. Not too sure that everyone would agree with you Carys.' Jayne snorted and the atmosphere in the room reverted back to the normally sarcastic conversations typical of their family. 'Certainly not the new owner of the Baglan house, or the headmaster of Baglan primary school or the landlady who banned him from her pub.'

‘But look at all the people who love him. Us, Taff, Krystie, Bob.’

‘Yes, you either love him or he gets on your nerves, no in-between!’ Jayne said. Her own feelings about Lucky certainly alternated between the two extremes. Despite this though, Lucky made their family complete, imperfect, but who of them were anything else?

‘He’s like our hero going off to have adventures in Port Talbot, picking up new friends along the way.’ Carys smiled, remembering her father’s assurances that their little dog was a wanderer, a natural explorer.

Lucky effectively ended the conversation about him by breaking wind and an unbearable stench spread through the room.

‘Oh no, Mucky Lucky,’ Jayne moaned as she left the room with her hand over her nose. Evan decided it was time for a bath and Carys went up the stables to check on the horses. Daniel remained oblivious. When Lucky left the house the following morning by himself, he headed in the direction of the bus station.

Chapter 19

Tari… Ops!

'Oh, Lucky, mun, get off me.' Krystie shouted at him as he licked her ear from his usual position in the car. Lucky yelped and was undeterred by Krystie ducking down in the drivers seat to get out of his reach. He was content and he was letting her know it. Krystie was barrelling down the motorway in her old Ford Sierra car, which was miraculously still running, with a cigarette in one hand and her other hand on the steering wheel. She did not have another arm to keep Lucky's tongue at bay.

'Krys, I think you'd better slow down, we have got a trailer on the back you know.' Carys pointed out to her as the speedometer in the car reached seventy miles per hour. Krystie abruptly took her foot off the accelerator and the tiny trailer behind the car started to swerve. Krystie swore and Carys rolled her eyes. This was not an unusual event when Krystie was in the driver's seat.

Lucky was eagerly looking out of the windscreen trying to detect where he was being taken today. Carys and Krystie had heard that there was a farmer selling some cheap hay. Always on the look out for a bargain, they borrowed a small aluminium trailer from Pete and went in search of a farm high up on the mountain overlooking Margam Park. Krystie turned off the M4 motorway and headed up a steep, narrow lane. She knew it well as half way to the top of the mountain was a sharp turning right where her cousin and his wife lived.

'We'll have to go and see Megan after we've got this hay, Carys.'

'Yeah, I know we haven't seen her for ages, don't get a chance to go riding with her as much now, do we?'

'It's not that we don't get the chance, Carys. It's because her horse is as mad as yours and neither of you can stop them when you're together. Too dangerous.' Carys shuddered as she remembered galloping towards the ten-foot high boundary wall that surrounds Margam Park with Megan on her horse along side. They had only just stopped their horses from barrelling into the stone wall and knocking themselves out.

Krystie interrupted Carys' flashback. 'Right, now this is the turning right towards Megan's, so the farm that we are going to should not be much further up the hill.'

'Getting a bit foggy now, Krys, can you see all right?'

'Not really, but don't worry, the lady told me that you can't miss this farm, it's the only thing up here apparently.' Lucky growled as white mist swirled around outside the car. He did not like it when he could not see where he was going.

Krystie continued to drive up the steep ascent and the tarmac road seemed to disintegrate, leaving a dusty, narrow pothole track. With the white fog so thick outside, neither Krystie nor Carys could see anything apart from a steel five-bar gate that emerged in front of them.

'She didn't say anything about a gate,' Carys murmured to Krystie.

'There's nothing else up here though, so it must be through there?'

'Difficult to say when we can't see anything though. Try it, shall we?' Carys asked. Krystie shrugged, wound down the window and lit another cigarette. Thick mist swirled into the car and Lucky growled. He stayed in the back as Carys jumped out and opened the gate. He was in no hurry to leave Krystie.

The fog continued to swirl around Krystie's car as she accelerated up the rough track beyond the gate. She drove slowly, trying to navigate the uneven ground safely. Lucky, Carys and Krystie were quiet as minutes passed and there was still no sign of any farmhouse.

'It looks like a tractor has been along here,' Krystie said as she desperately tried to peer through the fog. There were furrows starting to emerge either side of the track and as they got deeper the ground in the middle became higher. Grass and soil scraped noisily on the underneath of the car. Lucky yelped uneasily.

'Oh, be quiet, dog.' Krystie snapped, her patience quickly wavering.

'I think you'd better put the car on the side of the track, Krys' Carys suggested tentatively.

'What do you mean?'

'You know, like, stick the left tyres on the bank to the left and keep the right tyres on the middle of the track. It will stop the bottom of the car from scraping along the ground.'

'Oh, I don't like the sound of this,' Krystie said as she carefully steered the car so she kept as far left as possible. Krystie kept driving and the furrows got deeper.

'Carys,' Krystie said. 'I don't think there's any farm up here you know.' Carys had to agree with her. The fog was starting to clear and they could see that they were reaching the summit of the mountain with no farmhouse in sight.

'Do you think we should go back?' Carys asked.

'What… with this trailer on the back, I can't reverse something I can't see. It's too low.'

Lucky stopped growling and started panting, he could now see out of the windows again and although he had no idea of where he was, he was content that he had visibility. He yelped though when the car began to wheel spin and slipped, landing with a thump on the middle of the track. The back wheels spun wildly and clumps of grass and wet mud flew into the air and stuck to the car with loud thumps.

'Carys, I'm stuck.' Krystie shouted. Lucky started barking and attacked Krystie's seatbelt from behind her seat. With the bumps and bangs coming from outside the car it sounded to him that there was someone knocking to get in and he was going to defend it with his life.

Carys went to open her door but as she shifted her weight the whole car tilted to the left. Lucky was thrown from the seatbelt and landed in an undignified position on the floor of the rear seats. Carys and Krystie froze and gripped the door handles with white knuckles. They got out of the car slowly and carefully and Lucky leapt out with them. He ran around it looking for whatever or whoever had been knocking on it, but he found nothing. Neither Krystie nor Carys spoke as they surveyed the damage with white faces and open, gaping mouths. The furrows either side of the track had become so deep that when the car had slipped it had landed on the middle of the track making it impossible for all four wheels to touch the floor at the same time. The car was wedged up by the high middle of the track and rocked from left to right when pressure was applied either side. When the left tyres were on the floor there was at least six inches of ground clearance underneath the right ones.

'Oh well, look on the bright side,' Carys said to Krystie, her chirpy demeanour unscathed.

'What bright side can you find from this, Carys?'

'We've found the farmhouse. We drove straight past it. Look. It's down b' there. You can just see the roof.' Carys pointed about a mile down the track to a three-storey stone farmhouse that could only have been about fifty feet from where they had stopped to drive through the gate.

As Carys and Krystie stared down the mountain the thick fog swept further inland giving them a clear view of the sea and Port Talbot steelworks. The fog had descended for just enough time that they were unable to see the farmhouse and had ended up on the top of the mountain by mistake.

'Well you'd better go down to that farm house and get them to come and tow us out of here.' Krystie said to Carys as she lit another cigarette to calm her nerves.

'What do you mean, me? Aren't you coming?'

'No I am not, my nerves are shot to pieces.' Carys did not want to go to the farmhouse by herself so she thought carefully before coaxing Krystie.

'You know I heard that there were ghosts on the top of this mountain, from Margam Park, you know? Lots of supernatural activities and this is where they come.'

'Oh no, I'm not staying up here by myself, quick... come on, Carys. Lets get some help' Krystie shouted as she hurried down the mountain. Carys laughed as she followed Krystie to the farmhouse, Lucky bounding after them. Carys unhitched the trailer from the car and started to wheel it backwards down the track. She was glad that they had brought a small trailer and not the horse box or they would have really struggled to reverse it back to civilisation.

Carys knocked on the front door of the farmhouse with Krystie and Lucky close behind her.

'Oh, you're all the way up there, are you?' An elderly woman kindly acknowledged to Carys when she heard the predicament. 'The hay is only in that barn over there as well. You drove straight past it.'

'Have you got a vehicle to help us tow our car back down?'

'Well, my husband's gone out for the day today, luv, and he's taken the Jeep so he can't get up there to tow you out. Can you call someone?'

Carys and Krystie both had a few people that they could have called to help them tow their car back down the mountain. However, neither of them wanted to explain to anyone why they had driven a low clearance car up a desolate tractor trail and got it stuck. Carys settled on calling her previous employer, Hugh. He had discontinued providing a pony ride service and had taken another position working in Margam Country Park. He lived less than a mile from the farm that Carys and Krystie were stuck at.

Carys had her fingers crossed as she dialled his number

'Carys, good to hear from you. When you coming to visit?' Hugh boomed down the phone.

'Well... I was actually hoping you could come and visit me?' Carys replied. She correctly interpreted Hugh's silence as confusion and hurriedly explained where she and Krystie were.

'All right Carr, I'll be up now in a minute.' The line went dead.

'Well, is he coming?' Krystie demanded.

'Yeah, he said he'll be here now in a minute.'

'Well is he going to be here now, or in a minute, 'coz I can't take this mountain much longer.' Krystie lit another cigarette and Lucky continued to run around sniffing the land, which he was considering whether to make his new territory. As he explored, he made a mental note to try and find this exciting new place again.

Carys and Krystie both saw Hugh's beaming smile from behind the windscreen of his Jeep as he drove up the road and into the farm. When he pulled up in front of the five-bar gate his smile widened and the crow's feet around his eyes deepened as he laughed a greeting.

'Been doing a bit of off-roading have we?' he joked from inside his vehicle.

'Yeah, in a ruddy Ford Sierra.' Krystie exclaimed at him as she climbed in the front seat. Hugh laughed as he drove Carys and Krystie up the mountain and Lucky chased after them. He easily kept up with the Jeep as Hugh, even in a four by four vehicle, had to take care negotiating the potholes. Even Hugh began to get nervous when he heard the grass tickling the underneath of his Jeep.

'Are you sure you drove a car up here?' He asked incredulously.

'Course I did… look its there.' Krystie pointed the glowing embers of her cigarette towards her dilapidated car as it emerged into sight on the horizon.

'My God, how did you get up here?'

'My brilliant driving of course.' Krystie replied, her temper calming and sense of humour returning.

'My God!' Hugh repeated when he finally pulled up behind Krystie's car. It was tilted significantly to the left. 'This is going to cause some damage pulling that off there, mind you.'

When Krystie's car was the right side of the five-bar gate there were long bits of grass and clumps of soil extending from underneath the engine. Hugh waved goodbye and drove away chuckling to himself. Krystie continued to chain smoke as Carys loaded six bales of hay in the back of the re-attached trailer and Lucky resumed his position in the rear seats of the car. When Krystie drove out of the yard and headed back down the mountain lane, two of the bales fell from the trailer and Carys had to re-load them.

'That's it!' Krystie cried out. 'I've had enough. I can't go any further without a cuppa tea with loads of milk and sugar. A chocolate biscuit wouldn't go a miss, either.' A few minutes later, Krystie pulled up outside Megan's farm and demanded that she put the kettle on.

Megan welcomed her visitors with the hot, calming drink that Krystie needed and grinned while she heard a stammered explanation of the morning events. Lucky lay quietly, chewing on the lead that Carys had put on him. Megan lived in a beautiful stone farmhouse that she had faultlessly decorated, preserving the character with majestic, real log fireplaces and wooden oak beams and floors.

Lucky tensed when a large golden Labrador padded into the kitchen and flopped onto the floor only yards from him. Lucky whined and strained against his collar as

Carys held him back. Before Carys could ask Megan how well behaved the golden dog was, the lovely Labrador rolled over and shot a large paw out towards Lucky's face. Lucky also flopped on the floor, rolled over and stuck his legs up towards the ceiling, looking directly into the placid face of the golden dog from his upside down position. Carys was amazed when Lucky and Ben exchanged pleasantries without a growl or nip. Lucky lay comfortably alongside the bigger dog and they looked as if they had known each other for years.

'I can't believe that Lucky is being so good with your dog.' Carys exclaimed. Megan's usually cheerily demeanour faded and the light in her eyes faded and her smile turned upside down.

'Oh, Ben's such a good dog, but he's been in awful trouble with the farmers. He keeps chasing their sheep and I can't stop him from escaping.'

'Yeah, I know that problem.' Carys sympathized, although Lucky had never got into trouble for chasing sheep. He had chased them of course but he had always done it when the farmers had not been present to object. Megan continued to explain that the farmers had found Ben chasing their sheep on one too many occasions and they had told her that the next time they found him in their fields he would be shot. She was helpless to stop Ben from running away once outside so she was keeping him in the house until she found him another home.

'But it's awfully hard for him, I don't always have time to walk him enough and I swear that he is depressed.' As Carys watched Lucky snuggle up into Ben she had an idea.

‘He can come home and stay with me, if you want. Until you find him another home, I mean. Looks like Lucky would enjoy his company.’ Megan’s face lit up and she immediately agreed. Lucky was ecstatic to find that his new golden friend was coming home with him. Carys was secretly hoping that when she got Ben home and her parents saw how much Lucky liked him that she would be allowed to keep the lovely lab. Unfortunately for Lucky and Carys, Jayne went berserk when she found a large, glossy and friendly Labrador in her kitchen.

‘We can’t even control the dog we’ve got. No!’ But Jayne reluctantly agreed for Ben to stay with them until Megan found him a new home.

Lucky followed Ben around like a puppy would shadow its mother. He ate when Ben had food, played with the same toys, slept in his basket as opposed to on someone’s bed. Carys, who had long resumed the position of top female alpha after Lucky stopped pursuing Krystie, was unknowingly demoted again and Ben took her place. Lucky did not feel the need to leave the house unaccompanied because his hard work had finally paid off. He had successfully succeeded on expanding his pack.

The day that Megan came and took Ben to his new home, Lucky was gone by the afternoon. He wanted to find his golden friend but his search was in vain. When Jayne and Evan realised that he had disappeared they started to have discussions about his manhood, something that had never been questioned before.

When Evan had brought Lucky from Swansea dogs' home neither he nor Jayne had thought to get Lucky castrated.

'I bet it's his hormones that make him wander all the time, Evan.'

'Most probably.'

'I haven't seen any little Luckys running around though, have you? Maybe he doesn't work properly?'

'Well, based on the amount of times he's been caught in the actual act I would say that he hasn't got any problems going through the motions. Maybe we should take him to the vet's and get him done?'

'Oh, Evan! You can't do that, that's awful.'

'Why not? If that's the reason he keeps running away all the time.'

'Yeah but he's had them all his life, you can't take them away now, it wouldn't be fair to him.'

'Don't be so daft, it will take away his urge and he will stop wandering as much.' Evan disagreed with his wife.

'No. We can't do it. Anyway, even if he does stop… well… you know? He's been walking so much for so long that he would go out anyway.'

Carys had another idea to stop Lucky from wandering and it was due to his good behaviour while Ben had also been living with them.

'He needs a companion, Mum' Carys told her one-day. 'He's lonely and that's why he goes walking. He didn't run away once when Ben was with us.' Jayne predictably began to object to Carys' suggestion but after years of trying to ward off unwanted animals she decided to try and minimise the risk rather than eliminate it altogether.

Evan and Carys left Tyddyn one Saturday with a strict criterion from Jayne. If they were going to get another dog it had to be female, small and with no history of running away. They returned a few hours later with a dog very different to the puppy they had found all those years ago. She was a white, medium size mongrel dog with one tan coloured ear and freckles on her face. She had a soft, labrador's face on a beagle or terrier body but her legs were long giving her the height that Lucky lacked. She was apathetic, listless and her glazed eyes held no interest in her new surroundings.

Carys carried her into the back garden and the quiet dog lay on the grass where she was placed, warily eyeing her surroundings. Jayne came outside to appraise the new dog in the family.

'Hmmmm...' Jayne's eyebrows creased together and she drew in a deep breath before voicing her verdict on the new arrival. 'Well, she's not too big and she has a short coat. She certainly seems quieter than Lucky.' The white dog slowly lifted her head and retched until she vomited a small amount of lumpy liquid. When she finished emptying her stomach she slowly stood, moved a few feet and flopped onto the ground again with her head on her paws.

‘Hmmmm... Better than throwing up all over the carpet I suppose,’ Jayne sighed.

The lethargic white dog continued to lie on the grass, completely indifferent to her new home or the people moving around her. Evan and Carys took her to the vet and although she was given a clean bill of health, the vet warned that she had an upset stomach and they should expect some very nasty substances coming out of her from both ends. Lucky had disappeared the morning that Carys and Evan had gone to fetch their new dog. He stayed out that night and returned home on Sunday morning.

Lucky ran in through the front door and headed straight for the kitchen. He lapped some water from his bowl and froze, his ears flat to the back of his head and his hackles rising slowly as he inhaled the strange scent in his kitchen. He turned and saw a white dog lying in his basket under the kitchen table. She watched him quietly but did not move as Lucky ran up to her to sniff her over. Lucky lost interest in her and haughtily walked out of the kitchen and into the living room. He flopped in front of the fire and thought no more of the white dog in the kitchen. She did not have the same smell as Ben, she was not golden and she did not greet him as Ben had done.

Carys named the new dog ‘Tari.’ Jayne was glad that her children were older and there was no need for a naming ceremony. By the time Daniel realised that there was a new dog in the house she already had a name and he did not think to object to it. Tari stayed in Lucky’s basket for two days, only going outside to relieve herself and eating very little. Carys was getting worried about her but a few mornings after her arrival she came downstairs to find a completely different dog.

Tari greeted Carys with alert, bright eyes and she was eager to be patted and praised. Lucky did not think any more of the energetic white dog than he had of the quiet one. He ignored her completely and went out of his way not to be in the same room as her. Unlike Lucky, Tari did not have a danger list, she always did what she was told, did not try to chase or attempt to make love to the cat and had no interest in leaving the garden or the stables unless someone was with her.

She was a perfectly behaved dog with limited training. This certainly did not endear her to Lucky. When he found himself being shouted at by Jayne he stared at Tari with contempt in his eyes. He tolerated her but he avoided her company. Carys' plan to get another dog to motivate Lucky to want to stay in his home had backfired. Lucky continued to come and go as he pleased.

Lucky was increasingly becoming aware of the change of atmosphere in Tyddyn. Evan and Jayne were not always coming home to sleep in their own bed. Sometimes Evan stayed out and sometimes it was Jayne, but never together. Carys and Daniel did not have the same energy that they once had. They were both older and did not want to play with him in the way he wanted. He could chew as many of Jayne's hairbrushes as he liked and no one seemed to notice any more. The doorbell ceased to excite him and he had not had a newspaper girl to defend his family from in years. When he ran past Daniel and nipped at his trousers before racing away, Daniel did not scream and shout as he had once done. Carys did not take him out walking as often as he wanted and his family did not allow him in the car as much. To top it all off his family had brought a new dog into his territory and he definitely did not approve of her.

When Lucky and his family had moved to Tyddyn he had understood that his family were growing and no longer needed his protection as much. Most of his time had thereafter been devoted to expanding on his pack's territory and trying to recruit new pack members. Lucky loved his family and he still felt the same urge to protect them when it was needed, but that need was not so much any more. His little people had become big people and they had changed. It is rare that a dog has an epiphany and when it happens it is usually to make the association between a lead and a walk, the feeling of love and loyalty with a person or the difference between safety and danger. Lucky was having an epiphany of sorts but it was slow to happen and had been occurring over a long period of dog years.

Lucky missed his family not because they had gone anywhere but because he sensed they were going. They were growing up and, judging by the strange scents Evan and Jayne kept coming home with, they were forming packs of their own. Lucky knew what he wanted and that was a family, with little people that had lots of energy, newspapers and newspaper girls and walks and rides in the car nearly every day so he could fulfil his purpose of protecting his pack. Lucky was looking for a family like his used to be.

Chapter 20

'I Wasn't Kidnapped - I Ran Away.'

Lucky had wandered into Cwmafan and decided to try a different route to his usual. He headed up a steep hill and found a cluster of red brick houses on the opposite side of the road. There was a large, green verge running alongside and Lucky was delighted to see a group of little people kicking around a black and white cylindrical object. Lucky looked to the left, looked to the right and then ran across the road and headed straight towards the football.

He was pleased when the children did not shout at him but applauded and cheered when he bounced the ball madly around the green. He chased the ball for over an hour with his new friends pursuing him, patting him on the odd occasion they stopped for a rest. When the game was over and the children disappeared into different houses Lucky reluctantly returned home.

Lucky became a regular football player with the children from Ynysygwas and he revelled in the attention he got from them. He did not want to leave them so one evening he followed one of the boys to his house. He ran in through the door before the boy and was greeted by a woman who seemed to like him as much as the children did. Lucky stayed for an hour and had some tea but before dusk turned into night he was picked up and put outside.

'He can't stay with us, Tom' the woman placed her hands on her son's small shoulders. 'He's got a collar on, he's got his own home somewhere.' Little Tom said goodbye to Lucky and Lucky wandered back to Tyddyn.

Lucky still lived up to his nickname of Mucky Lucky and to Jayne's disgust he still returned home covered in excrement or some other nasty, smelling sludge. Jayne no longer had to ensure that her children had a bath but Lucky was a different matter. As soon as Lucky walked into the house stinking offensively, he knew by the way that Jayne wrinkled her nose and had her hands on her hips that he was be going to be soaked and scrubbed.

Once Jayne had locked Lucky in the bathroom, he knew there was no escape. Sometimes he struggled constantly but if he had walked particularly far that day he stood in the bath shivering, reluctantly accepting the strawberry shampoo being lathered into his coarse hair. As soon as he was out of the bath he would go mad, running around the house, rubbing himself up against the sofa and shaking the water from his coat onto everything and everyone possible. When Lucky became particularly hyperactive, Jayne sometimes forgot to put his collar back on.

Lucky was not wearing his collar the next time he went to Ynysygwas to see his friends. It was a different conversation between Tom and his mother later that evening.

'He can't stay with us, Tom' the woman repeated to her son for what felt like the hundredth time since Lucky had been visiting. 'He has a home.'

'But mum, he hasn't got a collar on. Maybe his family don't want him any more.' Tom said hopefully. Tom's mother groaned and agreed that Lucky could stay the night.

'But he's not staying tomorrow, he's going in the morning.' Tom reluctantly agreed.

Lucky stayed the night in Tom's bed and was put out in the morning but he did not go home. He went for a walk and came back to wait for his new friend and his mother. Without a collar on, Tom's mother had no way of contacting Lucky's real owners. This did not concern Lucky because Tom had a comfortable home, Tom's mother had mouth-watering food, which he was fed in abundance and he got to play football every evening. The fact that Tom's mother insisted leaving Lucky outside every morning in the hope that he would go back to his real home did not deter him or encourage him to leave.

Lucky had been gone three days and his real family had not been able to find him. Jayne had phoned all the dogs' homes but Lucky was not at any of them. The receptionist at Goytre dog pound had hung up very quickly after curtly telling Jayne that Lucky was not in residence and a good job that was too. It was Krystie who told Carys that she had sighted Lucky in Ynysygwas playing football with some young boys. Evan and Carys jumped into the car and headed up to the area to start knocking on doors.

It was late in the evening and the warm glow of the setting sun over Swansea bay was turning the horizon a deep, dark red. Carys began by knocking on the houses closest to the entrance of the estate but no one in the first two had seen or heard of a tiny, brown, scruffy terrier. In the third house a young boy told Carys that he had been playing with a small dog this afternoon.

'Try Tom's house' the little boy said as he pointed to a blue door further up the street.

When Carys knocked on Tom's door she spoke to his mother.

'I'm very sorry,' the woman apologised. 'I know he's usually got a tag on with a telephone number but he didn't this time and he usually goes after a couple of days.' Tom's mother directed Carys to a nearby field at the top of the housing estate and Evan and Carys went in search of Lucky and a boy called Tom.

It was nearly dark when Carys and Evan heard a rustling sound amongst a cluster of trees on the edge of a muddy, churned up field. The tinkling sound of a small stream running through the foliage masked the mumbling voices of small children. Lucky heard familiar footsteps and yelped. One of the boys hissed loudly.

'Quick boys, run, it might be the pound.'

Carys called out to reassure them that it was not the dog pound and that she was just looking for her dog. Lucky was attached to Tom by a dirty piece of fraying rope. He wagged his tail when he saw his other family but he made no effort to run to them. Tom reluctantly handed the old piece of rope with Lucky attached to Carys. She thanked him but picked Lucky up from the ground, untangled the rope from around his collar and handed it back to Tom.

Lucky hung from underneath Carys' arm and whined uneasily but his eyes did not leave Tom and his friends. He was not sure that he wanted Carys to come and take him away when he had been allowed to spend so much time playing with these children who matched his energy and need to chase a football. Carys thanked Tom for looking after her dog and turned to leave.

'Is he allowed to come back?' Tom asked. Carys thought carefully before answering the hopeful boy.

'Umm… I suppose... if he wants to that is? He tends to go where he wants to though. And he is my dog, so if he does come to play, can you just send him back home again? Or phone the number on his tag?'

'Yeah yeah,' Tom assured Carys. He watched as Lucky was carried away with a crestfallen expression on his face. Lucky attacked the seatbelt as soon as he was in the car for no good reason other than he wanted to.

'So we've got a part-time dog now, have we?' Jayne clarified when Carys told her about Lucky's sleepovers at the house up in Ynysagwas.

'Yeah but they had him on a lead so he couldn't have come back home if he had wanted to' Carys defended.

'Should have left him there. At least they care enough to put him on a lead.' Carys' mouth dropped open and she frowned so deeply at her mother's throwaway comment that Jayne quickly disappeared.

There came a day when Carys and Evan went to knock on Tom's door but Lucky was not there. Tom stuttered and fought back tears as he told Carys that he had not seen Lucky for over a month. As Carys said goodbye to Tom for the last time she heard him shout for his mother as he closed the front door. He was distraught that Lucky had been missing for so long but had not been to visit him. Carys expressed her sympathy for Tom to her father on the way home to Tyddyn.

'I mean, at least we are used to him going to stay with other people. Lucky was the only dog that Tom really had.'

'I'm sure Tom will find another waif and stray to play with, Carys' Evan sighed. 'The real question is exactly where has Lucky been for the past two days. Or, how many families has he got to visit?'

Lucky hobbled back to Tyddyn that evening, thinking that he might stay at this home for a few days before going to see his other friends. He did like this home but it just was not the same as it used to be. Lucky had always been good at reading body language and he knew that his family were changing. He knew it before Carys and Daniel but his loyalty to them was such that he kept coming back.

Jayne and Evan told their children they were getting a divorce in the spring of 1999, just four years after moving to Tyddyn. Carys was particularly shocked to find out that her parents had separated as a couple only a year after they had moved into the house with the stables. But with a modest combined income and a home that suited the family, they had come to an amicable agreement to continue living in the same house as man and wife. They remained friends and parents but began to date and so were both in long-term relationships with other people by the time they made the announcement to their children. Both had separate futures that did not involve living at Tyddyn. To Carys' horror, the house was put up for sale and a rollercoaster of events started and everything changed.

Chapter 21

Tiddles

The first thing that Lucky noticed was the disappearance of the person who, next to him of course, was second in command of the family and house. Evan made plans to take over a pub on the edge of Swansea City centre with his partner, Rhian. He moved his belongings out of Tyddyn and became a landlord in a pub twenty-five miles away. Lucky was taken to the Smith's Arms with Carys, Daniel, Sherry and Owen several times. The first time he ran into the pub he froze when he saw Evan behind the bar, surprised to see him out of context.

He quickly got over this shock and ran to greet him the same as he had always done. He yelped and wagged his tail wildly as Evan ruffled the coarse hairs around his neck. Lucky acknowledged Evan's new partner, Rhian, sitting on a barstool with half a lager in one hand and a cigarette in the other, but he did not understand the significance of who she was or why she was there. Since Rhian thought that anything with four legs should either be on a plate or out of her sight, she was content to allow Lucky to live in ignorance.

Whenever Lucky returned to Tyddyn after seeing Evan, he wandered slowly around the house. He noticed that the scent of the man who had been part of his family for so long was fading. Soon Lucky stopped expecting Evan to walk in through the door. A major part of his life had abruptly stopped.

Then, Big Black Cat's tail began to fall off in segments. The first time Carys came downstairs to find a small, black and bloody furry piece of tail on the kitchen floor she screamed thinking it was a dead mouse. Her heart sank when she remembered that she could not call on her father, the dead animal disposal man, because he was no longer there. Carys then realised that if it was a mouse it did not have a head or a tail. On closer inspection, she discovered that it was not a mouse at all. She followed the blood droplets across the floor and onto the kitchen counter where she saw Big Black Cat licking the wound of his much shorter tail.

Over the next few weeks, Big Black Cat's tail kept getting shorter as he slowly fell apart. Jayne took him to the vet and was advised to have him put to sleep. So it was that Carys, Daniel and Jayne had to say goodbye to Big Black Cat, the longest surviving animal in years of disastrous animal keeping since Carys and Daniel had been young children. Lucky was not able to chase or try to make love to Big Black Cat any more. Another part of his life had ceased to be.

Even the parties with the nice, friendly people who took him for walks in the middle of the night stopped. Lucky kept looking for all the cars parked along Cwmafan road to show him that his friends were gathering next door but none arrived. Dai was moving house and Delilah had resigned in her role as treasurer of the South Wales Transvestite order. There would be no more Hollywood beauties, women with middle aged spread or body builders in tight dresses tottering up the mountain road in high heeled stilettos with pretty, sparkling hand bags and earrings Another part of Lucky's routine had ended suddenly.

Lucky was taken often to a house where Jayne's scent was very strong. He also met her partner, Dylan. Lucky had a distant memory of Dylan from some of the parties held at Tyddyn. Dylan had been a friend of Evan and Jayne's for many years until they had separated. Jayne and he had become romantically involved a short while after. Lucky liked Dylan's quiet manner and the way that he gently fondled his ears but the house where this man lived was not his home and there were no little people to play with or cats to chase.

Lucky tried to spend time with Carys as he had always done. She still had the same friends whom he liked and she still went out riding on her mad, grey, long-legged animal. She even had a car now that Lucky was allowed to go in and she never screamed at him when he tore into the seatbelts. But Lucky was noticing a change in Carys. She did not shout at Lucky like she did at a lot of other people but she spent more time locked away in her bedroom. Lucky sat outside the door to her, whining and wondering why now, after so many years, he was not allowed inside with her.

Carys was reacting to the news of her parent's separating in a predictably selfish teenage manner. She was not upset to find out that Jayne and Evan had been separated for years and had long-term partners. Carys had liked Rhian from the first moment she had met her. Her step-mum to be lived with half a lager in one hand and a cigarette in the other, a sharp sarcastic tongue and a laugh that put everyone, including Carys, at ease. Dylan was an avid animal lover so Carys had immediately accepted and liked him.

Carys was reacting badly because her parent's divorce meant that the family home at Tyddyn was being sold. She was losing her stables, paddock and the home she had for her herself and her horses. Her grief and imminent sense of loss did not stem just from materialistic values though because she had recently made the decision to take Bu to a University over two hundred and fifty miles away. She would only be coming back for Christmas and in the summer holidays. But she had always thought that she would know what she was coming back to. Her parents had always been so dependable and supportive that she was struggling to reconcile the notion of being a family when they would all be living apart. Even though she had rarely spent any quality time with Daniel over the years, he had always been there, entertaining his family and anybody who visited the house whether they liked it or not.

Within time, Carys would come to appreciate the selflessness of her parents, continuing to live together despite their romantic separation in order to provide their children with the best upbringing possible. She would also be thankful for the time she had living at Tyddyn, a time she associated with true childhood. She would come to realise that a family like hers were far more important than the bricks and mortar of the house and stables up for sale. But her change in heart did not occur during Lucky's time with her and all he picked up from her was vibes of anger and resentment.

The only things that did not seem any different to Lucky were Jayne and Daniel. Daniel had been pleased to find out that once the house at Tyddyn had been sold he was going to move to Baglan to live with his mother and Dylan. Daniel could count the amount of times he had been up the stables on one hand and he only swam in the swimming pool if he was pushed in. His friends all lived in Baglan so the change of events suited him. Jayne's one consolation about moving house was that Daniel, with friends living closer, might start to spend more time outside his bedroom than he did within it.

This though was the only consolation for Jayne. She knew that she and Evan had done the best they could for their children and she, like Evan, did not regret the decision to move to Tyddyn or remain there despite their separating. She was also confident with the choice to move to Baglan with Daniel and Dylan. Daniel might be a slimmer lookalike of his father but he was just as, if not more than, organised and sensible as her and they were well suited to live together. But Jayne could not shake the sense that she had failed in her marriage and the empathy she felt for her despondent daughter made it difficult for her to always feel confident that what she and Evan were doing was right.

The hard decision had been made years ago, when she and Evan had decided to split as a couple but continue living together for their children. It had not been a dramatic affair but in a way the new beginning at Tyddyn had been the end of their relationship. The house had offered them freedom from the demands of carting their daughter back and forth to distant stables and Daniel just had an ever decreasing need for parental supervision. They found that when they were left alone as man and wife they just could not cope with each other - Evan always living for the moment and Jayne busy planning for the future.

But Jayne had always been the source of positivity, never ending patience and logical thinking and it was these core traits of her personality that enabled her to continue with the same daily routine until Tyddyn was sold and they could all move on. Lucky found that she was still the first to rise and let him outside, still fed him every day and shouted at him if he tried to nip at Daniel. While Lucky was sure that nothing of significance had changed with Jayne and Daniel, collectively they were not enough to make him want to stay.

Oneday, Lucky returned from one of his lonesome wanderings, having rolled lavishly in dark green sludge and animal excrement. Dried clumps of mud clung to his thick, coarse fur and he smelt like a cow farm in summer. He slunk in through the front door, already noticing that

Jayne's hands were at her hips and her nose was wrinkled. He tried to bolt past her but yelped when he felt her hands grab him and swing him into the air.

'Stinking, smelling, mucky Lucky's getting a bath.' Jayne muttered as she carried him upstairs into the bathroom. Lucky emerged fifteen minutes later smelling strongly of strawberry shampoo. He ran madly around the living room looking for someone or something to chase but no one was there. Evan and Big Black Cat had long gone, Carys was out without him and Daniel was in his room. Lucky stopped and looked around an empty living room and listened to an almost empty house.

He heard Jayne stomp down the stairs and waited until she was in his sight. Lucky cocked his head and his leg and peed on the sofa for the last time. Jayne's patience finally snapped and she yelled at Lucky

'Oh, for goodness sake, if you're going to do that you can get out, go on, out. Out. OUT!' Jayne grabbed Lucky by the scruff of the neck and hauled him into the front garden, slamming the front door so hard that the windows in the porch area vibrated menacingly. She paused, trying to figure out what felt wrong to her. She startled when she realised that she had forgotten to put Lucky's collar and nametag back on him and ran upstairs to retrieve it.

Lucky found himself outside, still dripping wet and unable to get back into the house. He stared up at the living room window and saw Tari's white, adoring face look out at him from within her home. He hobbled off the driveway, heading in the direction of Cwmafan with the sole intention of officially forming his new pack, new family, new life. He had fulfilled his duty as the leader of this family and he left knowing that they were all safe because of his efforts over the years. His held his tail high in the air as he sniffed his way along. He did not look back.....

When the house with stables and a pony paddock at Tyddyn was sold it was a quiet and subdued affair. Lucky had been gone for four months and despite his family searching the Welsh hills and valleys for him, he could not be found. Evan picked up Carys and Bu from Tyddyn at the end of September in a borrowed horse lorry while Jayne was in work and Daniel was in school. Carys had already said her goodbyes to her family and she was glad that she could leave Tyddyn and go to her chosen university with her horse without a scene. She had left a tear-stained note though, with a picture of Lucky with it, in the front porch area for the new owners of their house at Tyddyn. In it, she had told them all about the little dog who would not stay and who might one day come back to find his family. Jayne and Daniel moved out of Tyddyn the week after Carys had gone to university, the last of the Davies to leave Tyddyn.

It was eighteen months later, Lucky stretched out as far as his little body would allow, his front paws resting on the smallest of the little people. The only boy in the house was sitting in the middle, patting him on the head while Lucky's back legs rested on the oldest and tallest girl. The three dark haired, pale-faced children were all huddled together on a faded blue fabric, two-seated sofa. They all had their hands protectively on their dog as they listened to a woman who claimed to be the real owner of the tiny terrier who had come to live with them.

The mother of the three children sat on a wooden chair, the only other furniture in an otherwise barren room, and leaned forward. She was talking animatedly to the women drinking a cup of tea with the last of their milk. Lucky could not understand what was being said but he could sense how tense and anxious his family were. Usually they were always moving, talking, smiling and playing. That was why he had come to live with them, he loved their energy and they needed his protection. They all sat completely still now as the woman talked. Lucky was relaxed though, he had known this woman for years and he knew that she was not a threat.

'We looked for him for months but we moved house shortly after he left home and I have always worried about him. I didn't want him going back to our house one day only to find out that we had deserted him.'

'Look, we've known this dog for nearly three years. He was coming to stay with us on and off for ages before he actually came and moved in,' the mother said to Jayne as she fought back tears. She wanted to shout at this woman to get out of her house and leave her, her children and their dog alone. But she bit her tongue and reminded herself that the strange woman had mentioned that she worked for the council and she really did not want to get into any more trouble with authorities. She checked herself and started again.

'He used to have a name tag so we knew somebody owned him, but he always went again, so we did not worry. He came one day without a nametag and he's been with us ever since. I never took the number so I didn't have anyone to phone.'

'Yeah, he likes us,' the eldest girl, who was only nine years old said to Jayne. 'Are you really going to take him away? Do you work for the dog pound really?' and a tear started down her cheek. Lucky whined, jumped up from his sprawled position across all three children and rested his front paws on the girl's shoulder. He pushed his nose impatiently into her cheek. The little girl laughed and half heartedly tried to push him back down again but Lucky was persistent if nothing else.

Jayne smiled at Lucky's antics and continued to explain her reason for coming.

'Look, I haven't come to take him. I just want to know that he is OK and that he is happy, he made my children happy for many years you see.' Jayne paused and guilt consumed her. 'I actually feel guilty that he left. I remember the day exactly. He had come home stinking and I had bathed him and forgotten to put his collar back on him. He ran away and never came back and I have always felt that it was my fault.' Jayne sighed and in that moment exhaled all the remorse she had been holding onto since Lucky had left home. She felt better having confessed this even if it was to a strange family who did not know her.

Jayne had not told Carys how dreadful she had felt after Lucky had moved out. Even Daniel had shed a tear when he had realised (a few months later) that their little dog was not coming back. But it had been Carys who had cried unashamedly in front of her parents and Jayne also knew, behind closed doors. Lucky leaving had been hardest for Carys because it had made it all real and final for her; her parent's divorce, Tyddyn being sold, leaving to go to university, the end of an era. That was the reason why Jayne had not told Carys or Evan that she was coming here today. They would have wanted to come and they would have wanted Lucky back and Jayne was just not sure that was what Lucky wanted, or what was best for him.

'I just came to see if you were going to keep him, because if you weren't then I would have taken him home with me. I have some pictures… do you want to see?'

The two youngest children immediately jumped off the sofa and ran to grab the photographic evidence of their tiny dog's past.

'Look Mammy, it's him…'

'Yeah, it's our dog…'

The children's mother leant over and took the pictures of Lucky from her children. Despite her initial anger she could not help but smile when she saw the fluffy, oddly shaped terrier looking out at her from the photos.

'Well… It's definitely him, even though he looks younger in these pictures. Same ears, same long tail and the same funny face.'

The pictures were passed around from one child to another. Lucky stayed on the lap of the eldest girl. He could still feel her quivering underneath him. He knew that she was still upset and he was not going to leave her until she was smiling and laughing again. After all, she did belong to him. She was his responsibility.

'I just want to know that he is happy, that's all' Jayne said softly but as she stared at Lucky she knew that he was. The way he was stood on the oldest child reminded her of how he used to stand over Carys. He had done it from the very first day he had arrived and he used to look at Jayne, as he was doing now, with his big, brown and soulful eyes as if to say 'She's mine and I will look after her.'

'Look,' the mother said quietly as she leant towards Jayne and whispered with a broken voice. 'My kids adore him, don't take him away and he really is happy 'ere, he never runs away.'

Jayne tore her eyes away from Lucky and nodded.

'He does seem happy, I think that it is best that he stays.'

'Hurray...' the boy shouted and he jumped up, did a couple of star jumps and then ran around the tiny enclosed living room, a picture of Lucky still in his hand. Lucky yelped and jumped from the sofa to run after him. The other two children joined in, whooping and shouting that their dog was not going to be taken away from them. The children's mother relaxed her tense posture and exhaled deeply.

'Thank you' she said. 'And you don't need to worry because we would never let him go to another home.'

The silent implication that Jayne could not have cared for Lucky as much as they did was not lost on her but she was there to check on an old friend, not antagonise his family.

'Would you like to keep the photos?' she offered as a final good gesture to her. The children's mother gratefully accepted.

As Jayne stood to leave and say farewell she bent over and spoke kindly to the tiny, brown terrier running around with three small children.

'Well then, Lucky. Try and be a good boy from now on, yeah?'

'His name's not Lucky' shouted the youngest child.

'Yeah, that's not what we call him' the boy said haughtily.

'What is it that you call him?'

'Tiddles' the children shouted in unison as they continued their spirited dance around the sofa.

Tiddles cocked his head at Jayne's but was distracted when a small black and white cat nosed its way cautiously into the living room. Tiddles turned on his heel and chased the cat from the room, growling and yelping as he went.

'Tiddles,' Jayne muttered as she left. 'I knew I went wrong somewhere with that dog.'

★★★★★★★★★★★

'He looks very happy,' Jayne reassured her children and her ex-husband as she told them of her recent discovery. They were all sat around a table in the local workingmens club where Penelope and Pete's fiftieth anniversary party was in full swing. Carys was visiting from university to celebrate with her and Daniel's grandparents. Evan was gatecrashing as per usual, a welcomed tradition that he had formed since he and Jayne had separated.

'What's that, mum?' Carys asked as she leant forward to better hear her mother.

'I said, he looks very happy,' Jayne said louder, almost shouting over the music. She was momentarily distracted by the crowds gathering around the small dance floor in the function room, all clapping madly to the flashing blue and pink disco lights as aunt Lynne strutted around the dance floor, flashing her knees and thighs in her legendary impersonation of Tina Turner. She had adamantly stated at the beginning of the night that her sixty-year-old joints were not up to the job, but a few pints of cider had resolved that issue.

'I can't believe that you went without me, or didn't even tell me you had found him.' Carys said, a burning longing for her childhood dog vivid in her eyes.

'Look Carys,' Jayne said even louder as her extended family starting cheering the resident Tina Turner who had just got down on her knees and was shimmying her impressive cleavage to the crowd. 'I didn't take you because I knew you would want to bring him back home. He's got three children to play with, a cat to chase and he gets to go out every day for a walk, its Lucky's idea of heaven.'

'Are you sure that it was Lucky?' Daniel asked. 'But then again I don't suppose that there are many dogs that look like him, are there?'

'I do miss him, mind you, even after all this time.' Evan said and he inconspicuously wiped his finger around the bottom of his water filled eyes.

'Mum, Dad, we need to go and get him back, he's our dog,' Carys said and she gripped the edge of the table tightly. 'We spent ages looking for him when he first went and now we know where he is and you're saying we should just leave him there?'

'Carys, I miss him too but what are we going to bring him back to?' Evan sighed. 'You can't take him to university with you although I'm sure Lucky would be able to entertain himself enough in halls of residence. I can't have him in the pub because he won't like living on the outskirts of Swansea city. It's like a manmade concrete jungle and he's far too used to the freedom of the forests.'

Carys looked at her mother expectantly but Jayne threw her hands up, palm outwards and snorted.

'Don't look at me, his loyalties were always with you two.'

'But I miss him…' Carys repeated but her voice sounded worn because she knew her mother was speaking the truth. She watched as Tina Turner finished shimmying on the floor and was applauded back up onto two feet by her eager fans. Old greatgrandpa Bill was sitting patiently at the side of the dance floor, his false teeth in a glass of water besides him as he prepared to sing his family a song.

'Lucky's probably happy now that he's living with a family again. He was always happier when we were younger, he only really started to get into a lot of trouble a few years after we moved to Tyddyn, that was when we were growing up,' Daniel said. Carys and her parents were impressed with Daniel's unexpected insight.

'In the end, Lucky was a lot like us,' Evan said. Jayne raised one eyebrow and Evan hurried to defend himself. 'I mean, he grew up and moved on just like we all have. I bet he went to find another family because he knew that we were all going our separate ways. He was always a smart dog that one. And I'm glad as well, glad that another family can have just as much fun with him as we did, glad that Lucky has found another family who loves him as much as we did. I'm glad that I won't have to say goodbye the hard way but that I can remember him just the way he was, our little lovable scamp!'

Jayne raised her other eyebrow.

'Lucky was our lucky charm, he stuck with us while we were together and then when it was time he went to another family,' Carys said wistfully and Jayne's eyebrows nearly disappeared into her hairline.

'We had some good times though, didn't we?' Evan chuckled.

'My first ever memory is of Lucky running into the patio doors,' Daniel chuckled as he sat back in his chair and folded his arms conversationally across his chest. He acted and sounded very much like old greatgrandpa Bill who by the way, was still waiting patiently for Tina Turner and her fans to disperse so he could do his number.

'Attacking the letterbox,' Jayne groaned

'Running after the car over the Bwlch mountain,' Carys chirped up, instantly cheered by some of her most fondest childhood memories.

'Herding those sheep across the farmers' fields, remember that Carys?' Evan nudged her.

'I don't know what was worse, arguing a case of mistaken identity so we did not get sued or having to go and pick him up from the Baglan house and facing the irate owner.'

'Playing rugby for Tonna,'

'All my hairbrushes, chewed to pieces,'

'His crush on Krystie,'

'Going to work with Bob,'

'That angry woman at the dog pound,'

'His lifetime ban from the Riverside,'

'Partying with transvestites,'

'Good times, Carys, Good times, Daniel.'

'Eventful times, you mean Evan?'

'Yes, but all good,' and Lucky's family reminisced long into the night about his antics while Tina Turner drank more cider, old greatgrandpa Bill sang his toothless song and despite the fact the Davies family would finish the night by going to their separate homes, they were just that, a family.

Chapter 22

The Last Sighting

Jayne sighed and her head fell into her open palms. She was unable to catch the tiny, green parrot that was running backwards and forwards along the top of her new leather sofa. The little bird had far too much energy to go back into her cage willingly. She had spent the entire morning scampering up and down on the windowsill, looking out through the living room window into the front garden. She screamed and squawked every time a cat passed outside, raising her glossy green wings to flash a warning with her scarlet red patches that were usually hidden underneath her flight feathers. She was not going to allow any feline near her territory while she was there to protect it. Bitz considered herself to be top of the pecking order when it came to any person, any animal or anything and she could peck particularly hard.

She came to a standstill on the sofa, enjoying the feel and the sound of the soft leather as she cracked the material between her firm and sharp beak. She liked the way that this caused Jayne to jump up and shout at her

'No.' Of course, since the little green parrot had the ability to mimic, she just shouted straight back. She thought this was a great game to play.

Penelope sat across the room, a safe distance from Jayne and the parrot, drinking a cup of tea and giggling at Jayne's failed attempts to catch Carys' bird. Jayne sighed again and addressed her mother with frustration.

'It's just typical. I tell Carys not to come home with any more dogs, cats, horses, hamsters or any other farmyard animal. And what does she bring here? A parrot with more attitude than any other animal I have ever known.' Penelope giggled again but could not help challenging Jayne's opinion.

'What, even more attitude than that mad horse of hers..? She certainly can't have more attitude than Lucky had?'

'It's a close call.' Jayne grimaced as she botched another attempt to catch Bitz.

Bitz was thoroughly enjoying herself. She loved it when people played catch with her. She began running along the top of the sofa again, expecting Jayne to try and grab her. She stopped when she realised that Jayne was just standing in the middle of the room with her hands on her hips.

'Cheeky girl' the little green parrot squawked as she bobbed her head up and down.

'I'll give you cheeky girl.' Jayne spoke to Bitz sternly. 'You wait till Dylan comes home, he'll have you!'

'Oooooooh.' Bits screeched.

'Good job Dylan is able to control her, isn't it?' Penelope teased as Jayne rolled her eyes both at the parrot and her mother. 'Right then,' Penelope declared and she banged her empty teacup onto the coffee table and stood to put her coat on. 'Are you ready to go?'

'Goodbye. Goodbye. Goodbye.' Bitz screamed. Jayne looked pointedly at her mother and back at Bitz.

'I am ready, but as you can see I'm having a few problems here. That sharp beak of hers really hurts when she doesn't want to be picked up.'

'Well, come on, we're going to be late for lunch.'

'Goodbye. Goodbye. Goodbye.' Bitz continued to shriek. She stopped squawking, looked directly at Jayne and then turned her back on her and wriggled her bum and beautiful long tail. A large green and white blob of bird excrement dribbled down the mahogany brown sofa. Jayne's head fell into her hands, again and she moaned to Penelope

'She hasn't got as much attitude as Lucky, she's Lucky reincarnated... and just think of how long parrots live for!'

'Ha, ha.' said Bitz.

****

While Jayne was reliving Lucky's antics through a tiny, green parrot with attitude, Evan was having a drink with a few friends at the Red Lion pub in Port Talbot. He stood outside the front entrance leaning over the metal barrier, looking up and basking in the summer sunshine. He was starting to think that it would be better sitting, drinking and talking at the back. The front of the Red Lion faces directly onto the busy main road leading through Port Talbot and he could taste the exhaust fumes. The paved patio area at the back of the pub would definitely be an improvement than the noise of the constant traffic and road dust that Evan and his friends were inhaling. Evan decided against this though because despite the fumes he was enjoying people watching. Every now and then, Evan raised his hand to wave at a passing car when he recognised someone inside.

Evan and Rhian had been married for a long time and were still running their pub in Swansea but Evan was enjoying a day off from his responsibilities. His two friends, Dave and George, were also enjoying a day off work. So the three of them stood contentedly outside the Red Lion, watching the hustle and bustle of Port Talbot and chatting about life in general.

Evan was distracted from his conversations by a car horn he knew very well. He lifted his hand to wave even before he turned to see a large green and gold Mitsubishi Shogun accelerating loudly past the pub. He dreaded to think where and what Carys had been doing because her Jeep was covered in mud and sand. The windscreen was caked in large droplets of thick brown clumps of soil and fine dust which had been smeared around enough by the wipers that he could just see in, although he certainly did not know how Carys could see out in order to drive safely. Carys beeped her horn in quick succession and Evan thought that he could see her wave from behind the grime-covered windows.

'My goodness!' George clanked his pint onto the top of the steel barriers separating him from the main road. 'She had better take that thing through a car wash before she brings it to my place for an MOT next week.' George was Evan and Carys' mechanic, although with the amount of problems Carys had with her cars and the number of times George had to go and tow her home, she was a very demanding customer.

'I suggest you phone and tell her that before she is due to bring that mobile skip that she calls a jeep over to you, then.' Evan said drily 'You know what she's like.'

'Yeah I do. Still playing around with horses that's her problem, always in riding clothes and covered in mud.' Evan smiled, thinking of the amount of mud, hay and straw that their daughter tramped through the house after she had been at the stables.

'She still got that mad horse, Evan?' Dave asked.

'Yep. And he's still mad, he ran into a lamp post last week.'

'How did he manage to run into a lamppost? They don't exactly take up much room.'

'Yeah, well. What can I say?' Evan shrugged. 'He's just as mad as she is. Carys reckons he closes his eyes when he runs away with her and that's why he crashes into things.'

Dave and George were still laughing at the thought of Carys and Bu colliding with a metal pole when they heard another car horn beep.

'Oh look!' George exclaimed as he raised his pint up in front of him. 'It's Carys' mad friend.' Evan waved at Krystie as she drove past in a Jeep caked in even more mud than Carys' had been. Krystie was also a regular customer of George's mechanical services. Evan smirked

'Look out, George. If those two are going somewhere together you can guarantee one of them will break down. They'll be ringing you in a couple of hours.'

'Oh no. You're right, Evan.' George dramatically faked taking his phone out of his pocket and turning it off. 'Never mind, Evan. At least your son is half sensible.' Evan chuckled as he thought of Daniel. The son who, unlike Carys, had never given him any trouble when he was growing up and who had made the transition from teenager to adult with surprising ease.

As Evan relaxed on the cold, steel railings outside the old wooden door of the Red Lion he felt content, the warm sun a perfect contrast to his cold pint of cider. The conversation turned from his children to his previous night out with his wife and friends.

'That was a brilliant song you sang on karaoke last night,' Dave teased Evan. 'Nearly brought a tear to my eye.'

'No one does karaoke like Evan though, do they butt?' George chirped in as he held his pint aloft again in a silent gesture of cheers. Evan nodded his head in agreement. Dave and George entered into a very serious conversation about the best and worst karaoke songs of all time. Evan would have joined in but he was distracted by what looked like a tiny, light brown dog walking along on the opposite side of Station Road. The dog had an unusual walk. He looked as if he might have only had three legs because he was hobbling, sniffing every corner of every building as he passed.

Evan took his glasses off, pulled a handkerchief from his pocket and wiped them clean. When he re-positioned them on his nose he looked back up Station Road for the little brown dog. He had disappeared. Evan shrugged, making a mental note to stay off the dark rum until much later that evening. He turned his attention back to George and Dave's banter, swigged the last of his cider and interrupted their heated discussion.

'Come on boys. You drinking or what?'

'Yeah, and it's your turn, Evan, so cough up.' Evan put his hand in his pocket for a twenty-pound note and turned to take one last look up Station Road before parting with his hard earned cash. He froze, the bank note fluttering in the soft breeze. The little brown dog had walked past the Red Lion and turned off the main road, heading up a small lane in the direction of Cwmafan.

It was definitely a terrier, maybe a border terrier but not as big. Maybe a Jack Russell but his proportions were all wrong. His body was too long and his legs were too short. He was carrying his back left leg in the air. He hobbled along but despite this he moved quickly. His silver coat had flecks of brown in it and his tail was held high, pointing to the sky as he sniffed his way along the road.

'You getting these drinks, Evan, or what?' Dave broke Evan's astonished silence.

‘Lucky?’ Evan yelled across the road and down the alley to the little brown dog. Despite the noise of the traffic and the rumbling sound of the train behind the Red Lion the little dog stopped. He turned around and looked directly at Evan from the other side of the road. His overly large triangular ears pricked directly upwards and the hair around his muzzle was nearly completely white.

‘Lucky.’ Evan called again, this time more certain of the dog he was seeing. The tiny terrier stared at the man shouting and a distant memory stirred. He had lots of distant memories of people, places and events and he knew this man had once been a massive and important part of his life. The tiny terrier was tempted to retrace his steps to see the friendly man but his leg ached, his stomach rumbled and he had little people to play with and protect. He had somewhere else he had to be.

A large lorry slowly rumbled past the Red Lion and obscured Evan’s view from the little dog. When the lorry had passed and Evan was once again able to see down the lane, the tiny brown terrier had gone.

‘Evan, what is wrong with you? You cracking up or what?’ George demanded impatiently.

‘Get the drinks, George. I’ll be back now in a minute.’

‘Is that now or in a minute, Evan?’

‘Either… whatever.’ Evan walked around the railings in front of the pub and crossed the road over to the Grand Hotel. He half walked and half ran down the lane but he was staring ahead at an empty road. The tiny, scruffy, wiry haired silver terrier had disappeared.

Evan walked back to the Red Lion deep in thought. Could it be…? Was it…? Did he really just see Lucky? It was the summer of 2006, eight years since he and his family had moved out from Tyddyn and another eight before that when Carys had insisted they bring him from Swansea dogs' home. That would make Lucky sixteen years old, improbable, but also possible.

If it had been Lucky passing the Red Lion then Evan knew he could be anywhere by now. He could be on a bus to Swansea or catching a lift with a friendly face. When Evan returned to the Red Lion he took a swig of his freshly pulled cider and chuckled. He liked the thought of Lucky, a scruffy wiry haired terrier dog still with his own agenda and having adventures defending the highways and byways of Port Talbot.

THE END

To contact Cathryn Anne please email at:-
cathryn.anne@live.com

follow on Facebook – Cathryn Anne

follow on Twitter @Little_Welsh

You'll see him on the by-ways and the highways of the village,
Where the mountains rise with pride and the hillsides sing with courage.

His daily plight and duty is to protect his family,
Saving them from dangers, disasters and calamity.

He's the Alpha of his family that he thinks as his own pack,
On guard in case they need him for protection or attack,
But his duty doesn't stop at his home Port Talbot town,
As he investigates the perils and the dangers all around.

If only he knew his adventures gave them deeper troubles still,
Causing mayhem and desruction with his unruly mind and will.

But they love him all the more for his legendary stories and his tales,
As Lucky their Welsh Wanderer, wanders the hills of Wales.

by Angharad Rees